A
Plunge
Into
Evil

Kerrera House Press

A Plunge Into Evil

A Traveler 'n Wynter Greek Mystery

by

K. Scot Macdonald

Kerrera House Press

K. Scot Macdonald is the author of:

Novels
The Shakespeare Drug
In Justice Found
Mouse's Dream
The Grizzly Extinction Plot (as Liam Shay)

Non-Fiction
Deadly Dance: The Chippendales Murders
*Rolling the Iron Dice: Historical Analogies and Decisions to
Use Military Force in Regional Contingencies*
*Propaganda and Information Warfare in the 21st Century:
Altered Images and Deception Operations*

Macdonald, K. Scot.
A Plunge Into Evil/K. Scot Macdonald—1st Edition
p.   cm.
ISBN 978-0-9916653-5-8
Kerrera House Press
Culver City, CA
www.KerreraHousePress.com

First Printing: 2015
Printed in the United States of America

10 9 8 7 6 5 4 3 2

Dedicated to Lindy,
and to Jonathan, Ruth and AJ;
A long and happy life together.

Laws are partly formed for the sake of good men, in order to instruct them how they may live on friendly terms with one another, and partly for the sake of those who refuse to be instructed, whose spirit cannot be subdued, or softened, or hindered from plunging into evil.

—Plato

Greece

Kalampaka/
Meteora

Delphi

Corinth

Athens

Olympia

Naflion

Sounion

Kyparissia

Sparta

Pylos

Monemvasia

Mani Peninsula
Diros Caves

Rhodes

Santorini

Lindos

Crete

Your Traveler Excursion Guides

Scarlet Wynter (owner) and Jonathan Traveler (guide)

Your Fellow Excursionists

Hilda Rasmussen – Seattle housewife on her first trip abroad
Robert Rasmussen – Boyish museum sub-contractor
Dr. Peter Lodge – Psychology professor/dating website mogul
Petra Fox – Shy housewife; Dr. Lodge's daughter
David Fox – Ex-pro golfer; Golf equipment salesman
Gayle Garcia – US Olympic Team Physiotherapist
Michael Cohen – Forensic accountant
Charles "Chance" Sterling – Ex-fighter pilot; Yacht captain
Sonja Weaver – Model, actress; Chance's wife
Benjamin "Benny" Sartoris – A boisterous latecomer

Traveler Excursions
Your Greece Itinerary

April 17 to May 8, 2004

April 17: Arrive Athens, Corinth Canal, Nafplion

April 18: Palamidi Castle

April 19: Mycenae, Tiryns, Epidavros

April 20: Badron Gorge, Moni Profitis Ilonas Monastery, Monemvasia

April 21: Mystras, Sparta

April 22: Gythio, Diros Caves, Pylos

April 23: Methoni Castle, Neo Kastro, Kyparissia

April 24: Olympia

April 25: Chlemoutsi Castle, Tripolis, Delphi

April 26: Delphi

April 27: Kalampaka, Meteora Monasteries

April 28: Sounion

April 29 - April 30: Santorini

May 1 - 3: Rhodes, Lindos

May 4 - 7: Athens

May 8: Depart Athens

Chapter 1

Day 1: Saturday, April 17, 2004

Setting her Greece guidebook on her tray table, Mrs. Hilda Rasmussen took a breath, concentrating on forcing air deep into her body.

Her lungs refused to fill.

She inhaled deeply.

Nothing.

Another deep breath.

Nothing.

This couldn't be happening. Not now.

Turbulence buffeted the Olympic Airlines Airbus as it descended toward Athens. Even so, Mrs. Rasmussen felt full of a nervous energy as the clouds thinned and she thought she saw the ochre hills of Attica; hills that had felt the tread of Ajax, Achilles and Heracles, not to mention the lighter steps of Helen, Cassandra and Penelope. Joy flooded Mrs. Rasmussen's body. She had arrived—finally, after so long.

The Airbus leapt and dropped. Passengers' arms flailed like out-of-control windmills. The fuselage creaked. A baby screamed. Dull echoing bangs resonated from the overhead compartments as bags slammed against bulkheads.

Peering out the window, Mrs. Rasmussen strained to see Greece. She had to see Greece. Her repeated attempts to convince her husband, Harry, to take a trip to Greece, to Quebec, even to nearby Spokane had all ended in tear-drenched arguments and abject failure.

"Waste a money," Harry said. "Better save for retirement. Besides, who wants to sit on a plane for a million hours just to see old armless statues with a horde of sweaty tourists? You can see the same things in the comfort of our own living room on TV."

Some TV; a 15-year-old cathode-ray model that flickered in thunderstorms and never seemed loud enough, especially when she watched British mysteries on PBS with their wonderful accents.

The day her husband died, Mrs. Rasmussen vowed at his coffin-side to make up for all those lost years spent in soggy, gloomy, provincial Seattle. Freed of his miserly embrace, now barely a month later she was going to see Greece; if her body cooperated and if the plane didn't rattle itself into all its constituent pieces before they touched down in glorious Attica.

Mrs. Rasmussen's breathing grew shallower. She panted for air. It was, she told herself, just stress from the turbulence. The plane pitched, yawed and rolled between abrupt jolts. A soda plummeted to the floor, adding a sickly sweet smell to the jet's fear-laden atmosphere.

She sucked in a breath. It did little good. She still felt light-headed and starved of air. She finally had to admit what it was; asthma. Worse, it was a bad attack; one of her worst.

Mrs. Rasmussen loathed asthma. It never hurt. It just made breathing difficult. It made her feel weak, immature and unable to control her own body. At 69, you should have a real disease, diabetes, heart disease or cancer, not a silly condition that made you short of breath like an over-excited child.

Ignoring her lungs, she peered out the window; nothing but wispy white clouds. She yearned to see Greece. She had to see Greece. She would see Greece. Nothing would stop her. Not now. Not after decades of dreaming.

She struggled to take another deep breath. Her lungs screamed for oxygen even as her thinking began to slow. Anger, frustration and fear formed a tumultuous mixture boiling within her. She seethed at the injustice of her situation even as her much-loathed disease robbed her body and mind of oxygen. She sucked down air, but her lungs demanded more, as if they were receiving not even a single molecule of the life-giving substance.

Mrs. Rasmussen peered out the window as the aircraft dropped, shook and yawed. A portable music player fell to the aisle floor and skittered fore and aft before disappearing under a row of seats. Through the window, tinted green with age, she spotted the ground again. This time the clouds stayed away. She could see Greece. The dry, ochre hills looked warm and inviting. She pressed her left hand against the window's cool plastic to try to touch them. It was going to be a glorious trip.

She felt queasy. The rings on her fingers trembled, clicking on the window. The tremor spread up her arm. Even in her favorite new purple goatskin pumps her feet felt prickly, as if they were on the cusp of going to sleep. She wiggled each foot in turn; still prickly.

Finally with the gravest regret she resigned herself to using her inhaler, even though the drug made her heart race. Worse, it temporarily made her feel more nauseous than she felt when her asthma struck. Even so, the drug did work after five minutes or so. She slid her sleek new CD/DVD player, which she'd been too excited to use, into the pocket of the seat in front of her next to her unread novel, *Murder of My Aunt*, and reached down for her purse on the floor. She couldn't reach it.

The seat belt restricted her ability to bend, not that she was able to bend all that well without any outside restraints. She had to lose weight if she was going to travel the world, climb down into the Great Pyramid on Giza or to the top of El Castillo in Chichen Itza.

What a way to start a trip of a lifetime, trapped in a seat like a condemned murderer in an electric chair. She needed her purse. The plane jinked, weaved and dropped. The fasten seat belt lights were lit. Dare she unbuckle?

She struggled to inhale, but her lungs weren't drawing in enough oxygen. Dark tendrils of panic seeped throughout her brain. She knew exactly what was happening, yet sweat glazed her body. She must have her inhaler. Relief was mere inches from her outstretched hand.

She reached across her lap to undo her seat belt. Her right hand refused to cooperate. She couldn't undo the belt. She clenched and unclenched her fingers. They tingled as if asleep, muffling sensation and destroying her ability to control them with any degree of precision.

She needed help. Sighing, she looked across the aisle at her son. She loathed even having to consider asking him for anything. Why did the asthma have to strike now? In 10 minutes they would be on the ground and it would be no trouble at all to get her inhaler and banish her asthma for the rest of the day. Reluctantly, she realized she would have to ask for his help.

"Robert," Mrs. Rasmussen gasped. Robert had insisted she take the window seat and, when a seat remained empty across the aisle, he moved over to give her extra room. Whatever happened between them, he was nothing, if not considerate. She called again, her voice barely audible even to her, "Robert." Struggling to breathe, talking was an Olympian feat suitable for Heracles.

Enthralled by a DVD, Robert didn't hear her. The turbulence caused the plastic case for Agatha Christie's *Evil Under the Sun* to shimmy in a miniature dance on the tray table as he absently held it loosely in place with his left hand. How could he be oblivious to the gut-churning turbulence?

Frantically waving, Mrs. Rasmussen attracted the attention of several other passengers, but not Robert. Ensnared by their seat belts, passengers squirmed around to look over or around their seats to stare at her with a mixture of curiosity, concern and, in a couple of faces, disapproval. After an agonizing few moments, a blonde in the row ahead finally attracted Robert's attention and gestured at Mrs. Rasmussen. Robert turned, his dark eyes meeting hers.

"Inhaler." She gestured at her purse.

"What?" The DVD player's oversized red earphones were clamped over his ears.

"Inhaler!" She yelled with what she felt was her last breath.

The other passengers stared at her with concern, any hints of disapproval gone.

Robert pulled off his earphones and, leaning toward her, said, "Sorry, Mom. My ears are clogged." As if to prove it, he held his nose, closed his mouth and puffed out his cheeks to try to clear his ears in a Valsalva maneuver.

"Asthma," she gasped, clutching her chest, barely feeling her fine new silk blouse. The color in her vision had drained away, turning the world black and white. The rumbling hum of the Airbus's engines blocked out all other sounds. Her skin prickled, as if encased in velveteen. "Inhaler."

Intent on unclogging his ears, Robert still didn't hear her. She finally managed to force her fingers to undo her seat belt.

"Don't do that, Mom, we're landing." Robert cast her a stern look of warning. "You'll fall."

Silly boy; forty-three and he dressed and acted like a 12-year-old. Mrs. Rasmussen pointed again, emphatically, at her purse. She was running out of air. Why didn't he understand?

Robert frowned and then appeared finally to realize what she needed. He frowned his disapproval, but reached across the aisle for her purse. He could not reach it. Glancing up at the fasten seat belt sign and eyeing the erratically dropping and shifting floor, he hesitated with a put-upon look she knew all too well. Finally, reluctantly, he undid his seat belt.

The Airbus dropped. Robert fell to one knee. Recovering, he rose and grabbed her purse. As soon as it was within reach, she snatched it from him. She dug out her inhaler. Shaking it vigorously, knowing relief was seconds away, she put the end in her mouth and inhaled deeply.

Nothing.

In horror, she checked the counter on the inhaler; zero.

"In my bag," she managed to wheeze. An attack had never progressed this far. Her disgust at having to deal with the asthma, which had already evolved into controlled alarm, now transformed into panic.

Steadying himself with a hand on the seat top before him, Robert opened the overhead compartment, earning glares, angry gestures and shouted warnings to sit down from passengers seated nearby. Ignoring them, he dragged out her new red carryon. He just stopped another bag from rocketing out of the bin into his face before slamming the compartment shut.

"Sir, you must sit down," a stewardess who appeared in the aisle ordered. "The Captain has the fasten seat belt sign illuminated."

"My mother needs her inhaler," Robert said, unzipping the bag. "Without it, she'll die."

"Dying's not so bad," Race Traveler said.

"At least not until you try it," Scarlett Wynter said with a wry grin from the seat beside him. He could smell Penguin peppermints on her breath.

"You just need to see the potential in it," Race said.

"Explain that one and I'll marry you."

"Dying simplifies life. No worries about funding a long retirement. No need to see the dentist regularly. No more mortgage. Long-term plans? Forget it. Live for today, just like the self-help gurus recommend for a happy life."

Finished with yet another Sudoku, Race flipped the blank puzzle over onto the stack of completed blank Sudoku and crossword puzzles on his tray table. As he did so, he glanced up at one of the movies he was watching on the seat back monitor. Returning his attention to Scarlett, he said, "The key to dying is a modicum of health, and some money."

"Money's always necessary, but never sufficient," Scarlett said. "I guess I can see the simplifying aspects of dying, but certainly not of death. Who wants to die?"

"I said dying wasn't so bad, not death. So when's the big day?"

"In a few years."

"But you said—"

"I'd marry you, I didn't say when."

"Don't wait too long; the best things in life don't last forever."

"Nor do the worst." Scarlet cast him a saccharine smile. Eyeing the seven almost full miniature bottles of whiskey, rum, bourbon, and wine that jiggled and rattled on the edge of Race's tray table, Scarlett asked, "Aren't you saving your money to travel?"

"Found a stack of coupons in the lounge at JFK."

"Can I have one?"

"Take your pick. I am a disciple of new experiences, even if it's just one sip."

Scarlett chose a Riesling, tasted it and returned to the final pages of her novel, *Do Androids Dream of Electric Sheep?*

As he flipped channels to check that he had correctly guessed the endings of the three movies he'd been watching—he had, Race asked Scarlett, "Need a guide this fall?"

"With the war in Iraq, bookings are way down. If you want more work, you better make this excursion the trip of a lifetime for everyone on it." She rearranged her hair to better conceal the vivid auburn streak that ran from her part down to the ends and added, as if it was an inconsequential aside, "Paul asked to lead my next excursion."

"Paul doesn't know Ajax from Achilles."

"Few do, and fewer care."

"I make them care. I make history come alive: Paris' love for Helen—"

"More like lust."

"The boxers at the Olympic Games with brutal *himantes* on their knuckles, the miraculous construction of the cloud-touching monasteries at Meteora—"

"Where men can wear shorts, but women can't. You'd think monks would have a little more self-control."

"It isn't about self-control. It's about respect. Where was I?... The destruction of the Minoan civilization by the eruption of Strongili's volcano."

Scarlett drank her Riesling and said, "I guess you do have your good points; at least you don't talk in your sleep."

Race frowned, not following her.

"You talk in your audience's sleep."

"Yet, you still hire me."

"I have a soft spot for charity cases."

"Especially ones you've bedded?"

"Business will trump a one-night stand unless this excursion goes flawlessly. Everyone loves Paul, especially the older ladies."

As he considered ways to ensure a successful tour, Race saw a young man several rows ahead searching a red bag. A woman's arm reached up from an adjacent seat, flailing the air as if she was drowning.

Race flipped up his table. Ignoring the miniature liquor bottles and blank puzzles that spilled onto the floor, he slipped out and placed a hand on each seat back in turn to steady himself as he rushed up the aisle.

"What's wrong?" Race asked the young man who stood alongside a gasping lady with short, gray hair coiffed in a stylish cut. The woman's liver-spotted bony hands glittered with diamonds, rubies and garnets as she clenched and unclenched them on her lap.

"Asthma," the young man said. Dressed in jeans worn white at the tattered hems and a black T-shirt translucent from wear, the boyish-faced man could have passed for 18, except for his over-developed forearms, which were as thick as Race's thighs. "Inhaler's empty."

"Sirs, I'll have to ask you to sit down, now," the stewardess said. "I will assist the lady."

"She's my mother," the young man said as he searched his mother's red bag. Even through the lady's classic floral perfume, Race could smell the young man's nervous sweat like a siren of warning.

"Name?" Race asked.

"Mrs. Rasmussen, ah, Hilda. I'm Rob."

Mrs. Rasmussen's face was pale, her lips gray, her eyes wide. Her mouth formed a quivering puckered "O" as she gasped for air.

"Does she have another inhaler?"

"She does, but...." Rob shook his head as he gave up his search of her bag, his face the picture of despair.

"Please sit down, sirs, now," the stewardess ordered, braced against one of the seats as the aircraft dropped and yawed. "We're on final approach." She squared her shoulders and fixed Race with clear, commanding eyes. "If you don't sit, I'll have you placed in restraints."

"He's a doctor," Scarlett called from her seat, leaning out into the aisle, her long black hair with the auburn streak swaying like a velvet curtain.

Race frowned as he felt the plane angle down and bank to the left. What was Scarlett talking about? Ignoring her, he yelled, "I need an asthma inhaler! Now! Emergency!"

A moment later several hands shot up above the tops of seats brandishing inhalers. Race grabbed the nearest inhaler, checked the drug's name—a basic bronchodilator—shook it and, shouldering Rob aside, held it to Mrs. Rasmussen's mouth.

"Breath in deeply, Hilda," Race urged.

She inhaled with a long, deep breath and held the life-giving medicine in her lungs. Race waited a minute by his diver's watch and gave her a second puff. Relief flooded her face as she took full, life-giving breaths. Race leaned close to her mouth. He heard no wheezing or whistling over the jet's engines.

"Thank you," Mrs. Rasmussen said. She looked up at him with a look of immense gratitude, the tension in her body easing as her breathing returned to normal. "Thank you." Her wrinkled, ring-adorned hands found Race's left hand and held it tight.

"Please sit down, now!" The stewardess ordered.

Color seeped back into Mrs. Rasmussen's face. Race slid into the empty seat beside her as her son, still clutching her carryon, slumped back into his seat. The stewardess rushed back to her jump seat aft.

Race closed his eyes as he felt the tension drain from his body and his heart beat returned to normal.

Mrs. Rasmussen groaned. Race wriggled around in his seat to see her better.

"My chest. My arm," she mumbled as she repeatedly flexed her left arm, hand and fingers. She stared down at them as if they weren't a part of her.

CPR? No room. Race undid his seat belt, slid out and raced down the aisle, only narrowly avoiding falling in the brutal turbulence.

"Defibrillator?" Race asked the stewardess at the stern of the plane. He heard and felt the flaps deploy as they approached the runway.

Before the stewardess could answer, Race spotted the hard plastic defibrillator case amidst the shining metal galley drawers and cupboards. He undid the case's restraining latch and rushed back to Mrs. Rasmussen. Reaching her, he opened the case. He skimmed the instructions and turned the machine on.

"Help me, please," she gasped. "I have to see Greece. I've never been anywhere."

Race readied the machine as he double-checked the instructions as fast as he could read. There was an awful gasp and a wheeze. He looked at Mrs. Rasmussen. Her eyes were open, her jaw slack. Her face took on an ultra-relaxed appearance.

Race stopped. Defibrillators could return a beating heart to a regular beat, but they could not bring someone back from the dead. A bleak numbness flooded Race's body and mind.

Race turned to Rob, who looked over at his mother, her carryon still unzipped on his lap. Rob's face was blank, as if he couldn't process what he saw. Tears made tracks from his eyes down to his jaw, where they dripped onto his T-shirt, leaving dark splotches. Race heard something crack. Rob had crushed his mother's empty asthma inhaler in his right hand. A shard cut his palm. Blood dripped onto the thighs of his faded jeans. Rob didn't notice.

Chapter 2

"Mr. Robert Rasmussen said his mother brought three extra inhalers on the trip," Inspector Andreis Kanavou said as he stood with Scarlett and Race in the Athen's airport terminal.

"He certainly didn't find any of them," Scarlett said as if it was a personal affront. She glanced at her watch. The police had questioned everyone on the tour for two hours and Race knew she was worried. She had an itinerary to keep.

"We could not locate any of the inhalers either," Inspector Kanavou said. "Did you see any?"

"Just the one he crushed," Race said.

Kanavou nodded as he peered at Race, who listened in one ear on his music device to Stella Kali, a popular Greek *laïko*-pop artist. He held a novel he planned to get back to as soon as it was polite to do so, if not a little before.

Race thought Kanavou might be in his early forties, but his dark, ever-moving eyes gave him an alert, youthful aspect. His face had the look of a clay model that a sculptor had begun work on, got the general idea of a skull and face, and then walked away for an extended coffee break and a cigarette.

Kanavou asked, "How long will you be in Greece, Mr. Traveler?"

"We're on a three-week tour."

"Actually, we're leading an excursion," Scarlett said as she cast a disapproving look at Race. She smiled at Kanavou and tilted her head to the side, which set her black hair with the auburn streak swaying. "Traveler Excursions. We offer small, intimate, boutique tours." Glancing around as if she was about to impart a most personal secret, she leaned in close to Kanavou and said, her voice as breathy as Lauren Bacall's at her most seductive, "I wouldn't ask, but given the economy and the war, do you think you'll need to mention to the media that Mrs. Rasmussen was on our excursion? Her passing really didn't have anything to do with my little company, did it?"

A look of complete understanding on his face, Kanavou beamed back at her and said, "I doubt even the most sensationalistic media will be interested in the unfortunate, natural passing of an elderly American tourist."

Race noticed a frown flit across Scarlett's face before she asked, "Would it be alright, Inspector Kanavou, if we start our excursion now?" She smiled and gave her hair another swish; actions that would have convinced a miser to surrender his last penny.

"Of course, Ms. Wynter."

Scarlett turned to leave but stopped, turned back and said, "A natural passing?"

Kanavou nodded. "I forgot to ask, Mr. Traveler, you are a doctor?"

Race cast a disapproving glance at Scarlett. "I have a doctorate in logic."

"I was told by several witnesses that you are a medical doctor."

"A simple misunderstanding," Scarlett said. She glanced at Race and widened her eyes. She wanted him to say something, but he remained silent. Race hoped she would remain silent, but from years of experience he knew she rarely choose to exercise that particular right. She said, "Mrs. Rasmussen's son...."

"Yes, Ms. Wynter?" Kanavou pursed his thick lips, his dark gaze locked on Scarlett. She had that effect on men.

"I just wondered; are you going to investigate him?"

"For what, Ms. Wynter?"

"Manslaughter? Murder?"

Kanavou's thick lips took on a wry grin. "The coroner reported at this stage that all evidence points to the unfortunate Mrs. Rasmussen succumbing to a heart attack triggered by asthma. The ancient Greeks called such natural deaths Thanatos."

"No involvement by the Keres then?" Race asked.

"A violent death?" Kanavou asked, frowning. "Why? Did you notice something to suggest the Keres were involved?"

"The missing inhalers," Scarlett said.

"Easily misplaced at the start of a grand…excursion."

Scarlett nodded and said, "Thanatos it is, then." She sounded far from convinced.

As Kanavou walked away, Scarlett stooped to re-tie her hiking boots and get them just right according to her precise requirements. She and Race wore their boots on the plane to save space in their bags. "Do you think Kanavou will keep everyone in Greece after the tour?"

"Why?" Race felt drained and angry at himself. If he had acted faster, maybe he could have saved Mrs. Rasmussen. Maybe he should have tried CPR before the defibrilator.

"To investigate the murder of course."

"You heard Kanavou, death by natural causes."

Scarlett gave him a knowing look of disbelief. "I hope it doesn't ruin the tour."

"Scarlett, a woman just died."

"She was old and rich. She probably had a good long life. She had nice clothes, jewelry, and did you see her pumps?" Scarlett stomped on the marble floor to ensure her foot was well settled into her boot.

"Her son said she was 69, only about 20 years older than I am."

"But 40 years older than me," Scarlett said, drawing out the number with poorly suppressed glee.

"You have the sensitivity of a morgue attendant; besides, in terms of actual birthdays, I'm only ten."

"I don't think age works that way, even for leap-year babies."

"I can count my birthdays any way I want; so many people do, especially women of a certain age. Even you may, given time. So, I am ten."

"Then you're far too young for me."

"I like older women."

Scarlett started work on her other misbehaving boot. "Will Inspector Kanavou arrest Robert Rasmussen?"

"Not every son is Orestes."

"Who?"

"Son of Agamemnon and Clytemnestra; murdered his mother."

Scarlett looked up at him, holding his gaze as she always could. Finally he asked, "What?"

"I know you; you're thinking that son of hers couldn't find the asthma inhalers."

"A low percentage way to commit murder; what was the chance she'd have an asthma attack that would trigger a heart attack and die?"

"I'm not saying it was premeditated," Scarlett said warming to her theme. "It was bound to happen sometime. She's having a bad asthma attack. Her inhaler's empty. He makes it seem like he can't find any spares, even as he pockets them, and then dumps them before the cops question him."

"I thought you wanted this whole thing to go away without attracting any media attention."

"I do, but I also know you're thinking the same thing." Scarlett stood and, as they started walking down the concourse, said with expectant glee, "I bet they'll find she was loaded and he doesn't have a buck to his name. Look how he dresses: torn jeans and faded T-shirts at his age. He must be—what?—late thirties, early forties?"

"You could visit a nursery school and think a murder was in the offing."

"Ever hear of Leopold and Loeb?"

"They were university students."

"Kids compared to you." Scarlett grinned as she popped two of her favorite Penguin peppermints into her mouth.

"If you ever want to hear another proposal from me, you'll need to lay off the age jokes."

"I'm surprised you can still hear them."

"You're just happy the tour's name will stay out of the papers."

"After what happened in Slovenia, can you blame me?"

Race needed this job. It wasn't much, but it would pay for the summer in Europe if he was frugal on everything except sightseeing and sampling new food and wine. Besides, who else would hire him in his condition? Without this job, he'd end his life on some cold marble park bench in Piraeus, starved, sick and alone, having seen about as much of Europe as an agoraphobic monk.

"If you want Traveler Excursions to stay in business," Scarlett said, "we better keep our name pristine; so, no more deaths."

"My name."

"I paid our agreed-upon price for it."

"Dinner and a night at the Hotel Phoenicia; is that all a man's name is worth?"

"I didn't hear you complain any that night," Scarlett said, moving in close to stare up at him with her striking turquoise eyes that reminded Race of an Egyptian princess, her long, warm fingers stroking his cheek with a seductive intensity. "Besides, I have the contract, even if it was written on a restaurant napkin."

Race smiled, remembering that wonderful night in Valletta. Scarlett had an unrestrained enthusiasm in bed.

"Wish I hadn't drunk an entire bottle of Odyssey Grenache Rosé that night," Scarlett said, letting the Maltese wine's name roll off her tongue. "Of course, if I hadn't, I never would have agreed to your proposal." She stopped to test one of her re-tied boots.

"Why did you yell I was a doctor?"

"Just wanted the stewardess to let you help Mrs. Rasmussen. You have so much experience with lung stuff, and besides, you are a doctor."

"Just not the kind most people think of. Now the inspector thinks I'm the Great Imposter."

"Better than if he thought you were a murderer." Satisfied with her boot, Scarlett asked, "Should we let the tour use the restrooms or wait until Corinth?"

"We can hardly stop people using the bathroom after a 9-hour flight."

"We're already behind schedule and the airport restrooms are so small."

"Apparently the designers thought people would use the facilities with German efficiency."

Named for Greek Prime Minister Elefthérios Venizélos who led a Cretan uprising against the Ottomans in 1896, the new airport was designed by a German firm. It won a European Airport of the Year Award in 2004, just in time for Scarlett and Race's Traveler Excursion visit in April, not to mention the upcoming Athens Summer Olympics in August.

"If the bathrooms are busy, we'll never make up the time."

"Hardly anyone here," Race said, glancing down the nearly empty marble concourse beneath a white, metal latticework that supported the high ceiling. "Don't worry. The Corinth Canal has been there for more than 100 years, I'm sure it'll still be there even if we're behind schedule."

"Just as long as Inspector Kanavou doesn't decide that Mrs. Rasmussen was murdered and keeps us all in the airport for 100 years."

As Scarlett took roll, Race stood to one side. He enjoyed seeing her take charge as he listened to Greek Klephtic music on his second-hand music device in one ear, skimmed a new novel he had come across in the hospital in New York, *The Da Vinci Code*, and considered whether Robert Rasmussen stole his mother's inhalers before they boarded the plane and dropped them in a convenient trash can. Did he steal them from his mother's bag on the plane when she went to the bathroom and hide them in a seat back, an overhead compartment, a toilet or slip them into someone else's bag? How many places can you hide 2-inch inhalers on a 113-foot airliner? Worse, unless Inspector Kanavou seized the plane immediately, the inhalers would be gone forever as the jet was cleaned and prepped for its next flight. Race wondered if Mrs. Rasmussen had indeed been murdered or even just allowed to die. He hoped not, because if she had, it was going to be extremely difficult to prove either charge.

The tour had been booked for nine people, but with Hilda Rasmussen's passing and Rob handling her final details, they were down to seven. Always the businesswoman, Scarlett had researched each tourist to better cater to their likes and avoid their dislikes. Race wondered whether starting the tour with a death was on anyone's list of likes—maybe Robert Rasmussen's?

"I heard Sonja Weaver was on the tour," said an athletic woman bubbling with excitement, whose right wrist was in a black brace. From Scarlett's research Race guessed it was Gayle Garcia, a US Olympic team physiotherapist.

Race scanned the group, but failed to spot the luscious body and instantly recognizable face of the famous model/actress. Scarlett had crowed for a week after securing the booking. Even if Scarlett couldn't use Sonja's name or image to advertise, word would spread that the model had taken a Traveler Tour, or if Scarlett was lucky, a Traveler Excursion.

Scarlett called out each name in turn.

The dating website mogul, Dr. Peter Lodge.

"Present."

His daughter, Petra.

"Oh, yes?"

Her husband, ex-pro golfer David Fox.

"Yes, ma'am."

Physiotherapist Gayle Garcia.

"Yes, right here!"

Accountant Michael Cohen.

"Yes?"

Ex-fighter-pilot Charles Stirling.

No response.

Scarlett looked around and tried again; no response.

"Maybe he missed the flight," said David Fox, a tanned, muscular ex-pro golfer and current golf equipment salesman.

"Never missed a flight in my life," a confident voice boomed from afar, "even if I wasn't at the controls."

All eyes turned to behold a stunning couple cruising down the concourse toward them. Three bearded Orthodox priests in black cassocks turned as a handsome, weathered man strode alongside a curvaceous beauty who attracted every male eye in sight, whether orthodox, protestant or agnostic. Actress/model Sonja Weaver's perfectly symmetrical face with the famous pouty lips and cascade of reddish-black hair combined for a stunning entrance, as if the marble concourse was the red carpet at the Academy Awards.

"Mr. Stirling?" Scarlett asked.

"Chance, please," the man commanded, *noblesse oblige* personified.

Race noticed that Dr. Peter Lodge, the ex-professor and current dating website CEO, stared at Chance with a frown of concentration as if he was trying hard to remember something.

Chance Stirling had short-cropped, sun-lightened, black hair, just long enough in front to give it a wind-blown look, even in the airport terminal. His face had the appearance of warm stone, without a cell of fat. His cold, steady eyes attested to his two aerial kills in the Gulf War. Ex-US Air Force, Race knew from Scarlett's research that Chance was a yacht delivery captain part of the time and Sonja Weaver's husband all of the time.

For all his achievements and good looks, Chance was still just an accessory. Everyone focused on the model and ex-Playboy bunny turned movie starlet as she lifted a be-ringed hand in acknowledgement of Scarlett calling her name. Race knew Sonja was five years younger than her husband but for all her beauty she somehow looked older than the vigorous 38-year-old Chance. Sonja's wide eyes suggested sweet innocence, but Race saw in them vast experience at manipulating anyone she wanted, especially men.

With the roll complete, Race announced that if anyone needed cash they could get euros at an ATM across the concourse, which offered instructions in Greek and English.

As they walked past Race, Petra Fox whined to her ex-pro golfer husband, David, "I miss Macduff and Allegra."

"Sharon will spoil them rotten," David assured her with his soothing tenor voice. In khaki slacks, tasseled loafers and a red and black golf shirt, he moved with the fluid grace of an athlete. His short, straight black hair and skin the color of fine leather attested to Latino or possibly Native American blood in some branch of his family tree, well mixed with Anglo-Saxon branches and twigs. He was now a triathlete, Race knew, and at 43 looked shy of 30. David had been a pro at several clubs, taught privately, operated a driving range, and led tours of the finest golf courses in Scotland, Ireland and England. Now he toured the United States selling golf equipment by managing demonstration events at country clubs.

"We can't stay home forever just because of the dogs," David said, his smile widening as he gazed down at his worried wife.

"I like staying home," Petra whined, sounding far younger than her 42 years.

Race would have thought an outgoing athletic salesman-type like David would have married a buxom blonde with long tanned legs who was into the latest fashions. Petra was blonde and she wore simple black shorts, but they only served to display her unfortunately heavy legs. A loose-fitting polo shirt hid any curves she may have displayed. She looked somewhat ill and tired, her skin the color of cold oatmeal without a crystal of brown sugar. Race thought he saw traces of anger beneath her worried expression. David's sinewy arm possessively encircled her waist. In his other hand, he held his wife's white sweater and their carryon bags.

Race watched the couple walk past the ex-pilot Chance and his model/actress wife, Sonja. Holding out her neon red cell, Sonja told Petra, "Please use my cell to check on your dogs. I've spent a lifetime on sets from Tahiti to Cairo missing the ones I love." Her voice shifted down an octave and took on a seductive tone like molasses on diamonds as she added, "Hello, David."

Petra stared at the movie star as if a marble statue of Aphrodite had spoken, but David smiled and nodded hello, as if greeting an old acquaintance.

Sonja turned back to Petra, her neon red cell in her outstretched hand as her voice smoothly flowed back to a mezzo soprano and she said, "Please. It's all covered; one price whether I place one call to the States or a thousand."

"And she'll make every single bloody one of those thousand calls," Chance muttered. Race recalled that Chance had been stationed in England at Little Rissington for two years with the US Air Force.

As Petra stood to one side and talked with her dog-keeper across the Atlantic, Race realized the reason for the phone offer; Sonja chatted with David, standing as close to the ex-golfer as the most intimate of couples. While Race watched, the actress touched his forearm twice and upper arm thrice.

When Petra finished her call, Sonja accepted her cell back and sauntered off with her husband, Chance, who had been skimming his Greece guidebook. Even so, Chance hadn't failed to cast several proprietary glances at his wife as she chatted so intimately with David Fox.

"Can we get some snacks, David?" Petra asked, eyeing a concession across the concourse. "Do Greeks do vegan?"

"Do they take credit cards?" David asked. "I don't have any euros yet and the ATM has a line longer than for Masters tickets."

Dr. Lodge, Petra's father, who stood nearby, said, "I have euros."

Tall, wiry and white-haired with pale skin, Dr. Peter Lodge was 67. Over his shoulder hung a black camera bag which from its size and scuffed appearance suggested an avid photographer. From Scarlett's research, Race knew Lodge was an emeriti professor of psychology at Vincent College in Upstate New York. Lodge had started an online dating company, which had made thousands of marriages for users and a fortune for Lodge.

"How are you feeling, Dr. Lodge," David asked his father-in-law. "Long flight."

Lodge's face hardened, his lips forming a thin line as he snapped, "Fine."

Dr. Lodge handed Petra a 5-euro note and set off down the concourse alone. Scarlett and Race decided to avoid the busier bathrooms nearby and walked to the end of the concourse to another set. Race nodded to the Greek lady who tended the men's room and stepped into a stall. Having a middle-aged woman in the restroom to ensure it was clean and tidy had caused him some concern when he first heard about the custom, but now he was comfortable with it, although that comfort level didn't extend to using the urinal. He preferred the privacy of a stall.

"You treated me in a sordid way."

Race frowned, wondering who was talking to him and what he could have done to deserve such a criticism given his current situation.

"I did no such thing," a second male voice answered.

"Don't take me for a fool, Peter."

"I hope you didn't embark on this trip hoping to convince me to compensate you for some imaginary wrong you believe was done to you half a lifetime ago."

"I can see the only compensation I'll get is hearing you've died a long and painful death."

Something—or someone—slammed into a wall. The bathroom attendant screamed.

"How dare you," the second male voice snarled.

Race heard heavy footfalls storm out. Race finished his business, dropping the toilet paper into a wastebasket since paper of any size blocks the drains in Greece, and opened the stall door. Dr. Lodge stood at a sink, his camera bag slung behind him as he washed his hands. No one else save the agitated attendant was in sight.

Lodge asked Race, "Did you organize this tour solely to torment me with vile ghosts from my past or was it merely malignant chance?"

Lodge dried his hands and tossed a paper towel in the trash but missed. As Lodge strode out, the bathroom attendant cast a withering glare after the departing professor.

Outside, Race asked Scarlett, "Who came out of the men's room just before Dr. Lodge?"

"A member of our excursion." Scarlett looked down at her spiral notebook. "Michael Cohen, the accountant."

"Cohen didn't seem to have it in him." In his mid-fifties with a haggard demeanor, Cohen appeared in desperate need of a vacation or, Race thought with a sly grin, an affair. When Scarlett called out Cohen's name during the roll, the answer came in a faltering voice from the outer fringe of the group. Even so, Race had noticed that Dr. Lodge's head had swung around to stare back at Cohen.

Scarlett asked, "Didn't have what in him?"

"Cohen just had an argument with Lodge; gave as good as he got."

Scarlett's forehead furrowed and her turquoise eyes narrowed with concern. "I hope it won't spoil the tour for them."

"Don't you mean the excursion?"

"I was certainly not flirting with him," Sonja asserted, anger reddening her prominent cheekbones as Scarlett and Race approached their group at an exit. "Even if I felt the desire to, I don't have the energy after that hideously long flight. Did the pilot take us via Tokyo by mistake?"

"You sure as hell were rubbing up against him like a cat in heat," her husband, Chance said. His eyes were firmly on David Fox who stood with his wife, Petra, and their bags a few yards away—everyone else had used a porter—both studiously ignoring the marital spat. Even so, Petra looked far from happy, her face set in a tense scowl that would have frightened Achilles.

Sonja said, "I can't help it if you bumped me into him every step we took."

"I never even touched you," Chance said.

"Maybe if you did, you'd be of some use to me." Sonja turned on a high heel to stare haughtily out the glass doors toward the buses and taxis waiting for trade in the pale spring sun. "What a waste. I got myself camera ready on the plane and not a single reporter, photographer or cameraman in sight. Don't they have tabloids in Greece? Bruce positively assured me there would be coverage, or what's the point of coming on this hideous tour?"

"I wish you'd gone down with the *Lord of the Isles*," Chance said, "would have saved me a thousand days of cranial pain."

Once outside at their van, Race announced to the tour, "Thank you for choosing Traveler Tours—"

"Excursions," Scarlett corrected him with a pained look.

Race preferred the alliteration of Traveler Tours, but Scarlett had held out for what she argued was the more upscale sound of Traveler Excursions. The night in Valetta had sealed the name— Race would have agreed to any proposal she made that night—and it *was* her company. "We don't want just anyone to take our tours," she had said on more than one occasion. "You mean excursions," Race had corrected her on more than one occasion.

Race said, "Welcome to wonderful, intriguing, ancient—and modern—Greece."

David Fox and the physiotherapist, Gayle Garcia, using her uninjured hand, helped Beznik load everyone's bags into the van. Beznik, their driver, was a 21-year-old Romani-Greek Scarlett had met on an earlier reconnaissance trip.

"Let the hired help do the manual labor, David," Dr. Lodge urged his son-in-law, loud enough for everyone to hear, including the hired help: Beznik.

"Father, please don't say things like that," Petra Fox said, as she cast a look pleading for understanding at the others. "We aren't back in the nineteenth century."

"It's my pleasure to help," David said, his lithe frame easily hefting the largest bags into the van's rear cargo area. "I crave exercise after sitting so long."

"Take the greatest care with my luggage," Sonja told David as she set a languid hand on his shoulder. "I'd be utterly lost if anything happened to my cosmetics; they're all in crystal, of course."

Race wondered why Sonja Weaver, model and movie star, was slumming on their tour, even if it was an excursion.

"The pilot did mess up," Sonja announced, gesturing at the block-long yellow and blue Ikea store across the road. "He landed in Stockholm."

"Do you do much sailing?" Race overheard the dating website mogul Dr. Lodge ask Chance Stirling. Chance had donned aviator sunglasses to match his leather flight jacket.

"If I'm not flying, I'm sailing," Chance said.

"Do you own a boat?"

"Mostly sail other people's yachts."

Dr. Lodge nodded, his gaze downcast, thinking. Raising his gaze once more to Chance's cigarette-cowboy face, he asked, "I went on a cruise in the Mediterranean last year; most beautiful. Have you had the opportunity to sail the Med?"

"A fair bit, a fair bit."

Lodge nodded, yet Race got the impression he was agreeing with something far more important than idle talk about sailing.

Once all the bags were stowed and everyone was aboard, the diffident accountant Michael Cohen last of all, Race stood at the front of the van and, assuming his professorial voice, began his prepared introduction, "In Greece, you're at the crossroads of cultures and civilizations. Here you'll feel the grandeur of history and the warmth of being at the southernmost tip of Europe—and the sunniest spot on the continent. You'll discover the roots of modern political, social and philosophical thought; in short, you are in the cradle of Western Civilization."

Scarlett cast him a warning look from her front seat across from Beznik. What was wrong now?

"Greece has just over 11 million people, but it is extremely diverse," Race said.

Scarlett reached up and tugged Race's shirt sleeve. He bent down and she whispered, "That's enough. You're boring them."

"They're barely listening anyway." Everyone was stowing their carry-on bags and settling in.

"Case closed." Race hated it when Scarlett thought she was right, especially when she was.

"I'll shut up and they can guess what they're looking at the rest of the trip."

Abandoning the rest of his introduction, Race was about to sit down when Scarlett whispered, "Say something about Mrs. Rasmussen."

Race frowned, but Scarlett threw him a get-on-with-it look. Unfortunately, she was the boss.

"I've been asked to say something about Mrs. Rasmussen."

"Who?" Chance barked, looking up from his Greece guide-book.

"I believe she was the poor woman who died on the flight, was she not?" the accountant Cohen asked, looking at Chance with disbelief at his insensitivity.

"That flight came within a jolt of killing me," Sonja told David Fox, whom she had managed to sidle in beside. "The turbulence made me feel like when I played Dr. Kira Lee-Anne in my hurricane movie. It was…It was…What was it called, Chancey, darling?"

Chance just shook his head and continued to read his guide-book.

"*Twisted Love*," Gayle Garcia, the physiotherapist, called out with an eager smile. When everyone looked back at her, she sank back in her seat as if she had admitted to an addiction to trashy romance novels, professional wrestling and deep-fried Hershey bars.

"Wasn't a hurricane," Chance muttered. "Was a tornado."

Giving up, Race whispered to Scarlett, "No one cares if someone they don't know died."

"Unless they're famous—or rich."

Chapter 3

"Are you going to take the toll road?" Scarlett asked Beznik as he drove north out of the airport in Spata, south of Athens.

After the long flight, Race was glad he wasn't driving. He could rest, see some of Greece, sample some country music, Brooks & Dunn for the first time, and read his novel.

"The toll road is less nice," Beznik told Scarlett in a tone that implied only a blind Philistine would even consider such a route.

"We have to avoid the Athens traffic or we'll fall even further behind schedule; not to mention add to our gas bill."

Scarlett handed Beznik two euros for the toll. She handled all the money on the tours. Race knew she thought he was far too free with his money, but it wasn't like he needed to save for a rainy day; it had already poured in his life.

As Beznik reached 125 kilometers per hour on the toll road, the driver whispered over his broad shoulder, "Mr. Traveler."

Race pulled his ear buds out and leaned forward. Beznik confided in a whisper that the oil light had blinked twice. Race suggested stopping, but Beznik shook his dark head. "I just added oil. It will be fine. I will keep peeled eyes on it."

Race hoped Beznik was right about the oil. He was right about the route. A sunken road, the toll road offered views of blank concrete buttresses on either side of the six-lane thoroughfare. With such boring sights, Race closed his novel, found some soothing Enya on his music device and shut his eyes for a nap as he considered Mrs. Rasmussen's death and her apparently inept and, if Scarlett was to be believed, murderous son, Robert.

An hour later, as they disembarked at the Corinth Canal on the narrow isthmus to the Peloponnesus, Race set aside *The Da Vinci Code*—finished after his brief nap—and asked Scarlett, "Wasn't Beznik driving a tad fast?"

"Who got the speeding ticket outside Sienna?" Scarlett asked sweetly.

"We would have been run over if I hadn't gone twice the speed limit. Everyone in Italy does."

Scarlett popped more of her beloved Penguin peppermints into her mouth and said, "At least our van has the requisite crucifix and icon to keep us safe."

"Don't forget the evil eye," Race said, gesturing at the blue and white glass medallion dangling from the rearview mirror alongside a gold crucifix and a tiny Medieval painting of a saint flecked with gold. "They're the only things keeping Greece from just having the most dangerous roads in Europe, instead of the most dangerous on earth."

"I'll check our reservations in Nafplion. You take everyone over to the canal." Scarlett gave Race one of her warning looks and added, "Don't bore them."

"I've never bored you."

"I've just learned not to show it; a sign of respect for my elders."

"And betters?"

Scarlett couldn't get a signal for her cell, so Race watched his young boss stride across the parking lot toward the public phones in the restaurant area. He could watch her all day, coming or going. She had wonderful hips, shaped like an invitation.

Beznik opened the van's side compartment and took out a quart of oil. As the driver walked toward the front of the van, Race said, "You're dripping."

Beznik peered down at the shining drops on the pavement and inspected the container. "Leaks a little," he said and shrugged. Oil was smeared on his hands, but he didn't seem to mind.

"Should we call the rental company?"

"I will make sure the van operates, Mr. Traveler."

Leaving Beznik to his engine, Race announced, "Ladies and gentlemen, let me show you the wondrous Corinth Canal."

The physiotherapist, Gayle Garcia had already set off across the parking lot toward the canal with the dating website king Dr. Lodge striding along behind her, camera bag swinging at his side. They made for a striking contrast between her athletic vigor and his sedate, measured strides, although he certainly covered distance fast. In black track pants with white stripes on the outside of each leg and a navy blue sweatshirt, Gayle looked younger than her 47 years. She was well proportioned and tall for a woman, almost matching Dr. Lodge's long frame. Lodge wore a check button-down dress shirt and dress pants; a touch formal for a tour, Race thought, even if it was an excursion.

Race recalled from Scarlett's research that Gayle's boss for the Athens Summer Olympics had forced her to take the tour out of fear she'd been pushing too hard during the preparations for the games. Race wondered about the black brace on her right wrist; the result of pushing too hard on some athlete's sore back?

"Forgot my camera," Chance yelled, banging his hand against his forehead as if to punish his wayward memory. "Be with you in three."

Chance trotted back to the van. Beznik would let him in.

Catching up with Gayle and Lodge, Race led the way to the two-lane metal bridge that traversed the canal alongside a newer concrete span that carried the toll road. At the edge of the bridge he paused, waiting for the tour to gather around as he counted heads. Scarlett would never forgive him if he lost an excursionist.

"The Corinth Canal connects the Gulf of Corinth on the Adriatic"—Race pointed to the northwest—"and the Saronic Gulf on the Aegean Sea." He gestured to the southeast at the glittering waters of the storied sea across the road. "The canal cuts through the Isthmus of Corinth, making the Peloponnesian peninsula an island."

Everyone crowded forward to peer over the bridge's chipped metal railing down into the canal. Race had heard it was the most expensive three-mile ditch in the world, but refrained from reciting that tit-bit of information. Scarlett would frown on such levity with an excursion group; far more suitable for a tour.

"Says here it's 6.3 kilometers long and 63 meters deep with 8 meters of water, and was built between 1881 and 1893," Chance said as he returned with his camera and ever-present guidebook.

"True," Race said, then hurried on before Chance could steal more of his historical thunder. "The canal was planned by the Hungarian architects István Türr and Béla Gerster, who were also involved with early surveys for the Panama Canal. The Corinth Canal was started by a French company, which ceased work after only the two ends had been dug, due to a lack of francs. A Greek company led by Andreas Syngrou took over and completed the project, which was considered an engineering marvel at the time. It is cut down to sea level, avoiding the need for locks."

"Says here Nero started it with a golden pick," Chance said, looking up from his guidebook with an accusing stare as if Race had just uttered the blackest of lies.

"Actually, the tyrant Periander in the 7th century BC was the first to start a canal here," Race said with a smile. After years of teaching logic, he was well used to challenges by those who believed they knew more than he did; everyone liked to think they were logical. "Periander abandoned the project due to technical difficulties and instead constructed a simpler and less costly overland stone ramp, called the Diolkos, over which men could haul boats. Remnants of the Diolkos can still be seen alongside the modern canal."

"Says right here, Nero—" Chance began to read, earning a disapproving glare from Dr. Lodge.

"In the later years of the Roman Republic, Julius Caesar foresaw the advantages of such a canal, but never got far with the idea," Race continued, raising his voice as an exhaust-belching diesel truck sped across the bridge behind them. "Then, as Mr. Stirling mentioned, in AD 67 the emperor Nero ordered 6,000 slaves to dig a canal with spades. He took the first couple of swings with a golden pick, but I doubt he personally made much progress. The following year Nero died and his successor Galba abandoned the project as too expensive for even the empire's coffers."

Race spotted Scarlett speeding toward them. He rushed to wrap up his introduction. "The canal saves the 400-kilometer journey around the Peloponnesus for smaller ships wishing to go between, for example, Pireaus and the Adriatic."

"Doesn't look wide enough for a decent water hazard," the ex-golfer David Fox said, eyeing the deep, yet narrow canal. Sonja stood beside David, her long, reddish-black hair blowing free in the sea breeze. The hint of an exotic fragrance reached Race's nose.

"It's only 21 meters wide; too narrow for ocean freighters," Race said. "But 11,000 ships a year use it; mostly tourist boats." Scarlett was about to rejoin the group, so he hurriedly added, "At each end, roads cross the canal using submersible bridges that allow boats to pass."

"Very interesting," Scarlett said. "Now if you've all had your fill of Race's fascinating history lesson, please take an hour to look around. If we can all meet over at the restaurant promptly at 12:30, we can enjoy a fine lunch."

As the group dispersed, Petra held her arms across her chest, clutching her goose-pimpled forearms. "I thought Greece was hot," she said. A cool breeze blew in off the Saronic Gulf and an overcast sky allowed only occasional glimpses of the famous Grecian sun.

"I'll get your sweater," David offered.

"You can borrow mine, if you like," Chance said with a white-toothed smile. He took a gray U.S. Air Force sweatshirt from around his narrow waist and held it out to Petra.

"I could use a sweater," Sonja said. "Feels like Iceland in December."

"I'll get your sweater," David repeated to Petra, with a cool look of warning at Chance.

"I'll get it," Petra said, eyeing her husband and Chance as if they were ill-behaved schoolboys. She stalked off across the parking lot.

Chance held his sweatshirt out to Sonja, who waved it away with a be-ringed hand. "You can't expect me to wear that with this," she said, indicating with a sweep of her hand her gold sandals, white slacks, broad black leather belt, and snow-white silk blouse accented by gold earrings, bracelets and five-strand necklace.

Race hoped a night's rest would cure everyone of their jet-lag-induced grumpiness; at least he hoped it was jet-lag induced or it was going to be an extremely long tour.

With his music device playing a mix of 1980s hits, Race stepped over to look down into the canal. Layers of multi-colored rock were exposed like the edge of a child's encyclopedia with dozens of different colored sections. Bushes sprouted from the sheer sides like fluffy bookmarks as the canal gradually narrowed from top to bottom, like an inverted pyramid with its apex hidden beneath the water. The canal looked unnaturally straight, as if a Titan with an enormous scythe had cut a precise gash straight across the narrow isthmus with the precision of a meticulous surveyor. As wind rustled his hair, Race watched a cabin cruiser deep down in the narrow canyon of the canal cruise southeast toward the Saronic Gulf. Maybe if Scarlett finally said yes they could spend their honeymoon cruising Greece's wine-dark seas.

Race spotted the dating website king Dr. Lodge standing well back from the canal's edge taking pictures with an SLR digital camera atop a tripod. Lodge had attracted the attention of a female tourist. The woman was far younger than Lodge, but even from a distance Race could see her playing with the ends of her black hair and laughing, apparently enjoying the encounter immensely.

Race saw Beznik approaching, wiping his oily hands ineffectually on a red rag. As the driver drew near, Race asked, "Ever been through the canal?"

"Romani are known not for their love of the sea," Beznik said. "I got seasick on the Salamis ferry. My brother is in the navy, but he specializes in land operations."

"Scarlett got sick on a party boat on Lake Keuka in Upstate New York." Emerging from his daydreams, Race knew he had no hope of sailing any wine-dark seas with Scarlett at his side, unless he brought a hold full of Dramamine.

"The van is fine," Beznik said, "just an oil thirst.'"

"Where's the head?" Big, wide and imposing, Chance loomed over them, casting them into shade.

"I'll show you," Beznik offered, holding up his oily hands. "I must wash."

In the open area between the two souvlaki stands that comprised the dining area, one of which was closed during the shoulder season, Sonja eyed the bare concrete floor, marred white plastic chairs and nicked metal tables. "Is there anywhere else to eat?"

"I don't eat meat," Petra said.

"What about Corinth?" her husband, the ex-golfer, David asked. "Isn't it close? Must be some nice restaurants there."

"Sadly, we must stick to our schedule," Scarlett said. "We have much to see."

"Some of the best food is in the worst looking places," Chance said. "Maybe go the Greek salad route," he told Petra.

"I agree," the physiotherapist, Gayle said, peering at the menu, which was in Greek and English. "Better they focus on the food than the décor."

"As long as they are sanitary," Cohen said. The accountant rose on his toes to eye the kitchen behind the souvlaki stand's counter. "Do they use a rating system here for restaurants' cleanliness, like in the States?"

For lunch Scarlett drove a hard bargain, as usual leavened by ample flirting with the middle-aged manager. Based on the argument that she had brought the other tourists, Scarlett and Race feasted at half the advertised price on succulent, tender lamb *souvlaki*, vegetables bar-be-cued on a skewer over a charcoal fire, fries, and Greek salad. As he leaned back to savor his meal, Race wondered if the tomato in his mouth was even genetically related by a single gene to the cardboard-replicas for sale at supermarkets back in America.

"This bread is hard as a sand wedge," David complained.

"Soften it in the olive oil," Race said, pointing to a bowl. "Some say the custom dates to World War II when the Greeks had to eat stale bread, but it's probably far older than that."

After finishing his first course, Race ordered *stifado*. When he returned with the Greek beef stew with onions, garlic, and tomato sauce, Sonja said, "Wish I could eat like you. Every calorie I eat has to be burned off the next morning on the road or in the gym."

"I've always had trouble keeping weight on," Race said.

"Sounds like a dream," Sonja said, acting as if she was swooning at the very thought.

Race swallowed a couple of pills.

"Are those little beauties the secret of your ability to stay so svelte? Maybe I could try a few." Sonja rose to float over to Race.

"I don't think they'd work for you."

"Pretty please." Sonja draped herself over Race, her head on his shoulder. Up close she was even prettier than from afar. Her skin was like satin.

"I really don't think—"

"They're enzyme pills to help him digest food," Scarlett said, her words tinged with irritation and, Race hoped, jealousy.

Sonja frowned.

After silently asking Race's approval with a glance, Scarlett said, "He has cystic fibrosis; makes the mucus in his lungs and intestines thicker, so it's more difficult for him to extract nutrients from food."

Most CF patients take enzyme pills, which largely solve the digestion problem, but unfortunately in Race's case they didn't work perfectly and he still had to eat large meals to maintain his weight.

As Sonja retreated, Scarlett carefully noted the meal expense in her budget notebook and Race dug into his *stifado*.

"It's finally warming up," Petra Fox said, shedding her white sweater, which she had retrieved from the van before lunch. She had ordered a Greek salad with Romaine lettuce, plum tomatoes, English cucumber, green pepper, black olives, and feta cheese to meet her vegan requirements.

"I'll take your sweater back to the van," David offered. He had devoured every morsel of his lamb gyro, as if he hadn't eaten since his last triathlon.

"I can hold it," Petra said, placing her sweater on her lap and leaning back to bask in the sun, which had finally broken through the wispy cloud cover.

Scarlett told the group, "We have time for another look at the canal, if you wish."

"Nothing but a ditch compared to the Panama Canal, or even the Suez," Chance said. With a black felt pen, he checked off what Race guessed was the Corinth Canal entry in his guidebook. "What's next?"

"You must appreciate the technical feat it was to complete such a marvel more than 100 years ago," Dr. Lodge said, sounding every word the professor.

"Maybe," Chance said, "but I still don't have to look at it twice."

"Must have cost a bundle," the ex-golfer David Fox said.

"Shoot," Gayle said, digging through her purse with her good hand. "I left the euros I got at the airport in my carryon. Will they accept US dollars?"

"You'll get a poor exchange rate if they do," Scarlett warned.

"Beznik can give you the van's keys to get your euros," Race offered.

"Beznik can go with you," Scarlett said, eyeing Race. He sighed. Scarlett would have been security conscious in a nunnery.

Rising to join Gayle, David said, "I'll put Petra's sweater back."

Just after leaving the canal, Gayle asked, "What's that?" She gestured out the van's windows at a white butte with stark ruins atop it.

"Acrocorinth," Race said. "It was fortified by the Byzantines, who held it against the Crusaders for three brutal years. Then the Franks, Venetians and Ottoman Turks ruled it. It was the last line of defense before invaders could enter the Peloponnesus."

"When do we get there?" Chance asked, flipping through his guidebook undoubtedly, Race guessed, to find the entry for Acrocorinth.

"Could we have some AC, dear," Sonja called from the van's center row. "We're positively roasting alive back here." She fanned herself with a thick novel, which Race was surprised to see was George Eliot's *The Mill on the Floss*.

Beznik turned on the AC, although he frowned at Race. The thermometer on the dashboard read 74 degrees.

"I am sorry, but we aren't going to Acrocorinth," Scarlett said from the front passenger seat.

"Why not?" Chance demanded. Beside him, Sonja was making a call on her red cell phone. "Get off the damn phone, Sonja, enjoy the scenery." Sonja cast a patient smile at her husband, as one would a fractious child, and continued her call.

"We are visiting several other well-preserved castles and acropoleis, but we simply can't visit them all," Race said. "Greece has 17 World Heritage sites and thousands of historical ruins. You could spend a dozen lifetimes touring them all."

"How many of the 17 will we see?" Chance asked.

Race wondered if Chance had a checklist in his guidebook. "Mycenae and Tiryns, Mystras, the Acropolis in Athens, Olympia, Delphi, Meteora, and Rhodes."

"I'd have thought we'd be allowed to see Corinth," Chance said, sounding like a child deprived of candy on Halloween. "I mean, the guidebook says it 'boasts one of the most impressive, stunning and archeologically important acropoleis on mainland Greece.'"

Dr. Lodge, his ox blood leather carryon perched on his lap, the flap open as he rifled through the contents, said, "It should go without saying that such a site would be included as part of a comprehensive tour."

"But if, as Mr. Traveler said, there are thousands of such sites, how can we possibly see them all?" Cohen asked, his voice dropping into the barely audible range by the end of his tentative question.

"Can't see them all," David said, his arm around his wife, Petra. "I'm sure we'll see all the finest sites; that's what the brochure promised."

"There's an ancient quarry right there," Race said, pointing at a site. Centuries ago giant steps had been cut out of the slope near Clotea to extract blocks of rock. Today wildflowers bloomed amidst red, white and yellow poppies. The vanilla aroma of white heliotrope wafted through the van's vents. "It's probably not even in the guidebooks."

"Nope," Chance confirmed a moment later.

"Greece is riddled with thousands of such ancient sites," Race said. "Most are not large, overly special or well preserved, but attest to the wealth of peoples who have occupied all or part of Greece: Cycladians, Minoans—"

"Mycenians," Chance interrupted. "Dorians—"

"Athenians," Race said. "Spartans—"

"Persians—"

"Macedonians—"

"Romans—"

"Byzantines—"

"Frankish crusaders on their way to the Holy Land....Uh....."

"Venetians, Ottomans," Race said, eyeing the ex-fighter pilot, who appeared to have run out of names. Race was just hitting his stride. "Russians, British, and, finally, the modern Greeks themselves. Enough cultures to leave ruins to cover the world, let alone just Greece, which is only a little larger than New York state. Even so, Greece has more archeological museums than any country on earth."

"My God," Dr. Lodge exclaimed, "someone stole 1,200 euros from my bag."

Chance snorted. "Use a money belt. Only a doolie would leave a stack of cash in a van."

"It was zipped most securely in my bag," Dr. Lodge shot back.

"Was it wise to carry more than $1,500 in cash?" Cohen asked from the back row.

"I got a favorable rate of exchange from my bank in New York, so I took the opportunity to change all of the cash I would require for the trip," Dr. Lodge said, anger in his voice at being questioned about his choice of currency conversion options.

"Maybe you just mislaid it, Dad," Petra Fox said.

"Of course I didn't just mislay it," Lodge snapped back at his daughter. "It was here when we reached the canal. I extracted 20 euros for lunch and left the remainder in my billfold, and it is gone, too." He slapped closed his leather satchel and said, "It must have been the driver." Lodge's gaze bore into the back of Beznik's head as the young Romani-Greek drove along the twisting road through the low hills of Argolis.

"You can't possibly know that," Petra told her father.

"Do not presume to tell me what I know, Petra," Dr. Lodge said, sounding as if he was speaking to a seven year old.

Petra looked at her husband, David, pleading for support, but he remained silent.

Scarlett said, "I didn't see Beznik anywhere near your bag, Dr. Lodge."

"He remained with the van while we were viewing the canal," Lodge roared. "He could have taken it at any time."

"He must have done it," Sonja said and then added in a stage whisper to Chance, "After all, he is a Gypsy. At least, that's how it'd be in a movie—of course, it would turn out he was really a Gypsy prince, heir to all of Bulgaria or some such exotic place. Then he'd fall in love with a beautiful, but poor American, played by someone like me, and—"

"Oh, shut up, Sonja," Chance ordered.

Beznik remained silent, but Race could see the young man's neck and shoulders tighten under his pressed, white dress shirt.

"I trust Beznik completely," Scarlett said. "I have worked with him before and, besides, the van was locked while we were at the canal."

"He had the keys," Dr. Lodge said. "He let himself in. It had to be him." Lodge rose from his seat. "You! Driver! Return my money this instant! You thief! Brigand!"

Beznik took an instant to glance over his shoulder, glare at Dr. Lodge and then returned his attention to the narrow, gently winding road.

"You must be mistaken," Race said, keeping his voice calm.

"I demand that you search the brigand and his belongings," Dr. Lodge said, stooping to avoid hitting his head on the ceiling.

"Is that really necessary?" Scarlett asked. Her eyebrows turned down and her turquoise eyes narrowed as she tilted her head to the side, causing her glistening hair to swing out like an elegant curtain, displaying the eye-catching auburn streak. With such a look Race would have done anything she asked, but Lodge was well beyond any appeal, even a beguiling feminine one.

"It would clear the driver," Petra said.

"I believe you'll discover that only a judge can order such a search, or the police can do so if they have probable cause and there is imminent danger of contraband being destroyed," Cohen said. When everyone looked back at him with surprise, he added, his voice faltering, "That is, assuming Greek laws are similar to US statutes on the search issue. Does anyone happen to know?"

Everyone continued to stare at him.

Cohen swallowed and added, "I have a little legal training. I'm a forensic accountant. Didn't I mention it?"

"Not a word," David Fox said. "My dad was an attorney; wills and property law and such. Never touched criminal cases."

"I won't stand by while," Lodge began, before changing course and, turning on Scarlett, said, "If this is the sort of security provided on this tour, I will cancel immediately, demand my money back, and devote a significant portion of my time and money in the future to ensuring that anyone who even considers taking a tour from your slipshod outfit hears about the horrendous security provided for the paying clientele and the criminally unreliable staff you deem worthy of hire. I will see you and your puissant company bankrupt before the year is out."

Scarlett opened her mouth to respond, but Race could tell she quickly realized Lodge was in no mood for reason. Assuming her most conciliatory tone, she said, her voice betraying her reluctance,

"Beznik, we need to resolve this. I know this is a lot to ask and I hate to even suggest it, but will you please consent to empty your pockets and allow me to search your bag? It will help us clear this up right here and now."

"Seems a rude thing to ask a man," Gayle said.

Chance and Cohen nodded.

"Rather rude," David agreed. "I'd refuse; any man would."

"I will not," Beznik said. "I took nothing. You have no right, none at all."

"Bravo Zulu, young man, Bravo Zulu," Chance said with a broad grin, joined by nods from Gayle, David and Cohen. Sonja watched the unfolding drama with the aloof detachment of an actress waiting for the scene before hers to finish.

"You will regret this," Beznik told Dr. Lodge, his voice low and even, but filled with menace. "How dare you accuse me, just because I am Romani."

"I could not care less what you are, Romani, Gypsy, German or Gabonese," Lodge yelled back. "I only care that you are a thief."

"Dad, calm down, please," Petra urged, reaching out to her father for him to sit down. "It's just some money, pocket change, and you don't know who took it." Petra turned to her husband and said, "David, say something."

"Twelve hundred euros is far from pocket change," Dr. Lodge yelled, his eyes still locked on Beznik like a bird of prey's on a hare.

"Barely worth starting a war over," David Fox said, earning a look of loathing from his father-in-law.

"Enough, please," Race said. "We will leave this issue up to the police in Nafplion. Beznik, be so kind as to keep your eyes on the road. Dr. Lodge, please be seated."

Lodge did not move, glaring fixedly at Beznik.

Race said, "It is against Greek traffic regulations to stand while a vehicle is in motion, so please sit down, Dr. Lodge or we will be forced to pull over."

Lodge cast one last glare at Beznik, then at his daughter Petra's urging finally sat down.

"I didn't know you knew Greek traffic laws," Scarlett whispered as Race sat behind her.

"No better than Burmese traffic laws. Hopefully Lodge will have cooled down by the time we reach Nafplion."

"Maybe he'll even find where he misplaced his money."

Scarlett's cell buzzed. After a brief call, she whispered, "Robert Rasmussen's finished with the embassy people. He wants to rejoin the tour. Doesn't seem to be mourning his mother much."

"Everyone mourns in their own way."

"Some with a little extra cash to soften the loss."

They sped past fields of blood-red poppies. White, pink and salmon oleander sprouted amongst yellow broom. Jagged white rock outcroppings reflected the sun's stark rays now that the clouds had scudded on to the east. They passed white Greek Orthodox churches with reddish-orange tile roofs and blue domes, new two-story white-washed houses and crumbling grey stone farmhouses.

"Probably abandoned by families moving to Athens," Race said, trying to shift the tourists' minds from wallets back to Greece's sights. "Athens ballooned from 10,000 people in 1834 to 3.6 million in 2001 as Greece transitioned from an agricultural to an industrial nation."

"Was that a swastika?" Cohen asked, his head swiveling to peer in disbelief at what he had just seen.

"Greece has a wide range of political thought from the extreme right to the extreme left," Race said, "although the extremes are just that, extremes."

"There's a hammer and sickle to even things out," David called out with a boyish grin, pointing at red graffiti on a partially collapsed stone wall by the side of the road.

"Are communists legal here?" Chance asked. "I thought all of them had been relegated to the dust bin of history."

"Greece is the birthplace of democracy," Race said. "Even communists are allowed."

They passed a sign for Argos.

"Says here to avoid Argos," Chance read from his guidebook. "Confusing streets."

"It's a wonder the Argonauts ever got out of the city to join Jason on his quest for the Golden Fleece," Race said, "given that every street seems to be one-way in the wrong direction."

Beznik drove along streets past gas stations and homes, turning right and left and left and right past backyards adorned with rusted cars, twisting and turning in no apparent consistent direction. Just as Chance wondered aloud whether they were lost, Beznik maneuvered the van across railroad tracks, between two overhanging plane trees that brushed the van's roof, and out of the city of 30,000 onto a straight two-lane road.

Five minutes later they entered Nafplion—or Nafplio, Navplion or Nauplia. There were, Race knew, six ways to write the letter "E" in Greek, which only compounded the problem that since Greece has been ruled, invaded, occupied by or traded with everyone from the Cycladians and the Minoans to the Russians and the British, every city, town and historic site has multiple names in several different languages.

"Nafplion is on the Argolic Gulf in the first notch of the Peloponnesus just south of the isthmus," Race explained. "Only 140 kilometers from the capital, Nafplion is a favorite romantic weekend getaway for Athenian couples."

They passed through a series of 1980s-style glass and concrete apartment buildings before entering the old city with its two- and three-story white, tan and pale orange buildings. Blue and white Greek flags fluttered in gusts from off the gulf, while a dramatic cliff hemmed the city in against the coast.

Beznik turned left just before a Medieval city gate. The van's engine whined as it climbed the steep road that took them above the town of 13,000 to park at an abandoned hotel nestled in a notch in the steep ridge. Above the derelict hotel loomed Palamidi Fortress, standing stark atop an ashen massif, while slightly lower down and farther along the peninsula stood Akronafplia Castle.

"Why's the hotel abandoned?" David asked. "Prime location. I could drive a golf ball clear across Nafplion and into the gulf from here."

"It was state-run," Scarlett said, "part of a chain, Xenia, famous across Greece for apathetic service. Even its breathtaking location couldn't save it from abysmal customer service."

The tour gazed at the amazing views southwest across the sparkling waters of the Argolic Gulf and through the notch to the sea on the other side of the peninsula. As they disembarked from the van, a brisk wind twirled Sonja's silk scarf around like a whip. The crisp scent of the sea reached Race even as he caught the aroma of wild sage, rosemary and thyme. Across the parking lot, a gravel path led 50 feet down to Pension Marianna. A bright yellow two-story building with dark wood trim which looked as if it had been salvaged from a violin factory, the pension clung to the steep incline in the last row of buildings at the top of the city, just beneath Akronafplia Castle. Below, Race could see the harbor with its mini-castle, the Bourtzi, guarding the entrance, the shimmering marble town square, and Nafplion's narrow cobblestone streets forming an irregular lattice amidst the town's orange tile roofs.

"Should we hold Beznik?" Scarlett whispered to Race. "I mean, just in case."

"He's twice as strong as I am, doesn't have CF, and we're tour guides, not police."

"You look like you could take him," Scarlett said, patting the seat of his jeans.

Race grinned at the compliment and gave her a quick kiss.

"Where's the police station?" Dr. Lodge demanded.

"Dad, maybe we should wait and make sure the money isn't just misplaced," Petra said. She looked apprehensive, as if her father was on the verge of making a grave mistake. She had her arms wrapped across her chest, chilled by the sea breeze that hurtled through the notch in the peninsula like a wind tunnel set upon high. Her husband, David Fox stood beside her like a loyal, if reluctant, soldier.

"I am obliged to lodge a formal complaint against the driver related to the theft of my 1,200 euros," Dr. Lodge said. "I really have no choice, Petra. Law and order must be upheld."

"I'll find out where the police station is," Race offered, hoping to delay Lodge. The money might turn up in the meantime.

With a sour look, Dr. Lodge said, "I'll locate the police station myself, thank you very much."

"Maybe we could just reduce the price of your tour," Scarlett offered with an ingratiating smile, which Race knew was entirely put-on. She detested giving anyone money back.

"If it is ascertained that your company is at fault, I expect a complete and total refund," Lodge said. "I also expect your man to be locked away for a suitably long internment, and an apology from him, from you and from your company. If none is forthcoming, then I plan to use all of the considerable resources at my disposal to ensure that Traveler Tours receives the lowest available ranking on every website on the Internet." The ex-professor and dating website magnate stalked off across the gravel parking lot.

Race announced to the group, "You have a free afternoon and evening to explore beautiful, romantic Nafplion."

"Or to take a nap," Petra said. "Can we call Sharon and check on the dogs?"

"Oh, come on," David said. "We should explore. It's our first day in Greece."

Sonja was already on her neon red cell phone. Chance asked no one in particular, "What's the point of going on vacation when she has that damn thing in her ear the whole bloody time?"

Race was aggrieved to see the tour members pointedly avoid letting Beznik handle their bags. David and Gayle with her one good hand did the stevedore's share of the unloading. David even handed Beznik the young Romani's own bag as the ex-golfer gave Beznik a reassuring pat on the shoulder; so much for innocent until proven guilty.

Chapter 4

Day 2: Sunday, April 18, 2004

"I wanted to thank you, Mr. Traveler, for trying to help," Rob Rasmussen told Race early the next morning. They stood in the moonlight in the space between the pension and the castle wall, which provided just enough room for a row of pruned mall orange and lemon trees. A stone tower protruded from the wall, its niches and chinks providing homes for light-green moss, plants and shrubs, as well as perches for warblers and rock-thrushes, which chattered at the early-morning intrusion by the two humans. "I...I wish you had been able to save her, but I guess it was her time. She was old."

Robert looked tired and wan, his face the color of cold ash. He had arrived from Athens an hour before by hired car. Race wondered whether Rob, even in his forties, shaved more than once a week. His boyish looks were accentuated by baggy shorts with multiple oversized pockets bulging with only Rob knew what treasures, worn sneakers, sagging white socks, and a T-shirt, which Race guessed advertised a computer game depicting a knight locked in mortal combat with a red three-headed dragon. With his overdeveloped forearms, Rob looked ready for hand-to-hand combat himself, although one of his hands was bandaged from where he cut it crushing his mother's empty inhaler the day before.

The young man eyed Race, probably trying to guess his age. Rob said, "I mean, she was 69 and she'd been warned."

Was Rob about to confess to threatening his mother?

"Her doctor told her the asthma might trigger a heart attack. She had one 15 years ago."

"If she'd had an inhaler, I might....." Race glanced over at a blue-gray thrush as it landed on a nest 15 feet up the castle's stone wall. He looked back at Rob and asked, "Did you ever find your mom's backup inhalers?"

With deep furrows in his forehead, Rob's dark eyes peered out through slits as he shook his head. "I swear she had several in her carryon. She didn't want to risk losing them, so she carried them all on the plane to make sure she'd have them."

A black bird with red flashes, too swift to identify, swished past their heads on its way out to an early morning hunt.

"Did you search her carryon?"

"The police searched it, even stripped out the lining: nothing. Ruined now. She just got it, too; $265."

"Race, we should be going," Scarlett said as she appeared at the pension's back door. Her face was tinged red from her morning regimen of 60 sit-ups, 60 push-ups and 90 jumping jacks, as well as assorted stretches that Race could only marvel at when he was present. "Oh, Rob, I'm so sorry for your loss," she added with a glance at Race as if to ask, 'How sorry is he?' Turning back to Rob she added, "So very sorry." After a suitable pause, she asked, "Are you rejoining the excursion?"

"I plan to," Rob said, as if attesting to a plan to conquer Everest without oxygen in shorts, a T-shirt and flip-flops. "Mother wanted to see the sunrise from Palamidi Fortress."

Race wondered if someone who appeared so young could be a murderer, even if it appeared to be a murder of omission, not commission, although stealing someone's life-saving medicine was certainly a borderline case.

The jet-lagged tour members emerged from the pension and ambled up the gravel path lit by the pension's exterior lights toward the parking lot.

"Did you do your CPT?" Scarlett asked Race. "And your pills, or are you going to wait until breakfast?"

Race nodded about his chest physical treatment, which broke-up the mucus that formed in his lungs overnight, and said, "I'll do pills at breakfast. It'd be easier to keep tabs on me if we shared a room; save money, too."

"I'd rather save my heart."

"Have you?"

Scarlett just smiled as they followed Rob up to the parking lot. Dr. Lodge strode into view, his eyes narrowing when he spotted Beznik near the van. Beznik met Lodge's stare with a glare of unadulterated hatred.

"Sorry I'm late," the ex-golfer, David Fox, his hair wet, said as he and Petra joined the group at the van. "Had a quick jog down to the end of the peninsula. Wonderful paved path; spectacular."

Petra cast a look at Rob—was it fear or loathing?—and edged away from him to the other side of the group.

"Sonja's just showering after her morning jog," Chance said. "She'll be up in a minute. Damn cold this morning." He stamped his hiking boots and jammed his hands deep into his sheepskin-lined leather flight jacket. A thick guidebook, its pages well thumbed, was wedged under his arm.

David and the physio, Gayle helped Beznik load everyone's daypacks into the rear of the van. Race noticed that everyone kept a close eye on their bags and on Beznik.

"We should be going or we'll miss the sunrise," Scarlett urged as she looked at her watch. "Where's Ms. Weaver?"

"Here, my dear," Sonja called as she floated up the path, her outfit fluttering in the pre-dawn breeze. Even in the semi-darkness lit only by light from the pension, her bright red harem pants and low-cut purple blouse accented by a wide white belt and white leather sandals made her entrance memorable. A beaded necklace held a gold medallion nestled in the valley between her ample breasts.

"My God," Scarlett whispered to Race. "She can't make it up to the fortress in that, can she?"

"Whoever doesn't want to climb up to the castle, can wait and ride up in the van when Beznik brings up our bags and breakfast," Race announced.

"I shall walk," Sonja proclaimed, striding across the parking lot.

"Does she even have a clue where we're going?" Scarlett asked. "Did you tell Beznik to be at the castle promptly at 6:30?"

"Twice."

"Then he'll only be 15 minutes late," Scarlett said with a smile. "Greek time. Did Dr. Lodge go see the police?"

Race shrugged before setting off to lead the group. He had gone to the police station the previous afternoon, but even though they spoke enough English to understand what he wanted, they refused to tell him anything. Race hoped Dr. Lodge hadn't involved the police, but from the glares Lodge cast at Beznik, he guessed Lodge had reported his missing wallet. Race had to figure out what had happened to the wallet; if he didn't, the tense mood would ruin the tour for everyone and he would be lucky to ever lead another one.

With one earbud in to provide background music, Dire Straits' *Brothers in Arms*, and a novel, *The Shakespeare Drug*, in hand for any pauses during the day to read, Race caught up with Sonja. They led the way along the road, which meandered two hundred yards down the steep hill to the edge of the pre-classical town. In the light from the town, Race noticed the flawless skin of the actress striding with great purpose beside him. Sonja may have been past her prime as a model, but she was still a more attractive woman then 99 percent of the females on the planet could ever hope to be, even at the peak of their beauty.

"You set a brisk pace," Race said. Gayle and Sonja's husband Chance were keeping up with them, while the grieving Rob, the accountant Cohen, Dr. Lodge, Petra and her husband, David straggled out behind in a disorderly column, with Scarlett playing sheepdog to keep them somewhat together, moving, and on time.

"You must keep in shape," Race said. Sonja's perfume smelled of fresh-cut flowers with a strong base of old mahogany; feminine, yet with an unbreakable core.

"Five miles a day, six days a week," Sonja said, before adding in a throaty whisper, "Don't believe all that crap about models and actresses being born with those bodies. No one is, at least not past 25. Helps the image if you say it's all God and genetics; it's all about image, lover." She smiled, displaying a row of teeth like pearl tombstones.

They walked in silence for a moment, taking in the just discernable outline across the sleeping town of the serene Argolic gulf.

"Your wife—"

"Scarlett? She's not my wife."

"Oh, I thought..."

"I've asked her a dozen times; no luck."

"The age difference?"

"More her penchant for long-term planning."

Sonja frowned and waited for Race to explain. When he didn't, she said, "By the by, my bed last night lacked a box spring. Could you be a dear and look into it?" She cast him a warm look that made him believe, if only for a moment, that he was the only person in the world who mattered to her.

Emerging from her gaze, he said, "Most beds in Greek pensions just have a mattress set on wooden slats; practical and comfortable."

"Barbaric." Sonja shook her head and snorted with disdain. "No bathtub, either. I thought you said this was the cradle of Western civilization."

"The cradle, not the bathtub. Bathtubs are rare in pensions. You find them in hotels, though. Pension showers are usually a drain in the floor with a tile ridge around it. The shower curtain is optional, since the entire bathroom is usually tiled. Some places you shower with the water running down a drain in the center of the room."

"Room for more people, I suppose," Sonja said leering at Race. "Maybe you'll join me some time for a lather and hot rinse?"

"Tempting. Just remember to remove the towels and toilet paper before you shower—alone or with friends."

Sonja laughed, a lilting trill that seemed more of an act than a true response. She eyed the earbud in his ear and his book. "The ultimate multi-tasker?"

"I like to fill my days with new experiences."

"Sounds like my first husband, although his new experiences tended toward the young, flexible and slutty." Sonja glanced out over the sleeping city. "How did you end up a travel guide?"

"I was a professor of logic." They turned right, up the hill. "Then, rather late as such things go, I learned I have cystic fibrosis. I wanted to see the world while I still can."

She stopped and gave him a look of the greatest sympathy. "I am sorry. Can they do anything?"

"Far more than they could 20 years ago."

"How awful knowing that you're going to die; I don't think I could live knowing that."

Race refrained from mentioning that even actresses died.

"You must be very brave," Sonja said, peering at him as if he was a rare diamond.

"Bravery implies choice, of which I have almost none."

Race stopped and waited for the tour to gather at the foot of the stone stairs that zigzagged up the cliff to the fortress.

"Are you up to it, Dad?" Petra asked as she gazed up the cliff face at the illuminated walls of the castle 700 feet above.

"I'm fine," Dr. Lodge snapped. "When was the fortress constructed?"

"Fortifications on the mountain date back to the Mycenians, whose city we will visit later today," Race said. "The Byzantines also built a castle here, but the walls you see were erected by the Venetians in the 1500s, later modified by the Franks. Palamidi Fortress itself was built by the Venetians between 1711 and 1714. It immediately rendered the Venetian's Akronafplia, which it overlooks, militarily useless."

Gayle asked, "The Venetians made their own castle obsolete?"

"Better than an enemy doing it," the ex-fighter pilot, Chance said.

Dr. Lodge asked, "Are we going to be given the opportunity to tour Akronafplia Castle?"

"Not much of it left; Palamidi is far more interesting." Before anyone could argue, Race forged on, "Palamidi Castle played an important role in the Greek War for Independence, when Nafplion became Greece's first capital. Later the Nazis occupied the fortress during World War II. It offers stunning views of the city and the Argolic Gulf on both sides of the peninsula, but to see it, you have to climb 999 steps."

"No elevator?" Sonja asked, her head poised elegantly at an incline that favored her pert nose.

Race realized she was back playing her role; no longer a fit, strong young woman logging five mile runs, reading George Elliott, and interested in the lives of others, but a spoiled starlet, expecting everything and everyone to cater solely to her comfort. He said, "It might be best if you let Beznik drive you up."

Sonja threaded past several people to rub up against David Fox, wrapping her slender arms around his muscular left arm. Her movement reminded Race of a metallic liquid; graceful, smooth, slinky, and faintly dangerous. "David can carry me if I wilt. He's so strong and I weigh barely a trifle. His little wife won't mind me borrowing him, I'm sure, will you dear?"

Petra cast the actress a look that rivaled Medusa's stare.

As the group started up the steps, Race told Scarlett he was going to start investigating the missing wallet. He caught up to Dr. Lodge and after a few pleasantries, asked when he had last seen his wallet.

Concentrating on the uneven steps, which had twin depressions in the middle worn down by millions of footfalls over the centuries, Lodge said, "I spoke to the police. They will thoroughly investigate the matter, I am certain, identify and incarcerate the culprit. The Gypsy will be punished."

"I doubt it."

Lodge stopped, already breathing hard, and stared at Race as a pair of thrushes flitted past.

"The police are busy with the Olympics preparations," Race said. "I doubt they have much time for a missing wallet."

"I was assured it would be a top priority. I am certain the Greeks value their tourism industry, especially its image in the United States."

"A missing wallet won't stop people coming to the Olympics; not like it's a murder." Race needed Lodge's cooperation and he wouldn't get it if Lodge thought the police were going to find his wallet.

Lodge took a deep breath, peered with determination up the stone stairs and resumed his climb up the massif. Race stayed with him. It was easy to keep up. His lungs might be ravaged by cystic fibrosis, but he was in good shape. Before his tune-up in New York, Race had spent two months touring Europe, mostly on foot—cheaper, and you saw far more, besides the cardiovascular benefits.

"Did anyone see the money in your wallet?"

"How could I possibly know what other people saw?" Breathing rapidly and his face flushed red, Lodge paused on one of the many stone landings. Race wondered whether Scarlett should have asked each guest to sign a medical release of liability.

"I took no precautions to hide the money. I assumed, incorrectly and with inadequate foresight as it transpired that the tour you lead is safe and secure."

"Why did you leave your wallet in the van?"

Lodge pursed his lips and after a moment's reluctance said, "The wallet has some sentimental value. A gift from an old, dear friend. I did not want to lose it, the truth be told. I thought it more prudent to leave it in the locked van than risk some pickpocket relieving me of it. I have read that there are many such scoundrels in Greece at the major tourist sites."

"Not many people, let alone pickpockets, at the Corinth Canal in April."

Race followed Lodge as he began to climb again, now trailing the rest of the tour, which straggled out in an uneven column up the steep stairs. Lodge's camera bag thumped against his thigh with each step.

"I know you are trying to clear your employee, which is completely understandable and commendable," Lodge said, "but your driver—"

"Beznik."

Lodge gave Race a cool look of warning, like a leopard about to pounce. "Beznik"—he said the name with disgust—"was at the van while everyone else was at the canal. Beznik had the keys. Beznik must have stolen my wallet. In any case, as the operator of this tour, Ms. Wynter is ultimately responsible. If my wallet is not found and returned with all of its contents, including all of my money, I will do everything in my considerable power to ensure Traveler Tours never conducts another tour anywhere on this earth, ever."

"Excursions."

"Pardon me?" Dr. Lodge asked, his eyes narrowing and his nose rising in the air.

"Traveler Excursions, not tours; I'd hate for you to ruin some rival company with a similar name." Before the anger building in Lodge could burst forth, Race added, "Anyone might have stolen the money."

As if lecturing a class of freshmen, Lodge said, "I have given it some considerable thought. Neither Petra nor her husband, David has any reason to steal from their father. Petra even offered to cover the loss so we could avoid what she called this 'unpleasantness.' She has always been imprudent with money. The pilot, Chance Stirling and his wife, the actress, I would not even consider as suspects, given their wealth and, furthermore, he is an officer in the United States Air Force."

"Retired."

"I assume his honor did not retire with him. Robert Rasmussen stands to inherit, I assume, from his recently deceased mother, so why would he steal, leaving aside the question of who steals after having just lost their mother? As to Cohen, I do not believe he would do such a thing for what I am sure he considers trivial recompense for what he mistakenly believes I owe him. In any case, he does not have the wherewithal to raise his voice, let alone steal so much as a hotel soap. Which leaves one and only one suspect: Beznik."

"You're forgetting someone."

"You?" Lodge asked with a patronizing smile. "Ms. Wynter?"

Race shook his head.

Lodge stopped halfway up a section of stairs, one foot a step higher than the other. Race stopped beside him as a fishing boat far below sounded its horn. The ex-professor frowned. Lodge, his voice lower and far less certain, said, "Possibly, maybe....Gayle Garcia." Emotions flashed across Lodge's face: confusion, happiness, melancholy, and anger. "She had no euros to pay for lunch, but then she went to the van and returned with cash." Dr. Lodge peered at Race, but his eyes were seeing something far away. "And she hates me."

"Why?" Race asked. Did Lodge and the phsysio, Gayle even knew each other? She lived in Los Angeles; he lived in upstate New York.

Lodge started climbing again, much faster.

They stopped atop a tower on the stone finger of the fortress that ran down the mountainside on a prominent spur, pointing down at Nafplion like a scimitar about to cleave the city in two. The tower provided sweeping views of the harbor and the head of the gulf, at least in daylight; in the pre-dawn darkness there was just a vague hint of the coastline. At the head of the bay they could see the illuminated 6th century BC fortress on Larissa hill, the acropolis of Argos.

Race looked up. Even though they had reached the bottommost part of the fortress, they still had six or seven more sections of zigzag stairs to climb to reach the citadel.

As the tour set off again, Race asked Lodge, "Did you see anything on the plane before Mrs. Rasmussen passed away?"

"A mild commotion," Lodge said, the tension in his body easing as he was asked about something other than Gayle Garcia and his wallet. "Petra told that thirty-something child, Robert, to help his mother. She had to yell at him before he paid any attention." Dr. Lodge glanced up at Rob Rasmussen, who was boyishly leading the way, his grief apparently put aside as he bounded up the stairs. "He and his mother were in the row behind us. The whole incident rather upset Petra. She said something about the boy going too far, much too far. But ask her about it. I did not even realize they were related. Ten-hour flight and they did not speak a word to each other until the lady was dying; evidently no love lost there."

When they reached the top of the stairs, glistening with sweat, winded and thirsty in the quarter-light before sunrise, Race could just discern the walls, bastions, moats, battlements, and towers that formed the mighty fortress atop the peninsula's central ridge.

"Only 857 steps," Rob proclaimed, shaking his head in disappointment.

"Felt like eight thousand to me," Sonja said, dramatically dabbing at her glistening brow with a colorful scarf. Race noticed she wasn't even breathing hard.

"This is the Agios Andreas Bastion, named after that church," Race said, pointing at a tiny stone chapel. "Other bastions are scattered around the complex, all cited for maximum defense. They form one of the finest examples of early 18th century military engineering in the world."

David, Gayle and Rob set off to explore the vast site, dotted with clumps of prickly pear or cow's ear, Race was uncertain which. Petra, Cohen and Dr. Lodge were catching their breath, leaning against a rampart, admiring the view of the city lights in the darkness below. Chance tried to read a guidebook in the half-light, tilting it this way and that as he peered at its pages.

"Please be careful," Scarlett called after Rob as he bounded up a steep ramp supported by five stone arches to the top of the battlements far above them. "Dangerous areas are not roped off."

"Personal injury lawyers haven't discovered Greece yet?" Cohen asked between gasps for breath.

"What a cool place," Rob exclaimed with boyish glee from the rampart above. Race wondered whether the loss of his mother would hit Rob later—grief sometimes took time to appear—or maybe there was no grief in him.

Race led the others up the stone ramp in the diffuse light cast by the town below to the top of a wall that would offer the most dramatic views of the sunrise. Dr. Lodge took his digital SLR camera out of its protective case. The ex-professor stopped at a flat area and prepared to snap photos well away from the rampart's inner edge, which lacked a railing.

Race said, "The Turks took the castle in 1715."

"In God's name, how?" Chance asked, tearing his eyes from his guidebook to scan the defenses with his experienced warrior's eyes. "A kindergarten class with brooms could defend this place against a regiment of Marines."

"On these three sides the cliffs are unscalable, but over there"—Race gestured along the ridge toward the landward side—"the approach is far more gradual. The road comes up that way; the way the Turks attacked. They breached the outer wall, smashed an inner wall and broke through into the main fortress."

"Here comes the sun," Scarlett announced. All eyes turned to the east as the flaming orange orb spilled its light over the lip of the Aegean, casting glittering rays across the wine-dark sea.

As Scarlett and Race toured the well-preserved battlements, they stopped often to take in the views. On one side of the rugged peninsula, Nafplion's orange tile roofs spread out below them in the sliver of land between the massif and the sea, while on the other side, firs stood lonely sentinel on the strip of land between the cliff and the rocky beach.

Race said, "Nice place for a summer house."

"Not that you'd ever stay long."

"I might for you." He kissed her cheek, so smooth, soft and warm. He could smell her beloved Penguin Peppermints.

A woman's scream pierced the morning's serenity.

Race ran down a flight of worn stone steps two at a time toward where the scream had originated. He sprinted across an overgrown courtyard, dashed up a flight of crumbling stone stairs and reached the top with David Fox. They stood just outside a cannon embrasure. Within it, Rob crouched at the outer edge, his arms outstretched. For a moment Race thought Rob was knelt in prayer to the rising sun. Race stepped into the embrasure and only then spotted Gayle dangling from Rob's hands. Blood seeped from the bandage on Rob's right hand where he had crushed his mom's inhaler. Race could just see the physiotherapist's head as she hung out over the abyss. Pale faced and glistening with terror-induced sweat, Gayle's eyes were stretched wide open as she screamed.

Race and David rushed forward. They knelt on either side of Rob, whose arms quivered from the effort of supporting Gayle. Race grabbed Gayle's uninjured arm. David grabbed her other arm just past the black half-cast. A pebble fell from beneath Race's hiking boot, spinning down, down, down, and finally out of sight toward the rocky beach 700 feet below. Ignoring the deadly drop inches from his toes, Race said, "Lift."

The three men heaved. David's hand slipped. Gayle dropped three inches. She screamed. Race held on even more tightly to her other arm. Rob's muscular arms bulged from the effort of holding Gayle with the sudden added weight.

David reached down and grabbed Gayle's bicep with both hands, avoiding the cast. Race saw David's knuckles turn white; he would not lose his grip again.

"Lift," Race said, "now."

Race wheezed. He felt as if his lungs had been squeezed flat. His right hiking boot slid an inch on the pebbles strewn across the stone embrasure. Fearing he would fall over the edge and take everyone with him, Race pushed his heel down and stopped his slide just as his toe went out over the precipice.

"Lift," Race repeated.

Rob slid forward a couple of inches even as they hauled.

"Lift," Race urged.

Inch by inch the three men hauled Gayle up. Finally they hauled her onto the stone embrasure. She lay on her side panting as if she had just completed a triathlon, while being chased by demons.

"I thought it was a walkway," she gasped.

"It's a cannon embrasure," Rob said, his voice calm.

Gayle scrambled on all fours farther back from the edge. Rob helped guide her. They made an odd pair: Rob so boyish and youthful looking but with a layer of what could only be called baby fat all over his body, save for his muscular arms; Gayle middle-aged, but hard, muscular and, even shaken, moving with the smooth assured fluidity of an athlete.

"I walked out to take a picture," Gayle said between gasps as she sat against the wall well back from the precipice. "Suddenly I realized it ended in a cliff. Then, he...." She stared at Rob with an uncertain, dazed look.

"I grabbed her," Rob said. "I thought she was going to fall." Sweat glistened on his face, arms and neck. His T-shirt stuck to his chest.

"I didn't hear him come up behind me," Gayle said, her words coming out in a rush now. "He startled me and I fell." She kept looking at Rob as she slid on her bottom even farther away from the edge—and from him.

"I caught her and held on until you two arrived," Rob said.

A frown flitted across Gayle's face.

As the other excursionists arrived, Rob re-told the story. Scarlett was in full damage control, ensuring Gayle was alright and that the others would be extra careful from now on, even while stressing how safe Greece's ancient sites really are for visitors.

Race slumped against a wall. Wiping sweat off his hands onto the thighs of his jeans, he wondered whether Rob had tried to murder Gayle because she had seen him steal his mother's inhalers. If so, why hadn't she told Kanavou?

Scarlett made sure Race was alright, then whispered, eyeing Rob with a wary look, "I don't ever want to be alone with that kid."

"Just avoid cliffs," Race whispered. "And airplanes."

"Why steal 1,200 euros, Mr. Traveler?" Beznik asked as they unloaded breakfast from the van. "If I did, I would never labor in tourism again." Beznik set down a wicker picnic basket from the pension beside a rock block that would make an admirable dining table. Yellow, red and orange flowers bloomed nearby, adding splashes of color to the setting. "Hard enough to find work; no Greek trusts a Romani." He paused and considered as he looked at Scarlett and Race, who had one earpiece in to provide background music by an LA band called Signal Hill. "I think Lodge hid the money himself or never had it. He is just trying to be given a free tour."

Scarlett said, "He's a wealthy man."

"A liar. A fraud. He scratched out someone else's name on his camera bag; probably stole it."

Race swallowed an enzyme pill and bit into a chocolate bar. He was, as usual, hungry. "What happened at the van when we reached the canal?"

Beznik carried porcelain coffee cups, China plates and Odin ware utensils from the van and set them atop a red-checked table-cloth Race had used to cover the block.

"Everyone left the van," Beznik said, stopping and his eyes narrowing as he remembered. "I checked the oil. Then I unlocked the van for Mr. Chance to retrieve his camera."

"How long was Chance in the van?"

"I let him in and before I returned to the engine, he was off again. I went back and checked that the door was locked."

"He might have had time to steal the wallet," Scarlett said, "if he knew where it was."

Race finished his chocolate bar and said, "Chance wears a money belt."

"How can you possibly know that?"

Before he could answer Scarlett, Race coughed. The climb and the stress of helping to save Gayle had aggravated his lungs. He used an inhaler. Scarlett watched him with concern as Beznik un-loaded thermoses of coffee, tea and orange juice. Breathing well again but light headed from the bronchodilator, Race sat on a boul-der and said, "Chance called Dr. Lodge a fool for not using a mon-ey belt, so Chance must use one and he probably thinks everyone does. So I doubt Chance would think anyone would leave money in the van to steal. What happened next?"

Beznik said, "Mrs. Petra, David's wife, retrieved her sweater."

"How long did she take?"

Beznik shrugged.

"A minute? Two? Three?"

"She did not steal the money." Beznik smoothed the tablecloth and set out the cups, plates, utensils, and napkins with as much care and precision as if he was setting table at the finest restaurant in Athens.

Race asked, "Why so certain?"

Beznik opened the picnic basket and took out feta cheese, Ka-lamata olives, crusty bread, extra virgin olive oil for dipping, cheese and cream pies, spinach pies, and honey to sweeten the coffee. Next appeared cut-up fruit and yoghurt.

"Petra is Dr. Lodge's daughter," Scarlett said. "Why steal from him?"

Beznik looked at Race. "She did not steal the wallet."

"You were in the van the whole time she was aboard," Race guessed.

Scarlett looked at Race for an explanation.

"Petra defended Beznik at the airport after her father's comment about the hired help and she urged her father not to jump to the conclusion that Beznik stole his wallet." And, Race thought, she had a pretty face, long blonde hair and ample curves like an ancient Greek goddess, albeit probably more befitting a European than the thinner American conception of beauty. "I'm sure Beznik kept an eye on her in case she needed any assistance."

Beznik continued setting out breakfast as he said, "After Mrs. Petra left, I went to wash my hands with Mr. Chance. After lunch, I let Ms. Gayle and Mr. David into the van."

His breathing restored and the light-headedness passing, Race nibbled on a Kalamata olive; smooth and meaty. "How long were they aboard?"

"Mr. David sorted through their bags and found Mrs. Petra's. He put her sweater back and then he got out and we talked."

"Gayle was alone in the van?"

Beznik nodded.

"For how long?"

Beznik finished setting out the food, complete with a bouquet of wildflowers. Scarlett nodded her approval. Race inhaled the aroma of the fresh bread, just baked in a bakery in town; wonderful—the bread, and being able to breathe. He first heard and then saw the tour members strolling toward them across the broken and worn stone paths of the fortress's main courtyard.

"Ms. Gayle was in the van for some little time," Beznik said. "Ms. Wynter and Mr. Traveler, I am completely sorry it happened, but it was not my fault. I cannot watch everything all of the time. Lodge is a….I am poor and a Romani, so I am a thief to him, but I am most definitely not a thief."

"The wallet could have been stolen by anyone who went to the van," Scarlett said, "or maybe someone stole it when everyone was getting off when we arrived at the canal."

Beznik said with an undertone of malice, "You should question Mrs. Sonja Weaver."

"She didn't return to the van, did she?" Scarlett asked.

"She hung around the van on her mobile as if she was afraid I would steal it," Beznik said. "She and Lodge are one and the same—they think if you are poor, you are a thief."

After their picnic breakfast, of which Race had three helpings, Beznik drove everyone down to the pension for a free afternoon. On the short drive, Race noticed Chance checking off another entry in his guidebook, undoubtedly Palamidi Fortress. Scarlett rolled her eyes at Chance's score keeping as she popped Penguin peppermints into her mouth.

When they arrived in the parking area of the defunct Xenia hotel, a blue-striped Opel Astra stood gleaming white in the Grecian sun. As they exited the van, a broad-shouldered, dark man in a black suit with thin white pin stripes stood at the entrance to the gravel path leading down to the pension. Race recognized Inspector Kanavou from the airport.

As Race exited the van, Kanavou, cigarette in hand, approached and said, "One of the brothers at the pension reported that a man by the name of Brishen Beznik accompanies your group." Two brothers owned and operated the Pension Marianna.

"Our driver," Race said gesturing at Beznik, who with the ever helpful David and Gayle, was unloading the daypacks from the van.

Dr. Lodge strode over and introduced himself.

"Ah, Dr. Lodge. I am Inspector Andreis Kanavou, Ellinki Astynomia—Hellenic Police. I have the honor to serve in the Special Violent Crime Squad. I was requested to investigate the disappearance of your wallet."

"Not exactly a violent crime," Race said.

Kanavou gave Race a thin smile as he stubbed out his cigarette in the gravel of the parking lot with one of his black shoes. "Even so, with tourists involved, my superiors asked me to investigate to ensure that all that can be done, is done. It is an unfortunate time for tourism; the war and such."

"We almost cancelled," Sonja said.

"Silly," Chance said with a dismissive wave.

"I was worried, but can you believe my son forced me to come?" Cohen asked from the edge of the group. "He's used to all sorts of violence, anyway, of course."

Everyone cast him questioning looks.

"He plays e-sports, computer games for a living, you know?"

More uncomprehending stares.

"He plays in the Pro Gaming League in tournaments in Asia and Europe. Fifty thousand people watch him play on his own Internet channel, and the last tournament he was in had 15 million viewers online. He made mid-six figures last year, not counting endorsements. And, as I'm sure you know, the games tend to be violent, so he didn't think much of the war. Said it was boring on TV; nothing worth watching, just trucks and tanks and Humvees driving along dusty desert roads forever and ever; no climax."

Still more stares.

"Not that I have to worry about violence," Cohen rambled on in his quiet, tremulous voice. Having started talking, he appeared unable to stop. "I mean, I'm a black belt in taekwondo, second dan. Didn't I mention it? My son got me into it, something we could do together, like little league or bowling."

A shocked silence followed. Race would never have pictured Cohen breaking a silence, let alone boards. He wondered what other secrets Cohen was concealing.

Inspector Kanavou finally ended the stunned silence. "Greece is a peaceful, safe country."

"There's still a war on," Sonja said. "Terrorists could target Americans in Greece."

"The invasion of Iraq isn't going to have any effect here," Chance said. "It's two thousand miles away. May as well avoid Bali because of North Korea's nuclear program."

"I must reassure you all, you are as safe here as in any American city," Kanavou said as his dark eyes lingered on Sonja's pale beauty. Pulling his gaze reluctantly from her body, he assumed a serious countenance and asked, "Brishen Beznik, I must ask you, is this yours?" Kanavou held up a shiny, almost white wallet.

"It's mine," Dr. Lodge roared. "Where did you discover it?"

"Looks like a thousand other wallets," Sonja said.

"Far from it," Lodge countered. "It is made of a rare albino boa constrictor skin from the Amazon; extremely rare, even possibly unique."

"Probably endangered," Sonja told Chance, who chuckled.

"Do you recognize it, Mr. Beznik?" Kanavou asked, ignoring Sonja's wisecracks.

Sullen, his arms crossed over his broad chest, Beznik shook his head.

"After receiving permission from the owners of the pension and with a judge's warrant, a search led to its discovery in your room, in the side pocket of your bag."

Petra gasped and grabbed David's arm. She closed her eyes and appeared faint.

Lodge smiled and asked, "Did you recover my money, too?"

Kanavou shook his head. He took a piece of paper from the inside pocket of his suit jacket and, holding it out to Lodge, said, "Could you please check this inventory of the articles found in the wallet?"

Lodge snatched the list and a moment later announced, "My credit cards are all on the list, as well as my driver's license and AAA card." He paused and frowned. "I had a Bloomingdales gift card. You didn't find it?"

Kanavou shook his head. "Everything else is on the list?"

Lodge peered back at the inventory. "As far as I can recall, except for the cash. At least you can apprehend the filthy scoundrel and incarcerate him for a suitably long term."

"I told you the Gypsy did it," Sonja told Chance. "That's how it always is in the movies."

"Not anymore," Chance said. "It's always the white guy who's the crook."

"Mr. Brishen Beznik," Inspector Kanavou said, "it is my duty to have to inform you that I am obliged to place you under arrest for the theft of this wallet and of its contents on or about April 17, 2004, in or about the area of the Corinth Canal in the municipality of Corinthia, Peloponnese, Greece."

Chapter 5

Day 3: Monday, April 19

"A Dr. Jake Larson in Seattle," Race said as he sat on the bed in Scarlett's room. A novel, *The Eldorado Network*, lay open beside him. He skimmed its pages even as he spoke into the phone. In his free hand he held a buttered croissant he had liberated from the pension's kitchen long before breakfast officially started.

"Seattle?" Scarlett mumbled as she lay coiled under the blankets. No sunlight shone through the window. "You pound on my door, wake me, borrow my cell, and now you're bankrupting me with long distance calls."

"Deduct it as a business expense."

"You only get about 30 percent back, and you still have to pay for it. Go back to your room and use your own cell."

"Don't have one anymore; costs too much. I've already done my chest therapy and neb treatments, so get up or you won't have time to exercise."

"Not today, it's a holiday—somewhere."

Race answered the woman on the cell, "That must be him. Mercer Island, near Seattle? Can I please have the number?"

Race called Dr. Larson.

"Another call to the States?" Scarlett asked. Her head appeared momentarily from the sea of blankets to frown with displeasure before she snuggled deeper under the covers and hid her head beneath her pillow. "I'll never retire the way you're spending my money."

"My money; I'll pay."

"Our money, if we marry." Her sleepy voice emerged from beneath the pillow.

"You're accepting my proposal?" Race asked with mock excitement.

"I want to snore; let me sleep."

"You just have frigi-ped."

"What?" Scarlett croaked.

"Frigi-ped; cold feet."

A groan reached Race's ears. He patted her curvy hip that made an inviting shape beneath the blankets.

As the phone rang, Race finished his croissant and checked his watch. With the 10-hour difference, it was 3 pm in Seattle.

When the doctor's office answered, Race said, "This is Menelaus Pharmacy in Athens, Greece. I'm calling regarding a prescription for a Mrs. Hilda Rasmussen. She has requested a refill for her asthma inhaler, albuterol. Does she have refills left?"

The receptionist placed him on hold.

Another female voice came on the line and asked, "Will you be able to fill her prescription in Georgia?"

For an instant Race was nonplussed, but realized his story at the other end of the line had changed from one Athens to another. Recovering quickly, he said, "Of course. We just check your doctor's authorization number with a Washington State physician database."

"She has one more refill. She's used four."

"Yes, just recently, she said."

"Yes, she received three refills two weeks ago, all on the same day. Is she vacationing in Georgia?"

After his call, Race asked Scarlett, "How about a quick snuggle?"

Expanding her repertoire, Scarlett found yet another way to say no.

After breakfast on the pension's roof-top patio with its incomparable views of the bay and the storied Peloponnesus beyond, Race led the way up to the van. Sonja bounded aboard in front of Chance, who looked like a subject in a sleep deprivation experiment. Sonja told him, "A brisk jog is just the thing for jet lag."

Chance scowled.

With Beznik in jail, Scarlet said it was up to Race to drive.

"I don't recall such a role included in my job description."

"A future husband would help out his intended."

"Maybe for a few extra bucks."

"I can't afford to pay two drivers, even if one's in jail."

"How about a bonus if I get him out?"

"The bonus will be gratitude, from him and from me." She kissed him, soft and slow. He tasted peppermint on her lips. "But you can't read a book while you drive."

"Bet I can."

"Bet your job you can't."

Ten minutes later Race was driving through thankfully light morning traffic and listening to *Bob Segar's Greatest Hits, Volume I* in one ear as he wondered whether Rob had stolen his mother's inhalers. He also wondered who stole Lodge's 1,200 euros and his possibly endangered wallet? Race couldn't see how Beznik could have snuck onto the van to steal the wallet, let alone even known the wallet was in Lodge's bag. And why would Beznik leave the credit cards and take the Bloomingdales' card? Was Beznik planning a quick trip to the New World for a shopping spree at Bloomies? And was the stolen wallet related to the death of Mrs. Rasmussen? Race glanced back at Rob. His body was canted toward the window as he took in the Grecian countryside with interest; far from the picture of a grieving son. Everyone grieved differently, yet...

Guessing he would have to drive, early that morning as he performed his chest physical therapy and nebulizer treatments, Race had studied a map and memorized the 20-kilometer route from Nafplion through labyrinthine Argos to Mycenae. Even so, it was with relief that he spotted Mycenae's concentric stone walls on a rise at the base of a stark mountain on the edge of the Argive plain. Race parked and as the tour members stepped off the van, Scarlett handed out mini-flashlights.

"I presume the sun will continue to shine today," Sonja said with a patronizing smile. The sun rested just above the horizon, casting brilliant yellow-white rays across the sloping plain.

"If you should decide to go down the well," Scarlett said, "you'll need a light."

"Go down a well?" Sonja asked in disbelief as if Scarlett had suggested skinny dipping in a latrine.

"It's really a cistern with stairs, but it is dark."

"How exceedingly romantic," Sonja said with a coy giggle. "I'm sure my dear David can light me up when the need arises." She waved away the flashlight with a ring-adorned hand.

"Always wanted to come to Europe and go down a well with a movie starlet," David said with a grin.

Petra and Chance wore matching sour expressions as their flirting spouses followed Race across the parking lot and up an incline toward the famed Lion Gate. Two great stone slabs three feet thick and several feet taller than any man supported a 15 by 7 foot lintel. Above the lintel, carved into a triangular block of dark stone, two rampant lionesses stood tall with their forepaws resting on the raised base of a central pillar.

"The Lion Gate is the oldest monumental structure in Europe," Race said. "The lionesses were probably the emblem of the ruling family. Unfortunately, their heads are missing."

"Early souvenir hunters?" David asked. "Must be worth at least the price of joining every club on the Open rota—or maybe even buying every club on the rota."

"Mycenae was the first bronze-age European society and thrived between 1,500 and 1,200 BC," Race continued. "It was at its peak a thousand years before the rise of Athens, making the Mycenaeans as remote from Pericles and the Ancient Greeks as the Romans are from us. It was the seat of the legendary King Agamemnon of Trojan War fame."

Leading the way through the 10 by 10 foot dark-stone gate, Race looked up to see a couple of women in shorts and halter tops perched on a ledge on the back of the gate. A middle-aged man took their photograph from below.

"Should they be up there?" the accountant, Cohen asked, his eyes narrowed in a frown.

"Can we climb up there?" Rob asked, sounding like a twelve-year-old boy asking for a roller coaster ride.

"It's not like in the States," Race said, "you can climb all over many of the ruins in Greece. Until 1977, you could even walk inside the Parthenon."

"Just watch out for cliffs," Rob said with an impish grin.

Gayle eyed him and slid over to the other side of the group.

Just inside the citadel to the right, Race pointed out the 40-foot grave circle of flat, thin standing stones and royal tomb markers. "Heinrich Schliemann," he said, "discovered the ruins in the 1870s and unearthed magnificent gold treasures in the circle, which are in the site's museum, including the famous gold mask of Agamemnon."

"It's not really Agamemnon," Chance said, his ever-present guidebook in hand.

"Makes a better story than if it was some unknown ancient king," Race conceded.

"A good story trumps dry facts every time," David said.

Race led the way up the path to the ruins of the ancient palace, even as he advised everyone to drink the bottled water they had brought. It was already hot. Race wished he had worn shorts. Unfortunately, Scarlett required her guides to wear slacks and a polo shirt embroidered with the company logo. Excursion guides did not wear shorts. At least his lungs were clear. He only felt a vague tightness in his chest, which he hoped did not portend an infection.

Three tourists took in the view from the palace's 30 by 60 foot main hall. Only the stone-paved floor remained. Race gazed at the expansive view over the lower part of the complex with its more than 30 ancient stone foundations. Beyond the complex, olive trees sprouted like green mushrooms all across the white rocky Argive Plain. A few pine, aspen, cypress, fir, and beach trees struggled to survive in the arid soil. To the southwest a white line marked the edge of the glittering Aegean. To the west, mountains reared up like an impenetrable palisade on the horizon. The commanding location must have confirmed for many a king of ancient Mycenae that they were destined to rule forever from such an impregnable citadel.

Race perspired as he led the way up the rough, broken terrain toward the top of the complex. White stones reflected the sunlight into his eyes. In places the ancient wall surrounding the citadel was intact, but within it little remained save for the foundations of ancient stone buildings.

The group reached the well, which led via hand-cut stone steps 50 feet down to a cistern. The entrance formed by great blocks of stone was 4 by 6 feet with a triangular top. Chance took the lead down the steep steps, the light from his flashlight bobbing and swinging against the smooth, damp walls.

"Be careful," Scarlett called out, "the 99 steps are notoriously slick."

Oblivious to any danger, Rob rushed down right behind Chance. David was closely followed by Sonja, Gayle and Dr. Lodge, while Petra passed on the well. Cohen cautiously felt his way down the steps last of all. Standing just inside, Race found the dark, humid well mercifully cool after the searing heat atop the spur on which Mycenae stood.

Moments later, Chance strode back up out of the well.

"Nothing but a muddy, damp little room," he said, flicking off his flashlight as he re-entered the sun-lit world.

"Spring water's been collecting there from Mount Elias for 3,500 years," Race said.

Chance snorted and strode off in the same direction Petra had taken to tour more of the site. Since Scarlett was calling about their next accommodations, Race decided to explore. He was struck by the rear of Mycenae, where the spur fell away into a steep rift. Higher peaks overlooked the ruins, but they appeared unscalable and—crucial in ancient times—beyond bow range.

After his tour of the site under the sweat-inducing sun, Race found a comfortable shady spot against a stone wall near the Lion Gate and settled in for a jet-lag induced nap.

As Race drifted up out of his nap, a female voice behind his head urged, "It's the decent thing to do."

"I don't even know if it is my progeny," a male voice said.

"We can arrange a paternity test anytime you want."

Race wondered where the speakers were, then realized that just above him was a path along the top of the row of monumental stones he was resting against. As he awoke, he recognized the voices; Gayle Garcia, the Olympic physiotherapist, and Dr. Lodge, ex-professor and dating website CEO.

"Paternity test?" Lodge's daughter, Petra, asked in disbelief as she joined the fray.

"Not interested," Dr. Lodge said.

"You ignored my emails, wouldn't return my calls and refused to see me," Gayle said, her voice rising. "I thought I might be able to convince you to do the right thing if I discussed it with you in person."

"Quit harassing my father," Petra ordered, matching Gayle's raised voice.

Dr. Lodge demanded, "How did you even know I would be taking this accursed tour?"

"A little sisterly chat with your assistant on the phone and I found out all about it."

"One more flunky to add to the unemployment rolls."

"You're a bastard."

"No, I believe your son is."

"How dare you!"

Race was about to stand to intervene before violence erupted when he heard Scarlett's authoritative voice, "Excuse me, other tourists are trying to enjoy the ruins. Could you please continue your discussion later at a more suitable and private location?"

Race looked up to see Gayle shoot Petra a look of loathing, before the physiotherapist stalked away down the meandering path toward the palace.

As Scarlett walked away, Petra, not having seen Race below her, asked her father, "What was she talking about?"

"The woman is clearly clinically deluded, probably a paranoid."

"She seemed to know you."

"Delusions seem real to the patient."

Lodge and his daughter stared at each other.

After a long, tense silence, Petra said, "I can't believe you would do such a vile thing to Mom."

"Then do not believe it."

As they crossed the parking lot, a tour of Poles in dinner jackets, sweaters and slacks filed off their air-conditioned bus even as four more buses arrived. Race, listening to the opera *Thaïs* and skimming a novel, *A Piece of Cake*, led their excursion down the road. More tour buses passed them as Lodge, Petra and Gayle walked as far apart as possible, forming a triangle of loathing with the other excursionists marooned within it.

"Always good to be early," Scarlett said, eyeing the burgeoning hordes flooding off the buses like an invading army. "Nice to have the site almost to ourselves."

Some 300 yards down the road Race turned right. Ever-higher walls made of stones the size of refrigerators led 100 feet to a monumental doorway with a triangular opening the size of a panel truck above it.

Rob exclaimed, "Cool," and then added in a low voice, "Mom would have loved this."

"The royal Lion Tholos or beehive tomb," Race said. "The entrance would have been decorated in vivid red and green."

Built into a hill, the monumental six- by 20-foot entrance led into a burial chamber. Inside, from the stone-paved floor, rows of six-foot blocks formed rings until they reached a band of two-foot blocks. Above that band, foot-thick blocks formed gradually smaller circles until they met far above at the highest point to create a beehive shape.

Race said, "The tomb was the largest dome on earth until Rome's Pantheon was built 1,400 years later."

"I can think of some people I'd like to put in it permanently," Chance said. "Fit for a queen." He eyed Sonja, as she glided closer to David.

"It's empty," Rob said, disappointed.

"Please remember it's more than 3,000 years old," Race said. "Far older than the Roman Empire and the Great Wall of China."

"Similar design to the beehive houses on Skelig Michael and on the Ring of Dingle in Ireland," Dr. Lodge said, "albeit on a far grander scale, and built into the hillside instead of free-standing."

As he checked off the site in his guidebook, Chance said, "Just a big stone igloo."

"Our next stop is Tiryns," Race said as he drove the van up a narrow road through olive groves into what appeared to be a farm, south of Mycenae and just a few kilometers outside Nafplion.

"These ruins are far less ruined than Mycenae," Scarlett said.

"Aren't ruins just ruins?" Sonja asked.

"Far from it," Scarlett said as Race parked. "Mycenae is mostly just foundations, save for the Lion Gate and part of the walls."

"Don't forget the well," Sonja added with a smirk.

They strolled on a dirt path through a grove of plane trees to a wood hut. The dry, hot air cleared Race's nose, sinuses and lungs.

He felt good. Everyone paid their few euro entrance fee and Race led them along a tree-shaded path.

As Rob rushed ahead, David had his arm around his wife, Petra and appeared to be urging her to some action. She shook her head as she glanced at her father, before resolutely looking straight ahead. Race guessed David was trying to reconcile his wife and father-in-law. It was clear David was failing.

Sonja strolled along talking on her cell, while Chance glared at her between reading entries in his guidebook. Race hoped their next tour attracted a more amenable group; this group was as likely to kill each other as sit down to breakfast tomorrow.

"Homer called it 'Wall-girt' Tiryns," Race said, gesturing at the imposing walls that loomed above them as they emerged from the trees. "The walls are 2,200 feet long and up to 25 feet thick. The largest stones weigh 14 tons and the joins between the rocks are so tight you can't fit even a single piece of paper between them."

"How old is it?" Rob asked, shading his eyes to peer up at the ageless walls. "Can we climb on top?"

Before Chance could find the answers in his guidebook, Race replied, "Between 1400 and 1200 BC." They turned a corner and started up the long, broad incline between two stone walls toward the entrance. "You can climb wherever you want."

"Please be careful," Scarlett warned.

Cohen asked, "Who built it?"

"The one-eyed giant Cyclops, so the walls are Cyclopean," Race said as they emerged at the top of the fortress. "Less romantic scholars say it was the Mycenaeans."

Before Race could continue his prepared lecture, Scarlett announced, "Please take an hour to look around. A part of the site is being excavated."

"Why isn't there any printed information or signs about what we're seeing?" Chance asked.

"That's what I'm here for," Race said. Seeing his answer was far from acceptable, he added, "Greece has so many historic sites the Greeks don't have the money to print materials for all of them, let alone in all the languages of all the tourists who visit."

"Could just do English," Chance muttered.

As the group dispersed, Race meandered after David as the ex-pro-golfer walked toward where an archeology team in white hardhats was laboring. Sonja rushed past Race and caught up with David, her arm sliding easily through his. She hung onto him like a limpet on an especially choice rock.

"She craves adoration," Chance told Race, who had not realized the ex-fighter pilot had slid up alongside him.

"Most actresses do, I imagine."

"It's meaningless. They met at some pro-am golf tournament for an organ-donor charity he started. Sonja doesn't get much attention from being on the screen anymore; too old."

"Far from old to most people."

"Most moviegoers are between 12 and 24 years of age."

Race nodded and asked, "By the way, did you happen to see Gayle take any money from the airport ATM?"

"I had some euros from a sailing contract in Sicily, so I didn't use the ATM. But I wouldn't have noticed anyway; not my type. I go for blondes, for the most part."

After giving Race a firm pat on the shoulder, Chance set off toward a striking covered gallery of stone-framed windows, where another tourist was taking in the view: David's wife, Petra, a blonde.

After a tour of the site, Race borrowed Scarlett's cell and called Inspector Kanavou. "I talked to Mrs. Rasmussen's doctor in Seattle."

"How did you know his name?" Kanavou asked.

"It was on her asthma inhaler."

"You notice much, Mr. Traveler."

"As much of life as I can."

"An admirable trait for a detective."

Or for a dying man, Race thought, but pushed such depressing thoughts from his mind. "Mrs. Rasmussen ordered three bronchodilator refills two weeks before the tour."

"How did you gain access to her confidential medical information?"

"I lied."

The line fell silent as Race stared out over the olive groves below Tyrins with their gnarled trunks and silvery green leaves. As he inhaled their dry aroma, he could just see the glittering Aegean in the distance.

Kanavou said, "I will need to investigate the matter."

The inhalers, Race wondered, or his impersonation of a pharmacist?

"Please help me," Beznik asked Race that afternoon in the Nafplion police station after Race talked his way into seeing the driver. "Greeks hate Romani. They will do nothing to find the truth. I mourned my parents five years ago. My brother's in the navy. You are the only one who can help me. There is no one else."

After assuring Beznik he would do all he could, Race asked, "Do you know anything about stolen credit cards?"

"No, no, no. I have nothing to do with stolen wallet, stolen credit cards, stolen anything. In my life, I have never stolen anything."

"I understand, but if you were to find a credit card, alone and sadly forsaken, would you use it? I mean just to fill up the gas tank once on the credit card company's dime."

"No, no, no. I don't even own a credit card."

Crossing Nafplion's marble square on his way back to the pension, Race spotted Inspector Kanavou, who stopped to ask if he had seen Beznik. Race nodded.

"Do not waste your time," Kanavou advised. "He did it."

"Why so certain?"

"He had the wallet."

"But not the money."

"He spent it."

"In less than a day?"

Kanavou shrugged. "Hid it?"

"But left the wallet and credit cards in his bag to be found?"

"He took the cash, and had just not disposed of the wallet and credit cards yet."

"But plans to use a Bloomingdales' gift card? It's still missing."

"It fell out." Kanavou eyed Race, willing Race to agree with him. "Who else would take the wallet? If they can afford your excursion, why steal a wallet?"

"Greed?"

Late that afternoon as Race drove the tour 24 kilometers inland to Epidavros, the jagged white rocks and stunted olive trees of the coast gave way to stands of Cypresses, pines, firs, aspen, and white poplars. Poppies sprouted in profusion around irregular fields dotted with crumbling stone farmhouses. Interspersed across the rugged countryside were newer homes, open on the ground floor for parking and the storage of sundries, with one, two or three cinder-block floors above. Rebar pointed skyward from the roofs like skinny crenellations.

"Greek families often add floors as they add children," Race said. "Parents plan that as each child marries, they'll live on the new floor."

"The Greeks are an optimistic people," Chance said. "I'll give them that; always planning to build onward and upward."

"And give the next generation a leg up," David added with a glance at his father-in-law, Dr. Lodge. Staring out at the passing countryside, Lodge held his SLR camera ready for any don't-miss photo-opportunities.

When they arrived at Epidavros, Race led the tour into the shaded site.

"Around 400 BC, Epidavros was Greece's most famous healing center," Race said, "complete with mineral springs and an *enkoim-itiria* or sleeping hall where the ill were visited in dreams by the god of healing, Asklepios. The god revealed to the patient how to treat their disease. Given the sorry state of the Greek health system, wags have suggested they reopen Epidavros as a healing center."

"Not much left," Chance said, looking over the outlines of the foundations amongst the plane, pine, fir, and olive trees.

"Ruined ruins, then," Sonja said with a cheeky smile at Scarlett.

Chance said, "My guidebook says the museum is tiny, too."

"True, but we haven't seen what all the medical facilities paid for," Race said. They climbed a set of broad stone stairs and emerged from the trees at the glorious centerpiece of the ancient site: an intact 15,000-seat ancient amphitheatre. From the base of the theatre in the shade of the trees, Race explained that the seats were divided into two sections with an ambulatory or diorama sep-arating the upper section from the lower. Overhanging trees set close around the top of the 180-degree theater provided a natural backdrop for the theatre, which was built into a hill. Hard-packed dirt encircled by a ring of flat stones set flush into the ground and marked by a stone in the center formed the "stage."

"Please find a seat for a demonstration," Race said. "And please spread out."

The group dispersed throughout the rows of mottled, off-white limestone bench seats. Everyone stared down at Race with curious expressions, which attracted the stares of many of the other tourists admiring the theatre. Race withdrew a match book from his pocket. He stood beside Scarlett on the stone marking the center of the stage and, after a dramatic pause, struck the match. Race did not need to ask if everyone heard the match flare; the answer showed clearly in the amazement on everyone's face.

As the group gathered at their assigned seats, everyone marveled at the theatre's acoustics.

"It's the best preserved ancient amphitheatre in the world," Race said. "It forms a perfect semi-circle. The original Greek theatre had 34 rows and the Romans added 21 more. From the top you can see all the way across the Argive Plain to the Saronic coast."

Sonja said, "Put on a flop and everyone will be taking in the view, not the play."

"'Unlike Roman theatres, which sought to conceal the outside world,'" Chance read from his guidebook, "'Greek amphitheatres sought to bring the outside world in as an integral part of the playgoing experience.'"

"They succeeded wonderfully here," Dr. Lodge said. "Spectacular." He took several photographs of the view.

"The Roman Emperor Theodosiasis closed the theatre in AD 426 when he closed all pagan sites," Race said. "Pity."

"It says here a study by the Georgia Institute of Technology," Chance said, "'found that the design of the theatre is either an accident or the result of an advanced design; low-frequency sounds, such as the murmur of the crowd, are filtered out, while high-frequency sounds, such as the actor's voices, are amplified and reflected from the stage.'" He checked off the entry in his guidebook with a black felt pen.

Sonja asked, "What play are we seeing?"

"Euripides' *Medea*," Race said.

"In which Medea murders Jason's fiancé and father-in-law, before marrying Jason," Sonja said.

"Don't give it all away," Petra said, glaring at Sonja.

"Just a teaser," Sonja said with expectant glee. "Familial slaughter; always an audience pleaser."

Chance and Sonja, David, Petra and Dr. Lodge sat in a row, although Sonja sat far closer to David than to her husband. Cohen, who had avoided sitting beside Lodge, sat by Gayle one row back. Rob ended up next to Dr. Lodge, making a stark contrast between the statue-like Lodge and the fidgeting, always-in-motion Rob.

The play began as a nurse strode onto stage and said, "Ah! Would to Heaven the good ship *Argo* ne'er had sped its course to the Colchian land through the misty blue Symplegades, nor ever in the glens of Pelion the pine been felled to furnish with oars the chieftain's hands, who went to fetch the golden fleece for Pelias; for then would my own mistress Medea never have sailed to the turrets of Iolcos, her soul with love for Jason smitten, nor would she have beguiled the daughters of Pelias to slay their father...."

At intermission, as the night cooled and the crowd dispersed to concession stands at the base of the amphitheater, Race spotted Sonja standing alone just behind the last row of seats.

"Enjoying the play?" Race asked as he joined her. He inhaled the dry air, reveling in how good his lungs felt today; maybe the tightness had presaged nothing.

"Wish they had writers like Euripides in Hollywood," Sonja said. "Every actor would be hailed as a Olivier, Suchet or Streep."

They discussed Euripides and *Medea*, and then Race mentioned that he'd heard she had been near the van at the Corinth Canal.

Sonja's eyes narrowed and she tilted her head to the side, inspecting Race with great care. "Only before lunch," she said. "And, no, I didn't see any money on the van; Lodge's or anyone else's. Not that I'd notice anyway. Chancey handles all our money. I never deal with the stuff; filthy lucre and all that. Interferes with the art."

Race grinned. "But spending it has no such negative side effects?"

Sonja's face hardened, but then she laughed. Race wondered which role—the haughty, spoiled movie star or the knowledgeable, successful, hardworking woman—was the real Sonja, or was there a real Sonja?

"Did you notice who returned to the van?"

Sonja fingered one of the dry bushes that lined the top of the amphitheatre. "Lucky they have a sprinkler system. This stuff is drier than Palm Springs in August. I didn't see much. I was admiring the canal. A bore, but between you and me, I need the part."

Race frowned. Had Sonja come within 100 yards of the canal?

"My agent, Bruce, lined me up for a part in some Agatha Christie movie about a murder on a tour of Greece or Mesopotamia or some such horrible, hot, Third-World place. Be the role, get the role; Strasberg method and all that rubbish. I'll bury Bruce alive in a mountain of third-rate indie scripts if I don't get the damn part after suffering through all this; no offense. This kind of tour wasn't designed with someone like me in mind."

Race thought that not even Heaven was designed with Sonja in mind.

She stretched her back, displaying her ample breasts. "These seats are brutal. That Gypsy driver—"

"Beznik, and he is Romani. They don't like being called Gypsies."

"'A rose is a rose by any other name,' and all that, no?" she asked with a dismissive wave of her hand. "However he likes to bill himself, he was checking the engine when he let Chance and then Petra into the van. Petra got her sweater. She was in the van for only a few moments. Then Beznik went off to talk to you and wash his hands with Chance—splitting their ill-gotten gains in some suitably filthy bathroom stall, I suspect, to reflect their inner lack of virtue. We all had lunch, then David went back to the van to return Petra's sweater. Gayle went along, and Beznik let them in."

"How long was Gayle in the van?"

"Beznik and David were chatting in front of the van for a time before Gayle reappeared. I'd say three, maybe even four minutes." Sonja stared at Race and then the ends of her pouty lips turned up slightly as if she had just solved a difficult problem. "Then Gayle returned with euros to pay for lunch. Odd that."

"Did you see her get euros from the airport ATM?"

"No, but I was….I was chatting with David. We're old friends, you know."

"You remember all that?"

"An actor must be observant. Never know when you might notice something useful for a role. I am sorry."

"About what?"

"Your driver."

"Why?"

"He took the money, of course."

"But Gayle—"

She chuckled and tossed her head, which flung her hair in a reddish-black aura around her head. She rattled off her reasoning like long-rehearsed lines in a movie. "Chance would never steal; an officer's honor and all that. Why would Petra or David steal from their father; they'll get all his money sooner or later. Gayle thinks Lodge's bank account will spell salvation for their love child. Why ruin her chances by stealing a paltry sum from him? Cohen doesn't have the guts to steal a hotel pen, let alone a wallet. Besides, Gayle and Cohen still hope Lodge will recognize the righteousness of their claims and give them all they think they deserve."

"Cohen and Gayle have both argued with Lodge on the tour. Maybe they gave up ever getting any money from Lodge."

"Having come all the way to Greece, you don't think one rebuff will quell their optimism, do you?" Sonja gazed off across the broad plain lit by the last rays of the sun. "In any case, I'd be happy to make up the loss to smooth things over so we can all enjoy this trip as much as humanly possible. If I have to slum, I certainly don't want everyone around me miserable. Life's too short, don't you agree?"

Race agreed, but said, "Beznik would never accept."

"He might."

"He won't."

"Proud?"

"Honest."

"A nice belief for a boss to harbor."

"More than a belief. He could have stolen a car Scarlett rented on a previous trip a dozen times; worth far more than the cash in Lodge's wallet."

The audience began to return to their seats.

"By the way," Race asked as Sonja started back toward their seats, "did you see or hear anything odd on the plane from New York?"

"Other than that lady dying? Didn't see a thing, just you tearing around trying to save her; very dramatic." Then, putting on a look of great caring, she added, "I am sorry you failed; would never have happened in a movie. The hero always saves an old woman or two."

"Am I the hero?"

"Oh, dear," Sonja said, placing a languid hand on Race's shoulder, "everyone's the hero of their own story—or so the important people tell everyone so they'll feel important. Poor chumps."

Race followed Sonja as the actress floated down the worn marble steps back to their seats. She had provided a detailed description of what she had seen in Corinth, but he wondered if it got him any closer to figuring out who stole the wallet, and she had provided no help at all in determining whether Rob had murdered his mother. Worse, with Beznik in jail for the theft of the wallet and the initial report that Mrs. Rasmussen had died of natural causes, Kanavou would be of no help in solving either crime, if Mrs. Rasmussen's death was in fact a crime at all.

As they sat down, Sonja leaned back and, a graceful hand on David's shoulder, she whispered to Race in the row behind her, "I did overhear that lady who died on the plane and a young man, who I later learned was her son, arguing in New York as we were boarding; frightful row."

Race leaned forward. "What were they arguing about?"

Sonja paused, as any actress would before the money shot, and said, "The old lady said a wonderful line for someone about to be murdered, 'Robert, our relationship can't always just be based on money.'"

Chapter 6

Day 4: Tuesday, April 20

"The inland road is faster," Scarlett said as the tour gathered the next morning at the van above Pension Mariana.

"The coast road is infinitely more scenic," Race said, shading his eyes from the first rays of the sun as they lit the walls of Palamidi Fortress perched atop its massif.

"It takes longer, so less time in Monemvasia."

"They'll miss Moni Profitis Ilonas in the Badron Gorge, not to mention the gorge itself."

Scarlett considered, torn between unrivalled sights and her unbreakable schedule.

"Please," Race said, giving her his broadest smile.

After a sigh, Scarlett said, "Alright, but no stops for coffee or sweets."

Race drove around the top of the Argolic Gulf, munching on salty pretzels to keep his salt levels up as he listened to Eminem for the first time. Race wished he could clear Beznik so he could focus on sight-seeing, reading and listening to music instead of driving. Until then, he left his novel in his bag and stole glances left and right at the striking views.

"Not only do they have two castles above the town, but a third castle mini in the bay," Sonja marveled. "Such abundance could be considered gauche."

"Castle junior," Gayle said.

"The castle in the harbor is the Bourtzi, which means tower in Ottoman Turk," Race said. With a massive triangle of stone facing the sea and a single tower, the Bourtzi had its own tiny enclosed harbor on the side nearest Nafplion. Covering an entire islet, the Bourtzi looked like a stone cruiser with its superstructure forward on the seaward side and a low, flat area on the landward side pointing into Nafplion's harbor like a Damascus sword.

"Says here the Venetians completed the Bourtzi in 1473 to protect the city from pirates and invaders from the sea," Chance read from his ever-present guidebook. "The Greeks recaptured it from the Turks in 1822. Until 1865 it served as a fortress, when it was transformed into—get this—a residence for the executioners of convicts from Palamidi Castle. From 1930 to 1970 it was a hotel. Now it's a tourist attraction and hosts parts of the Summer Music Festival."

"Music festival sounds much nicer than the executioner's house," Petra said.

"A small price to pay for waterfront property," her husband, the ex-golfer, David said, "as long as you don't mind loping off a few deserving heads every now and then."

"How dreadful," Petra said.

"I'm sure the criminals deserve it," Dr. Lodge said.

As Race drove, they sped down the gulf's rugged, dry west coast. Widely spaced vacation homes dotted the rocky hillsides above scenic coves. The white houses with orange tile roofs contrasted with the ultramarine water, but matched the beaches, carpeted with white rocks worn smooth by centuries of waves. The villages of Miloi, Astros and Tiros nestled in rugged bays as if huddling against the approach of modernity. Goats roamed in the barren spaces between the villages, eking out a subsistence diet on the stark slopes. Any remotely flat area was covered with orchards of stunted, gnarled olive trees.

"We went to a great hole-in-the-wall *souvlaki* place last night," David said. "Just off the central square."

"The Greek salad and some sort of yoghurt was excellent," Petra said.

"The lamb was fabulous," David said, earning a pained look from his vegan wife.

"I saw a hamburger on the menu at the place we went," Chance said. "Even though we've only been here a few days, I was missing some good old American food, so I ordered it. Had a bit of trouble establishing communications since no one spoke English, but I think they understood the mission. I surveilled the kitchen to keep eyes on my burger and make sure they did it right. They fried up a patty, procured a bun, and applied some sort of sauce and lettuce and tomato. All was well. I took eyes off my burger and went to liberate a drink from a display case. When I returned, the burger was done, perfect, mission accomplished. Then the lady pressed my perfect burger flat and before I could intervene dumped it into a deep fryer."

Everyone laughed.

"Why would you come to another country to eat the same food you can get at home?" the physio, Gayle asked.

"You should always stick to the local food," Dr. Lodge said. "That is what they do best. In Italy, I only eat pasta, polenta and gelato. In Argentina, asado and empenadas, and in Singapore, Chilli crab. "

Chance said, "On my honor as an officer of the United States Air Force, retired, I will only consume Greek food the remainder of this trip; breakfast, lunch and dinner."

At Leonidio, Race turned inland. They drove along the edge of a V-shaped piece of flat land protruding in from the coast between a steep ridge and Mount Parnon. On the ridge stood three stone windmills. The flat land was covered with greenhouses, fields of tomato plants, and citrus and olive orchards. Around the fields Frankish-style stone mansions clung to the steep, rocky hillside, like rows of white boxes lining shelves in a closet.

"In most of Greece, save Sparta, towns are on hills," Race said. "Given there's little flat arable land in Greece, what there is must be used for farming. In fact, Greece is so hilly that it has no navigable rivers."

Race drove up through the town and into the square, which featured overarching fig trees and a rustic taverna with outdoor tables. Race slowed, but Scarlett shot him a look of warning.

"We have time," Race said, sotto voce.

"No. We don't."

"What's half an hour in a lifetime, even a short one? Besides, I'm hungry."

"You're always hungry."

"Let's make it democratic." Raising his voice, Race asked everyone, "Who wants to sample the local ouzo or a chilled Retsina?"

The vote was unanimous, save for Scarlet, who abstained although her sour expression left little doubt as to how she would have voted. The tour ordered Greek coffee, black tea with lemon, orange Fanta (Rob, of course), lemonade, Retsina, ouzo, and Amstel beer. Race had a Retsina wine, which came in a copper cup filled to the lip, the wine forming a convex curve that appeared to defy gravity. At one of the tables under a fig tree he sat in a silver metal chair at a table with Gayle, who waited for a steaming Greek coffee to cool enough to drink. Geraniums, honeysuckles and lemon trees in the gardens of adjacent homes added a nostalgic scent to the air.

"I'm trying to figure out who stole Dr. Lodge's wallet," Race said, sipping his wine, which was smooth and refreshing with a fruity after-taste.

"Served Lodge right," Gayle snapped. "Wish he'd lost everything." She picked up her white porcelain coffee cup. Holding it near her lips, she apparently sensed it was still too hot. She set it back down on the wood-slat table. "Probably lying anyway; probably never even had the money. He always was a smooth talker, a real player."

"Dr. Lodge said he knew you, but didn't elaborate."

Gayle gazed up at the red hills that reared up above the town, narrowing inland to form the mouth of the Badron Gorge. When she spoke, her voice sounded as if it was coming from far away. "Several lifetimes ago I won a scholarship to Lodge's college in upstate New York. I was so excited; all the way across the country, first time away from home—an adventure. It was great. I learned a lot, until I met him." She laughed; laughter laced with melancholy. "I guess he taught me a lot, too, about love and sex, and the vast gulf between the two. He convinced me I was the only girl for him. He said he'd leave his wife and we'd run away together—fat chance." Gayle glared down at her steaming coffee.

Race knew he shouldn't drink wine. It might interfere with the antibiotics he took to ward off lung infections, but a sip or three shouldn't hurt. To stretch his ration, he sipped his wine ever so slowly to savor every drop—and to give Gayle time to talk. After a pause, he asked, "Any ideas about what happened to his wallet?"

Gayle looked across at the other tables. Race looked, too. Petra, David and Dr. Lodge sat together. Scarlett was drinking Retsina with the reticent accountant and taekwondo black belt Cohen. Rob sat with Chance and Sonja, although Sonja appeared left out of whatever Rob and Chance were enthusiastically discussing with expressive hand movements, waving arms and exclamations, as if describing aerial combat.

Leaning close to Race, Gayle whispered, "Maybe Petra stole the money. She went back to the van. She was furious when she heard her wonderful, deified Daddy had a bastard child with me, a Latina." Gayle sipped her black coffee, which had finally cooled enough to drink—or maybe anger had dulled her senses.

"Petra doesn't seem like—"

"Do bigots wear a capital B embroidered on their shirts? Probably stole the wallet to get back at dear old dad."

Another long pause.

"Beznik unlocked the van for you—"

"For David and I." Gayle stared at Race, considering. "David put Petra's sweater back and I dug around for my wallet. I'd taken my money belt off the first day. It hung around my neck, but rubbed me in all the wrong places." She touched between her breasts. "I put it with my wallet in the bottom of my carryon; harder for a thief to find, but also harder for me to get at."

"How long were you in the van?"

"A few minutes." She shook her head, her unkept shoulder-length black hair spraying out like leaves in a dust storm. "My arm was hurting, so I dug out some Aspirin; had to find my water bottle to take them."

"Was David with you?"

"David was on and off fast. He burrowed through the stack of bags in his row like a terrier after a choice bone, until he found the right bag. Most of the time he was outside talking with your driver." Gayle thought for a moment. "I don't think Beznik could have taken the wallet then. He didn't even get in the van with us."

Gayle appeared not to have realized she had just implicated herself in the theft of the wallet: alone in the van for several minutes, emerging with cash to pay for lunch. Was she that naïve or was it a clever ploy to make it appear that the thought of stealing the wallet had never even occurred to her?

Race sipped his illicit wine. At least everyone seemed to be enjoying the stop. Scarlett needed to learn to slow down. The broad, spreading limbs of the square's fig trees provided welcome shade from the sun, which had long-since burned off the morning cloud and was pushing temperatures into the high 70s at the mouth of the red-rimmed gorge. Birds chirped, sang and squawked amongst the branches of the overarching figs.

Race asked Gayle, "Did you happen to see anything on the plane as we landed in Athens?"

"Sorry, no. I was asleep."

"It was turbulent."

"If you've traveled as much as I have with the various Olympic teams, you can sleep from takeoff to touchdown through a typhoon, cyclone or tornado—probably all three." Gayle shot a glance over at Rob, who now sat alone, his sneakered feet up on a silver metal chair, swigging his orange Fanta from a glass bottle. Chance and Sonja now stood by David and Petra's table, chatting.

"I'm sad the woman died," Gayle said. "She was the well-dressed older lady, right? Her son certainly fell far from the tree." Gayle's gaze flicked back over to Rob. "Dresses like a slob; never talks to anyone much."

"Shy?"

"His mother talked with me as we were boarding at JFK; seemed very nice, and so excited about the trip. Her son never said much to her; nothing like David Fox."

"You know David?"

"No," she said with regret. "At JFK Petra was in tears over something and David was so helpful and soothing; picked her spirits right up in no time." A wistful smile spread across Gayle's face.

Leaving Leonidio behind, Race drove inland up into the Badron Gorge. A river, now dry, had cut the gorge into red cliffs hundreds of feet high. Even dry, the river nurtured a dense canopy of trees that ran along its crumbling banks. The road twisted with hairpin turns and switchbacks as they climbed, rarely seeing another car.

Rob asked, "Are we there yet?"

"Not yet," Race said. "See the caves in the cliffs?"

"Some of them appear to have rock walls constructed in front of them like buttresses," Dr. Lodge observed as he peered through his camera with a lens the length of a child's arm.

"Shepherds use them as shelter," Race said. "Have for centuries."

Rounding a corner on the road they beheld an incredible sight: Moni Profitis Ilonas Monastery. Two-thirds of the way up a sheer rock face hundreds of feet above the narrow twisting road perched the white Monastery of Elona, as it was also known. A telephone pole stood incongruously at the top of the cliff like a bereft flagpole. Race stopped and the excursionists piled out of the van.

"You've got to be kidding," David exclaimed as he stared up at the gravity-defying monastery.

"Stunning," Dr. Lodge said as he readied his camera.

"How did they ever build it?" Chance asked.

"Awesomely cool," Rob said, scrambling atop a boulder alongside the road for a better view. "Looks like a Frank Frazetta painting in a comic book."

"The monastery was built on the site where a light was seen night after night high up on the cliff," Race said. "Since the mid-1400s, it's been a holy place with a water-filled cave that's said to cure many ailments. It also served as a hiding place during the Ottoman Turk occupation and both world wars."

"Wonder if it would cure my back," David said. "Could make it back to the tour if my back was 100 percent."

"Do I hear bells?" Cohen asked.

Rob was the first to spot earth-colored goats in the sandy riverbed far below with a shepherd meandering behind them, his head down, deep in thought.

"Looks like a picture out of the 12th century," Dr. Lodge said.

Rob laughed and exclaimed with delight, "He's using a cell phone."

"How in hell does he get a signal?" Chance asked.

"I've got a signal," Sonja said as a call she was making found a connection.

"Put your damn phone away," Chance roared. "Enjoy the bloody scenery."

Sonja shot her husband a patronizing smile and said into her cell, "Bruce, love, about that part in *The Chronicles of Narnia*…"

Photos taken and memories made, they drove on. After several switchbacks, they passed above the monastery.

"The monks welcome visitors," Race whispered to Scarlett.

Scarlett just tapped her watch.

Race told the group, "You can see the phone booth near the monastery entrance. It is said to have the finest view of any phone booth in Greece, down the gorge."

"Not another damn phone," Chance snarled, glaring at Sonja, who was back—or was it still?—on her cell.

After snaking their way 12 kilometers up through the spectacular red-walled gorge, they climbed out onto the Parnon Massif with its fir forests and broad meadows. They drove through the mountain village of Kosmas and down through Geraki, Vlahiotis and Sikia. The ancient villages seemed securely embedded in a quaint version of the Middle Ages, each with a tree-shaded square and rustic tavernas. Driving through Sikia, the road narrowed and narrowed again until, behind a rust-spotted, green tractor, Race was beginning to fear the van wouldn't fit between the white-washed stone houses.

"This can't be the right road," Scarlett whispered to Race. The tractor seemed in danger of wedging its fat rear wheels between the houses.

"Not like we have any turning options," Race said.

The farmer on the tractor looked back and frowned, which did nothing to boost Race's waning confidence.

"Maybe stop and back up?" Cohen asked.

"Let's keep going," David said with a devil-may-care grin.

"Maybe we should stop and ask directions," Gayle said, her good hand held up to her mouth.

"Do you not know the way?" Dr. Lodge demanded. "I would think you would have thoroughly reconnoitered the tour's route before beginning."

"Where's your sense of adventure?" Chance asked, giving Lodge's shoulder a good-natured slap, which only earned a glare from the dating website king.

Ignoring the backseat driving, Race drove down the narrowing channel of a street. Just as the cacophony in the van was reaching rebellious levels and Race was considering stopping to attempt to back up, they popped out the bottom of the village into the open.

They soon hit flatter, more open country and sped across Laconia to the coast. Turning south at the Myrtoan Sea, part of the
Aegean, they rounded a point to see a domed island looming just
off shore: Monemvasia. The island fortress showed nothing but
rock and a remnant of a crumbling wall high on its flattened crest.
Continuing along through Gefyra, a village strung along the coast,
Race turned onto the 200-meter causeway to the fortress.

"Monemvasia means single entry and the causeway is the only
way onto the Gibraltar of Greece," Race said. "During the summer,
cars are banned, but the rest of the year they're allowed across."

"Looks like a giant bowler hat," Dr. Lodge said, looking up at
the island.

Tired from the long drive and stifling coughs, Race parked in
one of the dozen angled spots where the causeway widened slightly
near the city gates. "Prepare to step back in time," he said as everyone exited the van.

Rob surged ahead with the energetic Gayle just behind. The
gate into the stronghold was in a stone wall wedged between the
cliff and the sea. Walking through the gate, Race felt a cool breeze
as he turned right and then left through a zigzag that prevented
attackers from moving quickly through the wall. From the dim
cool tunnel he stepped into the warm sunlight on Monemvasia's
main stone-paved street. The island was pedestrian only. Even a
Mini would have had difficulty navigating the narrow cobblestone
streets, let alone the even narrower alleys, most of which turned
into stairs as they snaked up the steep slope toward the fortress.
Restaurant tables with red-check tablecloths stood in marginally
wider sections of the street. Grape vines were interwoven through
trellises to provide shade for diners, although none were in sight.

"What an awesome fortress," Rob exclaimed as he took in the
scene down the Medieval street.

Chance looked back at the zigzag gate and said, "What a position. No one could ever take this place."

"It withstood Arab and Norman attacks in 1147," Race said,
"but the Frank, William II of Villehardouin took it after three years
of siege in 1248. He later built Mystras, which we visit tomorrow."

"What's a Frank?" Cohen asked.

"A Germanic people from the lower Rhine river area," Race
said.

"Amazing anyone could conquer it," Chance said. "Must have been an epic siege."

"With unimaginable suffering," the physio, Gayle said.

"Beautiful location for a sea-side estate," Sonja said, gazing south between a stone house and a white-washed Orthodox church at the azure Aegean.

"No room for a driving range, let alone a golf course though," David said.

"Some 40,000 people lived in Monemvasia at its height in the 14th, 15th and 16th centuries, with the Byzantines, Turks, Franks, and Venetians holding it at various times as a major trading center," Race said as they strolled up the main avenue that inclined gently as it paralleled the shore. "Today, with a population of about 50, some of the houses are abandoned, while others are being restored to shelter the tourist horde that invades every summer."

Scarlett and Race checked everyone into their rooms while the excursionists explored the lower town and the fortress above it. Race's lungs were starting to restrict his breathing, so he found two local boys to haul everyone's bags from the van to the rooms for 20 euro. Since Scarlett loathed the debit side of her balance book, he told her their hotel, the Malvasia, provided the boys. The hotel offered unique rooms in various quaint buildings through-out the old town. Race and Scarlett's rooms were side by side in a white-washed building with dark-wood shutters. The rooms were low-ceilinged with wood-beams and white stone fireplaces with decades' worth of soot coating the mantels. Eyeing the fire extin-guishers that stood nearby, Race was relieved the night would not be chilly enough to warrant a fire. Small windows cut through the thick walls overlooked the sea.

"After I clear my lungs and drug up, let's go explore," Race said as he unpacked his mechanical precussor, which would shake the phlegm from his lungs.

"You should rest," Scarlett said as she sat on his bed reviewing the next day's itinerary. "It was a long drive."

"I've been sitting too long."

"I don't want you getting run down."

Race stopped his unpacking, looked at her and said, "Scarlett, I'm not going to spend the rest of my life resting."

She met his stare, but said nothing.

A half hour later, they were striding up the steep, narrow streets toward the top of the island. Massive stoneworks supported the path that zigzagged up the cliff, which looked impossible to scale, let alone if there were any defenders armed with anything more than pebbles. They paused to take in the view of the tightly packed town below. A church with a circular roof stood out amidst all the rectangular orange clay tile roofs clustered on the incline between the base of the massif and the Aegean. Cypresses poked up like natural flagpoles from amongst the buildings and lush vegetation that flourished throughout the town.

"How did 40,000 people ever cram into such a small area?" Scarlett wondered.

"Many would have lived up on top," Race said.

Fifteen minutes after they started their climb, Race's lungs laboring, they reached the fortress's main gate of 6-inch thick planks bound with iron bolts. The fortress encompassed the entire top of the massif. The area was relatively flat, widening to 300 meters and stretching almost a kilometer back toward the coast. From where they stood just inside the gate, they could not see the edges of the plateau. It took half an hour to trek across the island, winding their way toward the mainland along narrow paths past dozens of ruined stone buildings, a long-abandoned Byzantine church, and the early blooms of violets, narcissus, peonies, primroses, tulips, poppies, and anemones.

They finally reached the highest point on the island, which was nearest the mainland. A lonely, weathered stone arch and the remains of a cluster of crumbling buildings stood nearby. Scarlett took pictures as the wind whipped her hair, her auburn streak flapping like a pennant. Race could smell the sea 900 feet below. As he admired Palaia Monemvasia Bay and the white houses of Gefyra along the coast, Scarlett asked, "Did you ever take pictures much?"

"Used to, so I could remember places I'd been."

"Not anymore?"

"I want to live so I won't need photographs to remember any day."

Finished with her photography, Scarlett led the way as they trekked back across the island. They came upon David Fox sitting alone on a tuft of grass watching the sun slip toward the wall of mountains that formed a palisade along the Peloponnesian coast. The sleeves of his dark blue windbreaker snapped in the breeze.

David said, "Petra and her father are down taking endless pictures of that ruined church."

"The Church of Ayia Sophia," Race said.

Scarlett and Race made small talk before Race decided it was as good a time as any to ask about the stolen wallet.

"Shame about the cash, but I don't see any reason to ruin Beznik's life," David said. "Seems like a nice kid. I'm sure if he apologized, all would be forgiven."

Scarlett's expression hardened as she said, "He did not take the money."

"If he just admitted it to Lodge, we could forget the whole damn thing and get on with the trip; have some fun in the sun."

"Beznik would never admit to something he didn't do," Scarlett said.

Race asked, "Why do you think Beznik took the money?"

"He's poor," David said, spitting out the despicable word. "Look at that cutter-rigged sloop," he said, standing as he shielded his eyes to better view a fully-rigged sailboat as it tacked from a cove just down the bay. "Must be 50-foot at least. Magnificent." He watched her for a long loving moment.

Race said, "What happened when you returned to the van at the Corinth canal?"

With a sigh, as if it was onerous to remember such mundane things, David said, "Beznik unlocked the van for Gayle and me. I put Petra's sweater back and got off to talk with Beznik."

"About what?"

"I wanted to learn about the real Greece, where the best spots are to eat and drink and such, but we ended up talking cars. Young men are the same the world over: fast cars and faster girls."

"Beznik didn't get into the van?" Race asked.

"No." David gazed at the sailboat then frowned and said, "Gayle took a while in the van. Don't know what she was doing." Tearing his gaze from the sloop, he said, "She didn't have euros for lunch, and when she returned from the van she had the euros to pay."

"She said she got money from her wallet."

"Seemed to take her a long time." David paused. "I saw her at the ATM at the airport." He stopped again, frowning with concentration. "No, I....I can't be sure, but I think she was in line for the ATM, but then got tired of waiting and walked away. No, I'm pretty certain she didn't use the ATM. She walked over to a concession and was looking at a candy display when Petra went to get a snack."

He turned to watch the sailboat as a breeze filled its white sails.

Scarlett said, "We seek to make every excursion a trip of a lifetime, but Petra doesn't seem to be enjoying herself. Is there anything we can do to help her enjoy the excursion more?"

David laughed. "Fly her dogs over here first class."

Race asked, "Did you notice anything on the plane related to Mrs. Rasmussen?"

"Her son ignored her," David said. "Petra, who's far from easily riled, finally yelled at him to help his mom. I hadn't even realized they were related. Kudos to you for trying to save her life. Wish I knew first aid and such, but other than sprains, strains and dehydration from triathlons, I'm not much use for anything beyond a paper cut. Probably faint if I saw a dead body."

"Did you see anything else on the plane?"

"Lodge chatting up the stewardess—got her number as usual, even if she was a third his age—and Petra reading some book on dog training by a bunch of monks. Not the best company on a long flight, but what are you gonna do? For better or for worse, for richer or poorer, in sickness and in health...."

When Scarlett and Race arrived at one of the only open restaurants on the island just after 8 pm—the time Greeks usually begin to consider thinking about dinner—they said good evening to Dr. Lodge, Petra and David Fox at one table, Chance and Sonja at another, and, seated alone, Gayle Garcia, who politely declined their invitation to dine with them. The excursionists were the only customers. At their table on the flagstone patio, Race and Scarlett had a view of the Aegean in one direction and the pink-hued castle atop its rock in the other.

The waiter, a Brit, as many waiters in Greece are, said, "We were running three dinner sittings for the Easter holiday and we'll be positively knackered after the May 1 holiday, but right now there are almost no tourists, so most restaurants shutter."

For 10 euro and the promise of business from future tours Scarlett negotiated a dinner for two of *fasolada* soup filled with white beans, tomato, carrots, onion, and parsley to start, followed by lamb gyros, fries, *souvlaki, daktyla* bread, and white wine.

Race overheard a waiter ask David at the next table, "What can our chef make you tonight?"

"Rich," David replied with a grin.

"Where are Cohen and Rob?" Scarlett asked Race, always concerned about her excursionists.

"Some fine seafood restaurants over in Gefyra."

"Or after murdering his mother, Rob is on the first plane to somewhere Greece doesn't have an extradition treaty with."

"North Korea? Cuba? Iran? Not the best places to spend your inheritance, however you got it."

"Better than rotting in a Greek jail."

"Maybe they have a cell on Santorini with a nice sea view."

The lamb was cooked to perfection, tender enough to melt in their mouths. The *souvlaki*, which they shared, featured vegetables that exploded with flavor as they bit into them.

As Race ate, he heard Dr. Lodge say, "I thought all Greeks would be dark haired and brown eyed with olive skin. I have seen everything from blonde to black hair and from pale white skin to almost black."

Since everyone from Romans to Venetians, Franks to Byzantines, Brits to Russians had passed through Greece over the centuries, Race knew there was an immensely broad range of contributors to the Greek gene pool.

"I just hate how every Greek male above the age of 12 smokes," Petra said.

"As do many of the women," Dr. Lodge said. "Hard to find them dates in the States if they smoke."

"But they dress like Parisian models," David said. "Far sexier than American women."

"I'll say," Chance said, overhearing from his table. "Some beauties over here, and they know how to show off their best assets." Sonja glared at him, but he didn't seem to notice.

While everyone ate, a cat appeared to beg, making the rounds from table to table.

"I wish they treated their dogs as well as they do their cats," Petra said. "People leave plates of fish out in the streets of the villages for stray cats, but I've seen dogs all skin and bones; so sad."

"Sharon will take five-star care of your dogs," David reassured his wife, patting her hand on the table top and kissing her cheek.

As the sun set over the coast in a spectacular array of colors, Race offered the stray cat a chunk of lamb from his *souvlaki,* which was quickly accepted. In less than a minute, he was surrounded by five strays in a range of colors from ghostly white to midnight black. Race glanced at Petra, the vegan, and received a sad look in return.

As Race wondered if Petra frowned upon the feeding of meat even to felines, David said, "Please excuse her. She's bereft without her dogs."

As if on cue, a sad-eyed droopy black Labrador retriever ambled through the doorway from the restaurant to the patio. The dog was 15 and deaf, and belonged to the waiter, who said the dog was Monemvasia's unofficial mascot. Petra greeted the mascot warmly with pieces of David's lamb gyro. Veganism apparently did not extend to canines.

Still hungry after his first course, Race ordered a Greek salad and *moussaka* with eggplant, beef, onions, garlic, tomato sauce, oregano, and a rich cheese sauce.

"How's your weight?" Scarlett asked, watching Race take more enzyme pills to help digest his *moussaka.*

"Close to my target," Race said, and then asked Scarlett about her future tour plans to change the subject.

"I've been running the numbers to consider expanding from two to four excursions a quarter, and…"

As they finished their dinners, a light rain began to patter on the patio. As it gained in volume everyone hurried inside, the last rays of sunlight now gone. Inside, the Lab curled up next to Petra, who scratched him with loving, attentive and experienced fingers. He did not look like he had too bad a life, even if he wasn't a cat.

As everyone lingered over Greek coffee at candle-lit tables inside, Race heard David tell his father-in-law, who already had his new wallet out, "I'll pay."

"I will pay," Dr. Lodge said.

"You lost 1,200 euros yesterday," David said. "Please let me cover dinner."

"Our treat, Dad," Petra added, placing a hand over her father's to stay his hand. "We insist."

After a pause, Dr. Lodge slid his wallet back into his pocket and with great formality said, "Thank you."

The trio rose and headed back to their rooms, followed by Chance and Sonja. Moments later, as Race and Scarlett walked past their tables, Race noticed David's tip: a 20-euro note. At Chance's table, a single euro coin glittered in the candlelight.

Race and Scarlett strolled through the darkness back toward their rooms. The worst of the rain had moved on, scenting the air with ozone and leaving a sheen on the stone-paving which gleamed in the illumination cast by the widely spaced streetlights held in Medieval metal frames. The few store owners still open for business gossiped before their narrow store fronts as they stretched out the process of closing for the day. Light from their stores cast shadows across the narrow cobblestone street and against the wall on the other side. Race smelled Greek coffee wafting from the cups held by the shopkeepers as they clicked worry beads called *komboloi* and chatted and laughed with each other. The town was silent with no cars or machinery, and the narrow streets and aged, uneven stone buildings made Race imagine he had been transported back to the 15th century.

"Look," Scarlett hissed.

Race looked to where she pointed, her hand close to her body, index finger extended as if she did not want to be seen pointing. Race saw a corpulent shopkeeper take an ornamental dagger, which sparkled with gems in the store's stark light, from a display stand just outside the door and step inside with his last customer of the day: Rob Rasmussen.

Moments later, as Race and Scarlett watched, Rob emerged carrying a white plastic bag, which bounced heavily against his thigh. Rob strode their way a few steps, saw them and, with a curt nod, turned on his sneakered heel and headed back deeper into the darkened town.

Race said, "At least he wasn't on the first flight to Pyongyang."

"What's he buying daggers for?" Scarlett asked. "And why'd he bolt when he saw us?"

"More like an about-face than a bolt."

Grasping Race's arm tighter, her head flicking left and right to scan the shadow-filled street, Scarlett said, "First he kills his mother, then tries to push Gayle off Palamidi Fortress, and now he's buying daggers. We have a psychopathic killer on this tour. We should tell Inspector Kanavou."

"Kanavou said Rob's mom died of natural causes, and Gayle just lost track of where she was standing."

"What was Rob doing sneaking up behind her?"

"He wears sneakers, how else can he approach someone? Is he supposed to belt out show tunes at all times?"

As they strolled back toward their rooms, Scarlett said, "Maybe Gayle saw something incriminating on the plane when Rob murdered his mother."

"Such as?"

"Rob disposing of his mother's inhalers somewhere."

"Why didn't she tell the police?"

"Maybe she doesn't realize she saw something important."

"Then why kill her?"

"Rob's afraid she'll realize it's important."

"Then why save her from falling off Palamidi Castle?" The cool, moist night sea air prickled against Race's bare arms. "What are you reading now?"

Scarlett frowned. "*Beyond a Reasonable Doubt* by C.W. Grafton; Excellent novel, by Sue Grafton's father. I like it better than most of her novels. Why?"

"A mystery?"

"Murder," Scarlett said, rolling the word off her tongue with great relish.

"You should read something else tonight. I have *Aunt Julia and the Scriptwriter*. It's good; a comedy about a scriptwriter for South American soap operas who finds that what he's writing for the show is beginning to happen in real life."

"Why should I read it tonight?"

"Help you realize the difference between fantasy and reality, and stop seeing murder everywhere."

"Not murders, just one murder and one attempted murder—oh, and the theft of a wallet. I didn't imagine that, did I?"

Scarlett unlocked the door to her room.

"Come in for a bit," she said, "but lock the door behind you. I'll jam a chair under the handle after you leave."

"I doubt Rob will come in the night to murder you, but if you're worried, I could spend the night."

"Tempting, but I think we should keep our relationship all business."

"If it makes you happy, feel free to pay me."

Chapter 7

Day 5: Wednesday, April 21

The tour met for breakfast in an arched room sunk half underground beneath one of the hotel's many scattered buildings. Chance reported that Sonja was late.

"Probably misjudged her jog," he said as he poured himself Greek coffee. "She said she was going to cross the causeway and jog along the coast five clicks, but she may have gone farther—or more likely, she called someone on her damn cell, lost track of the distance and found herself half way to Athens."

"I'm on vacation," David announced. "Only a little light training for me, and no cell phone; hate the damn things."

"He does Ironman triathlons," Petra added. "First in his age group at Kona last year."

"Really must they insist on the foul habit of smoking?" Dr. Lodge asked as the ex-professor eyed a couple eating breakfast just down the narrow white-walled room.

"It is legal here," Race said as he finished *The Times* crossword.

Scarlett said, "I'm sure you can sit away from them."

"I will still smell the disgusting odor, not to mention be exposed to the dangerous chemicals and carcinogens in the fumes," Dr. Lodge said with a look of grim distaste.

Race wondered if he wasn't the only one with bad lungs.

"Can I see that when you're done?" Chance asked Race, eyeing his London newspaper.

Race held the paper out to Chance.

"I thought you were doing the crossword."

"I'm done."

Chance frowned, eyeing the blank crossword.

"He does them in his head," Scarlett said.

Chance laughed. With a smile, Scarlett offered Chance a wager. Chance accepted and, picking up his pen, Race wrote in all the answers to the puzzle without pause. Staring at the completed crossword, Chance handed over 20 euros to Scarlett.

"I should get a cut of that," Race said.

"You will; it'll cover some of your wages."

After breakfast, the group gathered with their bags on the town's main pedestrian street. Rob showed off his dagger to everyone, before carefully wrapping it in a white T-shirt and stuffing it in his bag.

"Better check that for the flight home," Chance advised with a grin.

"I can't believe he showed everyone that thing," Scarlett whispered to Race.

"Maybe he doesn't plan to sink it into anyone's chest."

While the tour members took some last photos of Monemvasia, Scarlett and Race with help from Gayle, bad wrist ignored, started schlepping the bags out the ancient zigzag gate to the van. They passed a donkey train entering the town. Each donkey's worn and battered leather saddle had a wood shelf on each side with a rock block strapped to it.

As he reached the van, Race started to cough. He set the bags he was carrying down as the coughing wracked his body. He staggered over to the low stone wall that overlooked the sea. Between coughs, he spat out phlegm laced with blood into the sea below. The coughing would not stop. He felt Scarlett's arm around his shoulders and heard comforting words from her and Gayle, but he kept coughing. Pain radiated throughout his chest with each cough. Then, as suddenly as it had started, the fit passed. He spat out a final glob of ugly, green phlegm discolored with streaks of blood.

"Do you need to stay here and rest?" Scarlett asked. "You could catch up with the tour in a couple of days."

Race breathed deeply, took a swig of water from a water bottle he carried and, spitting it out, said, "I'll be fine."

Race insisted on accompanying Scarlett and Gayle back for the second load of bags. He hated letting CF control him. As they stepped out into the light from the zigzag gate, a sun-weathered Greek approached along the narrow street leading a donkey train loaded with the rest of the tour's suitcases.

"Figured we could use some help," David said with a Huck Finn grin as he ambled along behind the donkeys.

"Let us cover the cost," Race offered, earning the briefest of concerned looks from Scarlett as her frugal nature conflicted with her desire to maintain her gold-standard of customer service.

"No, no," David said, waving off the offer. "My pleasure. Besides, makes a great story; well worth the price of admission. Might come back and start a business here, buy some donkeys and whisk tourists' bags to their cars."

"Looks like he has a corner on the carry trade," Race said, nodding toward the weathered workman who led the donkeys. "Yesterday he had a dozen donkeys carrying supplies in for a reconstruction project."

"Maybe I can get a job with him, then," David said. "Worse things than working outside under a Grecian sun. All I need is an interview and I'm in; done it a dozen times."

"Do you have any donkey experience?" Race asked with mock seriousness.

"Plenty with the two-legged kind."

Two-hours later they arrived at the capital of Laconia and the home of the greatest military society in history: Sparta. The ancient warrior city, which has never been sacked, sat in a broad valley guarded by the Aegean to the south, Mount Taygetus to the west, Mount Parnon to the east, and hilly uplands rising to 1,000 meters to the north. Race drove up the valley from the south through orchards, passing open trucks laden with oranges. A citrus scent filled the van. As they approached a military base just south of the city, Chance raised his camera.

Race said, "Please no photos of the base."

"Just one recon shot?" Chance asked, having put down his guidebook for once. "A Spartan military base; it's too good to miss."

Dr. Lodge said, "I would prefer to stop for a photograph. It would make an interesting conversational image."

"It's illegal," Race said.

"The barracks among the fruit trees do look idyllic," Petra said.

"Yeah, just one shot of famous Sparta's military base?" Rob asked, raising his camera.

"Without pictures, nothing's real," Sonja said.

"Please don't," Scarlett insisted. "A few years ago some British tourists whose hobby was 'plane spotting'—a competition to collect the most airplane tail numbers—were sentenced to prison just for writing down the tail numbers of military aircraft on public display at a Greek air show. If they'd taken photographs the sentence would have been twenty years."

"That sucks," Rob said, but he, Chance and Lodge lowered their cameras.

"Sounds a little extreme," Petra said.

"The Greeks have been invaded dozens of times over the centuries," Race said.

"It's a tough neighborhood," Chance said. "I'd be hyper-vigilant, too."

As they entered Sparta, Race drove between multi-story, cinderblock houses and apartment buildings with varnished wood shutters. Olive, mulberry and orange trees provided shade and greenery.

"Nice wide streets and lots of flowers," Petra said. "But the apartment blocks are pretty drab."

"I hope you did not include Sparta on the itinerary merely because it is famous," Dr. Lodge said. "I was on a tour of Britain that included Stratford upon Avon; apparently included merely for its historical link to Shakespeare, instead of for any intrinsic sightseeing value. The main street reminded me of an American strip mall."

"We didn't come here for Sparta," Race said.

"Then, if you don't mind saying, why'd we come here?" Cohen asked from the back of the van.

"For that." Race pointed to the west. Extensive ruins carpeted a vast swath of land on a steep spur of Mount Taygetos. "Mystras."

Only a couple of the buildings still sported orange clay tile roofs, but scores of stone walls attested to the vast size of the Byzantine city. Pencil cypresses stood in rows, as if subdividing the expansive site. Plane and fig trees provided shade, while stalks 10 feet high topped with yellow flowers competed for colorful dominance with the red, yellow and purple wildflowers that bloomed in abundance across the rocky site. Even in the van, Race could smell wild sage and thyme.

"Wow," Rob said, staring in awe up at the ruins that spilled down the mountainside like the remains of an avalanche. "Cool."

"Beautiful," Sonja said, "the poppies against the white stones. The ruins. Wish we could film a movie here, a romance. I'll call Bruce." She took out her cell.

"Magnificent walls," Chance said. "What a position."

Cohen asked, "Who built it all?"

"The Franks in 1249," Race said. "The Byzantines took it and they lost it to the Turks in 1460. The Venetians took possession in 1687 and the Turks recaptured it in 1715, before it was burned and abandoned. It's now a World Heritage Site. We'll park at the top—you can park at the top or bottom—and walk down through it. I'll pick everyone up at the bottom."

As Race maneuvered the van up the serpentine road, he coughed, earning a concerned look from Scarlett, but the spasm passed. He parked and, entering the site through a stone gate larger than a four-bedroom home, led the group several hundred yards up the slope to the citadel perched at the pinnacle of the ruined city.

"The despot lived here, ruling over the Byzantine Despotate of the Morea," Race said. "As Mystras grew in importance and became the seat of government for the area, the city added first one and then a second set of walls. Among the dozens of ruined stone buildings, I recommend the Convent of Pantanassa, which has been operating since the 1300s. It has impressive 14th century religious paintings."

"It must have been a mighty power in its day," Dr. Lodge said as he rummaged in his camera bag.

"In the 13th century it was the second most important city in the Byzantine Empire after Constantinople," Race said. "The second home of the emperors."

"It's the picture of what Disney would draw for a ruined fortress and city," Petra said with a childish smile of delight. "Straight out of Scheherazade and *One Thousand and One Nights.*"

As the group dispersed, Scarlett and Race wandered around the citadel, peering over the walls down the sheer cliffs that had protected Mystras for 750 years. Coming around an eroded stone column, they found Rob slumped atop a stone wall. He stared out at the view of the lush valley below with the braided Eurotas River, its banks crowded with trees, snaking down the valley. The new city of Sparta, built in the 1830s when Mystras was abandoned, stood along the river.

As they approached, Rob said, "Mom would have loved the view." His legs dangling over the precipice, he acted as if he was sitting on a stool at his local diner. "She would have loved you, too, Mr. Traveler. All that stuff about history and such; just loved it."

"We are terribly sorry she isn't with us," Scarlett said.

"Maybe it was a good time to die; just before you get something you've always wanted," Rob said. "The expectation of a thing is often better than the thing itself, isn't it?"

Race nodded, and glanced at Scarlett.

Scarlett leaned against the ancient waist-high stone wall beside Rob. Race stood near enough to grab Rob if the young man did something rash. It was more than 40 feet down to the jagged jumble of rocks, boulders and dislodged stones at the base of the wall.

"I wish I'd noticed her sooner," Rob said, his voice hoarse. Each word seemed to require almost more effort than he could bear. "It was a long flight. I was watching that…that damn movie."

A crag martin with white flashes on the underside of its wings flitted up and over them before banking and plummeting down the mountainside, its wings tucked as it accelerated faster than Race's eyes could follow.

"I made sure she ordered extra inhalers," Rob said. His sneakered heels hit the rock wall as he swung them forward and back, faster and faster, forward and back, harder and harder. "I made sure she packed them. I made sure she had them on the way to the airport. I stowed her bag at her feet, so it would be within easy reach, just in case. I know they were there. I know it. I know it. I know it." His heels kicked back into the wall again and again. Puffs of dirt and stone erupted from each strike. He seemed intent on being the one who finally leveled the walls of Mystras.

"Do you have any idea what happened to the inhalers?" Scarlett asked, her voice soothing and gentle, like a nurse checking on a terminal patient.

"No," Rob said. Leaning back, he sighed again and looked up at the snow-topped mountains above Mystras. Then he looked down the mountainside at the ruins of the partially restored palace in the upper city, and the middle and lower cities, each forming a broad crescent of ruins around the mountain. "Guess I should look around a little."

He slung his legs back over the wall and hopped down onto the uneven ground. White rocks, some jagged, some worn smooth with time, the elements and tourists' boots, protruded at irregular intervals, endangering ankles and knees. Even so, Rob set off at a rapid pace toward the citadel entrance as if he'd completely forgotten what he'd just been talking about.

Just shy of the entrance, Rob slowed and called over his shoulder, "I heard you're trying to figure out who stole Dr. Lodge's wallet. I'd ask Mr. Cohen."

Race wondered how Rob could know anything about the wallet. He'd been in Athens taking care of his mother's final arrangements when the wallet disappeared.

Rob said, "Petra said something about seeing Mr. Cohen hanging around the van at Corinth."

Race and Scarlett stopped to rest on the remains of a foundation that provided the excellent qualities of a bench, their backs against a stone pillar. In the refreshing shade, they shared a water bottle. Scarlett nibbled on beef jerky and trail mix from their daypacks, while Race ate salt-and-vinegar chips and pretzels to maintain his salt levels. It was a beautiful day for sight-seeing, in the mid-70s with a gentle breeze ruffling the tall grass and the leaves of the plane, cypress and mulberry trees.

Scarlett asked, "How are the lungs?"

"Better than this morning."

"Infection?"

Race shook his head. His lungs felt tight, but nothing like an infection—not yet.

"Maybe you should see a doctor in Sparta or Pylos."

Race nodded. For a time, they sat in companionable silence, legs extended, touching from hip to boot.

"I think you may be forgetting a key aspect of our deal," Dr. Lodge said, his voice relaxed, confident and controlled. From the crunch of footsteps on gravel, Race realized that Lodge and someone else were walking along the path just above and behind Race and Scarlett's prized pillar.

"Equal partnership; that was our deal," Cohen said.

"Between a full professor and an accounting sophomore? I know sophomore means wise fool, but you were far from wise then and you must be a fool now."

"I hope you rot in hell," Cohen roared and Race heard his heavy foot falls recede down the gravel path.

"I think here in Greece that would be Hades," Dr. Lodge called after his nemesis before laughing.

Scarlett whispered to Race, "Time to talk to Cohen about a wallet?"

"He certainly has a motive."

Their high-rise hotel stood in the northern part of Sparta with stunning views, depending on which way a room faced, of Mystras and Mount Taygetus, Mount Parnon, the uplands that separated Laconia from Arcadia, or the broad valley in which Sparta had raised its undefeated warriors for 250 years.

After dumping their bags in their rooms, Race and Scarlett rode down in the single-car elevator, which was barely large enough for two.

Race leaned in to kiss Scarlett, smelling Penguin peppermints on her breath. She shifted her head so he missed her lips. "Stop it."

"Why?"

She looked away at the wall six inches before her eyes.

Race asked, "You like me, don't you?"

Silence.

"You like me."

Finally she nodded. He smiled, until she said, "But I don't want to love you."

"Why not?"

She turned her head to stare at him with a look that said he knew why not; cystic fibrosis and all it entailed for the present and the future.

The elevator reached the lobby, swinging from their weight as it stopped. Spilling out of the elevator, they found Inspector Kanavou and Rob sitting in the lobby. A uniformed police officer and another man in a suit, probably another detective, stood discretely off to one side, but well within earshot.

Trying to push Scarlett's rebuff from his mind, Race stopped on the pretense of tying his hiking boot near the padded chairs in which Kanavou and Rob sat.

"I should have helped her," Rob said, his long dark hair swaying as he shook his head. "It's my fault."

Race glanced at Scarlett, who raised her eyebrows and gave him an I-told-you-so look. Scarlett already saw Rob as the poster boy for matricide.

"Rob," Race said, rising, "maybe you should consult an attorney before the inspector interviews you."

With his deep-set alert eyes Kanavou cast Race a look of warning. Rob turned his head to look up at Race as if he was struggling to return from a far distant place. Rob said, "I want to help."

Kanavou said, "If we can complete this interview now, it would be in the finest interest of the case and of your mother."

"This is Greece, Rob," Race said. "Their laws are different. I wouldn't want you to say something you shouldn't."

"I just have some routine questions to ask to complete my report," Kanavou said. "Nothing of importance; no need to go to all the expense and time of finding and retaining a barrister."

"I don't need a lawyer," Rob said. He still sounded distant, as if lost in some far-off place.

"I'm no lawyer, but mind if I sit in?" Race asked with a cheery smile as if asking to join a friendly poker game.

Kanavou, his lips set in a grim line, said, "As long as you just listen."

Race sat in the third of the four padded chairs that formed a seating area in the lobby. Kanavou took out a cigarette, earning a disapproving look from Rob. Kanavou replaced it in the pack and slid the pack back into his inside suit jacket pocket. Instead he took out a string of black *komboloi*, which he proceeded to work with his left hand one bead at a time. After expressing sympathy over Rob's loss, Kanavou said, "We thoroughly searched the plane. We found no inhalers."

"They had to be on the plane," Rob said with a frown. "I saw them at security in….in New York." His frown deepened. "Or maybe it was in Seattle. In New York, Mother and I left the security area for lunch because we had a long wait between flights."

"Did your mother have any enemies?"

Rob looked at Kanavou as if he was insane.

"Rivals?"

"She was a housewife."

"We have learned that you and your mother argued in Seattle at the airport just before you boarded the flight to New York; heatedly. Is that true?"

Rob hesitated and for the first time, as he chewed his lower lip, he appeared to consider the gravity of the situation. "Mr. Traveler, do I have to answer?"

"I'm not a lawyer, Rob." In his jeans with the faded thighs and frayed cuffs still dusty from Mystras, loosely laced sneakers and black T-shirt with a dragon on it, Rob looked about 12 years old. Race said, "Maybe you should consult a lawyer."

"I'm not guilty of anything."

"If you answer my questions, we can clear this up right now and you can continue with your tour," Kanavou said. "What was the subject of the argument?"

Rob pursed his lips, rubbed his hands on his thighs and after a glance at Race, looked straight at Kanavou and said, "None of your business."

"I'm afraid it is, Mr. Rasmussen."

"Rob, please," he said automatically.

Rob and Kanavou stared at each other, neither giving way. Kanavou was calm, composed and at ease, while Rob was clearly upset, his long-fingered hands playing tattoos on his thighs as he repeatedly bit his lower lip as if it was the source of his distress.

"Do you have any idea what happened to your mother's inhalers?" Kanavou asked.

Rob shook his head.

"We know she filled a prescription for three inhalers just before she left Seattle."

Rob stared at the floor.

"Who stowed your mother's carryon?"

Rob looked up and hesitated. "I did."

"So you were the last person to touch the bag that contained her inhalers."

"I just helped push her bag under the seat in front of her."

"Witnesses say you tried to use the toilet in first class during the flight. Why?"

With a crooked grin Rob said, "I had to go."

"There are toilets in the rear of the plane for coach passengers."

"The one's in first-class were closer."

Kanavou stared at Rob for a moment as he continued to work his *komboloi* with his right hand. "Your father passed away just over a month ago. Can you tell me what happened to him?"

Rob cast a pleading look at Race.

Before Race could say anything, Kanavou hurried on. "The case report from the Seattle Police Department states that your father was on the roof of his house during a rainstorm repairing a leak. He fell and landed 23 feet below on a flagstone patio. He was pronounced dead when he reached the hospital." Kanavou paused and stared at Rob before he added, "The report states that at the time your father fell to his death, he wasn't alone. You were with him. Can you tell me about that night?"

Rob took a loud, deep breath, sniffed and bit his lower lip. He stared down at the marble floor between his sneakers. Race heard the hotel clerk across the room entering something in a computer, the keys clicking in the silence. After a few moments, Rob looked up at Kanavou, his face set in a hard, cold mask of rigid control, as if he was a child about to try to maintain an absurd lie in the face of a disbelieving parent. "I don't remember that night."

"Are you an only child, Mr. Rasmussen?"

Rob hesitated, glanced at Race and then nodded.

"Is it true that with your father dead and no siblings, you are your mother's sole remaining living heir?"

As they hurried across the street in a misting rain to a taverna for dinner, Scarlett asked Race, "Should we have mentioned that Rob tried to push Gayle off Palamidi Castle?"

"Let Kanavou investigate his own crimes."

"So you agree there are crimes, like the murder of Mrs. Rasmussen," Scarlett said as Race held the taverna's glass door open for her. "I wonder why Rob didn't say anything about his father before?"

"The subject didn't exactly come up," Race said as they stood at the counter. "What was he supposed to say, 'Hi, I'm Rob and my father fell off a roof and died last month.'"

"Have you at least figured out who stole Lodge's wallet? I thought you were going to talk to Cohen."

"No chance yet."

"Well, at least I wish you'd clear Beznik."

Race considered Scarlett's suggestion. Then he smiled, kissed her on the cheek—smelling her subtle, flowery perfume mixed with the scent of Penguin peppermints—and said, "That would be far easier than figuring out who stole the wallet."

"Sounds like the same thing to me." Scarlett turned to the board that displayed the menu in Greek. "If you can't figure out who stole the wallet, who murdered Mrs. Rasmussen or what really happened to Gayle at Palamidi, can you at least decipher the menu?"

Chapter 8

Day 6: Thursday, April 22

Race and Scarlett rode the tiny elevator downstairs for breakfast. Race did not try to kiss her and he did not even try to justify his silent reserve by telling her that his lungs felt tight. He prayed it did not portend an infection. Sometimes it did; sometimes it didn't. He couldn't tell at this point. In either case, he needed to finish the tour and get paid so he could do some more sightseeing when he felt better. As for his silence, Scarlett didn't seem to even notice as she perused her itinerary.

Sonja was late, yet again, for breakfast, but appeared in time for the hour drive south between pine-tree studded hills to Gythio.

"Founded by Heracles and Apollo, Gythio was ancient Sparta's port," Race told the tour as he drove into the much-photographed harbor town. "Today it's a charming fishing village with reputedly some of the most beautiful women in the world."

Dr. Lodge leaned forward, his eyes scanning the sidewalks as he asked, "We are stopping, I presume."

"We have to stop," Chance said with a wolfish grin as he too went on high alert for females. "With intel like that, we have to perform a thorough recon."

"I support that motion wholeheartedly," David said, earning a pained expression from Petra.

Cohen's face flushed red, while Rob appeared to be trying his best to ignore the conversation as he stared out the window at the sea.

Sonja asked, "Are we also going to stop in the town with the most handsome men in the world?"

"We're already here, baby," Chance said, flinging his arm around Sonja and giving his wife a long, lecherous kiss, which she fought off as best she could as the others laughed.

The sun sparkled on the shimmering blue water as white fishing boats with splashes of red, yellow and blue paint bobbed in the harbor. The famous Kranai lighthouse stood on its namesake islet just beyond a stone breakwater that arced around the harbor. Pastel colored four-story hotels with ground-floor cafes sporting colorful canvas awnings lined the waterfront promenade. Pine, plane and chestnut trees shaded cushioned wood café chairs invitingly set out for customers.

Race asked, "Shall we stop for coffee?"

A chorus of 'yes' from the men drowned out screams of 'no' from the outnumbered women.

As they exited the van, Race whispered to Scarlett, "Never fear, I'll keep us on schedule."

"You've never been on time in your life."

"But I've always had fun being late. Maybe we can stop at the Isle of Marathonisi on our way out of town."

"Why?"

"It's where Paris married Helen and, if you'd be so kind, you could marry me."

"After what happened to them?"

Scarlett led the way to a nearby *kafenio* or coffee shop. Race explained how to order Greek coffee *sketo* (no sugar), *metrio* (equal portions coffee and sugar) or *gliko* (more sugar than coffee). Then they sat at wood tables under an expansive plane tree. Race bought chips and pretzels, as well as a gyro from a street vendor. He was, as usual, hungry.

As he swallowed his enzyme pills and ate, Race tried to ask a few more questions about Mrs. Rasmussen and the stolen wallet, but the men were focused on ogling women and the women were taken by the harbor view. He tried to ask Cohen about Lodge's wallet, but again got nowhere; even the shy Cohen was on watch for the most beautiful women in the world.

After their stop, they pushed on to the Mani Peninsula, the middle peninsula of the Peloponnesus' three southern peninsulas.

The road was as twisted as the Gordian knot and often narrowed to one lane for both directions. The dark, rugged mountains and rock-strewn fields attested to the inhospitable nature of the Mani region, whose name means 'dry' or 'treeless.' On the hills, lonesome goats searched for sustenance amidst the white, jagged rocks with little apparent luck, befitting the peninsula's status as the poorest region of the Peloponnesus.

"The Mani area was well known for bandits and feuds with almost no government control," Race explained as he drove, wishing Beznik was not languishing in jail. Driving and talking was tiring, and it cut into his reading time, not to mention making it far more difficult to see the sights along the way. "For centuries Mani houses were built for defense with two- and three-story towers for safety."

"That structure," Dr. Lodge said, pointing at a cream-colored house with a tower, "does not seem by appearances to be any older than my alleged son."

Gayle cast a look of loathing at him.

"In keeping with tradition," Race said, "even new houses are built in the same style with a tower."

"Whole place looks deserted," Sonja said, eyeing the broad expanse of rocky terrain that rose to the base of a range of steep mountains. She was dressed more conservatively today in tight jeans and a white T-shirt sans jewelry, any hope of paparazzi snapping her picture apparently gone.

"Sixty-thousand people lived on the Mani peninsula 200 years ago," Race said. "Now there are only about 5,000; most migrated to Athens."

"Looks like a poor man's Cortona or San Gimignano," Dr. Lodge said.

"Are we there yet?" Rob asked for the third time since they left Gythio.

"Nearly," Race said.

Twenty minutes later Race announced, "Welcome to the Diros Caves."

The group filed off the van just above a white-stone beach in a secluded cove. Three fishing boats bobbed at buoys, the land rising steeply on both sides above the beach. At the head of the cove, the terrain rose gently and a two-story stone house commanded what must have been a splendid view.

Race said, "The locals believe the caves stretch all the way to Sparta."

Chance, reading his guidebook, said, "Says here they've only been explored 5 kilometers."

"Exaggeration never hurts sales," David said with a grin. "Something several of my former bosses never understood; fools."

Race noticed that Petra and Dr. Lodge cast David a stern look, as if he had divulged a dark family secret.

As they walked toward the cave entrance, Petra said, "I don't really like enclosed places."

"Come on," David urged. "It'll be fun." He propelled her toward the entrance. "Just like something out of Disney."

"This is going to be great," Rob exclaimed, his police interrogation of the night before apparently forgotten.

At the entrance, the group walked down a broad sweep of stone stairs into a gallery with dozens of stalactites and stalagmites stretching back into the darkest reaches of the cavern. Cool, damp air mixed with a hint of various minerals engulfed them. Strategically placed lights lit the scene just enough to create an otherworldly scene. Weathered boatmen handed out well-worn orange life preservers that must have dated from the 1950s and began to help the tourists into flat-bottomed boats.

"Do you expect me to ride in a boat with him?" Cohen asked as a boatman attempted to seat him beside Dr. Lodge, who already sat, camera ready, in a flatboat. Race noted that Lodge and his daughter, Petra, were not sitting together; still divided over his alleged fathering of an illegitimate child with Gayle?

The boatman appeared not to understand Cohen and, with a reassuring smile and a firm hand on Cohen's forearm, drew the accountant toward the boat.

"No," Cohen yelled, his voice echoing throughout the cavern. For once, he did not speak in the form of a question. Raising a hand held rigid like a blade, he crouched like a fighter ready for battle. The boatman just stared at him.

"I'll sit there," Scarlett offered, and slipped in beside Dr. Lodge.

The first boat full, the boatman used a long pole to push off from the rocky ledge that served as a dock toward a low, narrow tunnel on the far side of the underground gallery. Race noticed that Sonja had managed to sit beside David, while the reluctant Petra ended up alongside Chance. Both couples appeared to be talking and flirting, although not with their spouses. Race sat next to the forensic accountant, Cohen in the stern of the second flatboat, which had three rows of wood seats worn smooth from long use. The physio, Gayle and the boyish Rob sat in front of them. As their boatman pushed off with his pole, Cohen apologized for his outburst.

Race admired the stalactites and stalagmites that ranged from white to pink to yellow, and probably even more colors he knew his color-blind eyes could not see. Strategically placed lights floated on buoys along the route to aid observation. Exclamations of "Ooh," "Wow" and "Ahhhh" drifted back from the boat ahead, and from Gayle and Rob in front of him.

"Would you believe I haven't seen Lodge in years?" Cohen said. He only briefly glanced at the incredible geological sights around him. "Lodge was a new prof then, one of the youngest full professors at the college. I was studying to be an accountant."

"He was a psychology professor?"

"I had to take an elective, ended up in his course. He heard I was in accounting and asked me to do the books for his new dating company."

The boatman leaned far out from the stern to push them through a narrow passage. The boat barely fit, its sides scraping on the rock walls worn smooth by the countless passings of wooden gunwales.

Cohen asked, "Would you believe Lodge was a real ladies man?"

"Bastard slept with every pretty co-ed in every one of his classes," Gayle spat as she swiveled her head to look back at Cohen and Race. "Wish the bastard was dead," she added before she turned back to watch the passing subterranean scenery.

Race felt a tickle in his chest. He suppressed a cough.

Cohen lowered his voice, forcing Race to lean closer to hear him. "I used to think Lodge went into psychology because every girl on campus took it as an elective and he could talk about sex all the time. He taught dating theory, sexual deviance and preference choice: why people choose the things they do."

"Like spouses?"

Cohen nodded. "He used psychological theories to start his dating company, basing it on personality traits to match people, instead of letting people just pick based on looks. Romance and love have been extensively studied; just most people ignore the findings because they contradict what most people believe. It isn't like in romance novels or the movies; likes attract likes. Two people who dislike each other on their first meeting aren't going to see each other again, so romance will never happen. It worked; the clients were more than happy, marriages resulted and business grew. We transitioned it onto the Internet and it exploded."

"Sounds like a dream."

"It was, until he offered to buy me out." Cohen cast an evil eye toward the boat ahead carrying his nemesis.

Race coughed, coughed again and kept coughing, his hacking reverberating off the cave walls and returning to him, foreshadowing his own mortality. He took out a tissue to hack into, twisting in his seat so Cohen would not see the nasty green phlegm even as its vile smell assaulted Race's nose.

"Are you alright?" Cohen asked as Gayle and Rob turned to stare at Race.

Race nodded, even though he felt as if he was about to vomit. It had happened before during a coughing fit. Then, just as he wondered what the boatman would say if he vomited in the boat, let alone in the pristine water, the coughing eased and finally stopped. Race's breathing slowly returned to normal. He hoped Scarlett had not heard him.

After several reassurances from Race that he was fine, Cohen, who appeared to want to tell his story to someone, continued. "Lodge paid me what I thought was a reasonable sum, then turned around the very next day and sold the company to a New York media conglomerate for ten times what he paid me."

They had to lay back flat to glide through a low passage. The rock ceiling almost brushed their noses.

As they slipped out the other side into an expansive multi-colored gallery, Cohen said, "Don't think I'm the only one he screwed. Lodge found a loophole in the non-competition clause of the sale agreement and promptly started a new online dating service that was an improved version of the site he'd just sold." Cohen snorted. "He's lucky that conglomerate didn't hire some fifth-dan black belt to take him to the roof of their 86-story headquarters and toss him off like a Frisbee."

As they were poled through another immense cavern, Race asked Cohen, "Why did you came on our tour?"

"Would you believe my son set it up? He found out Lodge was coming and thought if I talked with him, I could get...get..."

"Compensation?"

"No, it's too late for that. I realize that now." Cohen and Race looked out at a perfectly still pool with brilliant red, yellow and orange algae and lichen clinging to the bases of a dozen stalagmites. "Just some closure, I guess. My son thinks I dwell on the past. Don't all young people think that of the old, but what else do we have? The past is alive with everyone who was ever important in your life. At a certain point, it seems the dead outnumber the living."

Race agreed. He had lost too many friends and acquaintances to CF. But he did not want to live in the past; he had too little present left to waste a second of it.

"My son kept insisting," Cohen said. "'End it one way or the other,' he said, 'once and for all.' Finally, I gave in and said I would go on the tour with him. Of course, the day after we booked the tour, a tournament invitation arrived from Seoul—$1.5 million prize money, so here I sit alone."

The boatmen expertly maneuvered them through the caves from one magnificent gallery to another as Race recalled that Cohen's son played computer games for a living. As they entered yet another chamber, Race asked, "Did you see anyone take Lodge's wallet?"

"I should have stolen his wallet, bag and everything else he has," Cohen said. "But I didn't. Didn't think of it, truth be told. Guess I'm just not that petty. Besides, he owes me millions not hundreds."

Race watched and listened as water dripped down a stalactite and onto a stalagmite forming ever so slowly as it rose through the golden-yellowish water toward its stalactite mate and creator.

"I wish the bastard was dead," Cohen said. "Should be dead; Can you believe he's already had two strokes? I bet his daughter Petra would be a damn sight more amenable to a settlement than he will ever be."

The boatman guided their boat through another low passage-way. Everyone was once again forced to lie flat to slip under the low arch.

"This hasn't exactly been a great tour for you," Cohen said. "First that lady on the plane, the stolen wallet and then Gayle almost falling to her death, what next?"

"Did you see anything on the plane?"

"I was a few rows back from the poor woman who died. I did overhear her on the way to the restroom. She stopped to talk to a couple with a baby. Cooed and oohed and ah-ed over it. Said something about not having grandchildren and never expecting any. Guess she'd given up on that son of hers ever even getting married." Cohen leaned in close to whisper, "Rob doesn't look like he has enough money to support a decent wardrobe, let alone a wife and child. Not like Lodge. That bastard has enough for a harem, and the way he chatted up that stewardess on the flight, you'd think he was trying to build one, one stewardess at a time."

Cohen glanced at the back of Rob's head ahead of him. Rob exclaimed with delight as they cruised across a multicolored pool. He was paying no attention to them. Cohen whispered, "Did you hear Petra screaming at Rob to help his mother? She was furious, as if it was all his fault. Didn't you hear her?"

At the end of one arm of the magnificent caves, the flatboats bumped against a rock ledge and the boatmen helped everyone disembark, collecting the life vests in the process. The tour walked up broad stone ledges that formed stairs and emerged into the warm sunlit world above the cove. Race's eyes adjusted to the daylight as the tour trouped along a wooden walkway several hundred yards back to the parking lot. He breathed in the refreshing sea air, which seemed fresh and alive after the still, cool air of the caves. Scarlett rushed to Race's side to make sure he was alright; she had heard his coughing fit.

"I told you I get claustrophobic," Petra told her husband, David. Looking far worse than Race felt after his coughing fit, Petra was green and shook like a feather in a sirocco. "Why'd you make me go?" Petra whined. She stopped to retch and then vomit over the railing onto the beach below.

"You'll be alright," David reassured her. "Take it easy. It's over."

"I don't feel alright. I didn't want to go."

"You can't come all the way to Greece and miss all the sites."

Chance stopped to comfort Petra, his gruff voice taking on a comforting timbre, while David, looking frustrated, stood off to one side with Sonja. The movie star leaned in close to the ex-golfer as they chatted in whispers.

As Race reassured Scarlett that he was recovered, they walked to the van and brought out baskets full of crusty bread, ham and several types of cheese, spinach pies, and Greek yoghurt. Everyone found places to sit along the low whitewashed seawall to enjoy their lunch to the gentle rhythm of the knee-high waves on the shingle below. Petra recovered her color, but didn't eat anything. Race, with much longer experience of recovering from illness, ate a hearty lunch with plenty of crusty bread dipped in olive oil, supplemented with chips, pretzels and jerky from his stash.

After lunch as Scarlett and Race walked along the seawall, Race took her hand.

"Don't do that," she said, whipping her hand away. She noticed his hurt expression and said, "Your hand's oily."

Race stared down at his hand. He thought a moment and then realized something. "I need your cell."

"Not another call to Seattle."

"Your phone, please."

"Wipe your hands off first."

Moments later, Race was on the phone with Kanavou.

"While Beznik worked on the engine and everyone was at the canal," Kanavou said, "he must have unlocked the van, stolen the wallet, and returned to the engine before anyone noticed."

"As everyone got off the van, his hands were already oily from carrying a motor oil container, so his hands were oily from then until just before lunch. During and after lunch he was with the rest of the tour. If he stole the wallet before lunch, he'd have had oily hands when he did it, which begs a key question."

"Which is?"

"Does the wallet have oil on it?"

Listening to the German artist Black in one ear on his music device, Race drove on the twisting, lonely road north up the Mani peninsula. Lined for the first hour with waist-high stone walls, the road wound past olive orchards which alternated with rock-strewn fields that appeared fit only for the hardiest of goats. The tour's route then rose through rugged mountains on roads designed by a doodler; switchbacks and hairpin turns required Race to slow at times to a walk, especially since on many corners the road narrowed to a single lane. At each turn, Race prayed he wouldn't meet a car coming the other way. Luckily there was little traffic. Even so, the number of shrines along the verge to people killed on the road jumped from one or two every ten miles to one or two every ten feet on the sharper corners.

A dog appeared loping along the middle of the narrow road.

"I hope it's not a stray," Petra said, leaning forward. "Can we help him?"

Race was about to reply when a flock of sheep ambled into view, followed by an elderly woman dressed entirely in black and with a determined look peering our of a face made of crinkled leather.

"At least some of their kind work," David said with a grin at Petra, only to be rewarded with an icy stare.

Race stopped as the sheep engulfed the van. In moments, like a receding tide, the sheep, the dog and the woman flowed on their way to wherever they were headed with such purpose.

Soon after, as they wound around yet another hairpin turn, Petra called out, "Can we stop? Now?"

"Not really anywhere to stop," Race said. The road perched on a narrow ledge cut into a cliff. There was no shoulder.

"I really don't feel well," Petra said, her voice faltering.

Race glanced back. Petra was pale and grimacing as she took short, sharp breathes. With no traffic, Race drove a moment more to a straight stretch of road between two hairpin turns. He edged over to the side of the road as far as he dared and stopped.

Petra was out the door before the van stopped rocking on its suspension. She vomited against the base of the cliff beside a patch of orange poppies. David gave her a water bottle to rinse out her mouth as he rubbed her back and whispered sympathy.

After four more stops for a motion-sick Petra, they finally came down out of the tortuous mountains to a broad plain where Kalamata nestled its 50,000 souls amid olive groves at the head of the broad Messenian Gulf. Tramp freighters swung at anchor on the placid waters.

"With wet winters and dry summers," Race said, "Kalamata boasts famous olives for eating, not for making oil."

Race navigated through the canyon-like streets between 5- and 6-story homes and apartment buildings, and then out the other side of the city and back up into the hills.

Four hours and 19 of Rob's "Are we there yet?" questions after they left the Diros Caves they reached Pylos. The coast curved out into the Ionian Sea to meet a crescent of jagged islands that formed the magnificent sheltered harbor of Navarino Bay.

Race parked in a vacant lot and the tour walked a hundred yards down the road beneath squawking gulls to their pension overlooking the perfect bay. Below them, the neat, compact town was laid out in a saucer-shaped piece of land cradled by an amphitheatre of hills. Pencil cypresses stood silent sentinel throughout the town. Race smelled the sea and heard the chug of a fishing boat above the cacophony of the gull symphony. Their pension was The 12 Gods. A stone set before the entrance listed the 12 Greek gods for which it was named. As Race began to read the names, an ear-splitting screech rent the air.

"What was that infernal noise?" Dr. Lodge asked.

"A rooster," Race said, looking across at the next property. "Lives next door."

Lodge stared at Race.

"Not exactly the high rent district," Sonja said. "Isn't there a Four Seasons in town?"

"You can't even see the high rent district from here with a telescope," David said. "Haven't seen a golf course since we landed."

Race said, "Greeks don't play golf."

"Not even the rich ones?"

Later, in her room, Scarlett told Race that Dr. Lodge had reminded her that he would take it as a personal mission to ruin Traveler Excursions unless he was completely satisfied that Beznik was justly punished and his 1,200 euros returned. "You must find out who stole his money."

Having passed along the dire warning and with a free afternoon, Scarlett took a nap. Race sat on the patio outside their rooms and halfheartedly read Somerset Maugham's *Up at the Villa* as he munched on chips and pretzels, listened to Tom Petty's *Greatest Hits*, and puzzled over Lodge's wallet, as well as whether Rob had murdered his mother and attempted to murder Gayle.

Deep in thought, Race gazed at the bay and the islands beyond, which had once been one island, broken by centuries of waves into islets. One islet was the site of a contingent of Spartans' last stand. He hoped this would not be his last tour.

Race's thoughts were interrupted by a coughing fit. It felt as if a pair of balloons were filling his lungs, refusing to allow his body to take in the oxygen it craved. After the fit passed, Race was about to return to his theories on the missing wallet when Scarlett asked from the patio door, "Going to see a doctor?"

"I'm fine."

"When you're not coughing up a lung."

"I've got two."

"See a doctor."

"It's not an infection."

"It might be."

"When I know, I'll go."

"You a medical doctor too, now?"

"I can't clear Beznik from a hospital bed."

"Or from a grave." Scarlett met Race's gaze and held it. Race looked out at the view.

Scarlett sat down and swiped a couple of pretzels from Race's bag on the circular table between them. "I think Rob let his mother die," she said. "Motive: he inherits. Means: he knew she had asthma and it was life-threatening. Opportunity: he was the last one to touch her bag and was with her when the back-up inhalers disappeared."

"Is Rob the type of man to murder his mother in a way that requires the utmost patience?" Race asked. "How often had Mrs. Rasmussen had asthma attacks, and how many would have been fatal if left untreated?"

"Only her doctor would know, and I doubt he'll chat on the phone about it to a doctor calling out of the blue from Greece."

"Let alone a doctor of logic." Race munched pretzels as Scarlett asked about the missing cash from Lodge's wallet. "Even with Beznik cleared," Race said, "which I expect to happen as soon as

Kanavou looks closely at the wallet and finds no oil on it, we aren't short on suspects. Chance was alone in the van."

"But he returned to the group pretty fast. Besides, he's rich. Why would he steal a wallet?"

"A chance to teach Lodge a lesson about using a money belt?"

"David?"

"Gayle was with him in the van, and why steal from his father-in-law?"

"Gayle was in the van long enough to steal the wallet," Scarlett said. "She had no euros for lunch, went to the van and returned with euros; Lodge's money?"

"No one seems to have seen her take money from the ATM, but people usually don't flash money around after withdrawing it."

"Did you learn anything from Cohen?"

"He hates Lodge, but he didn't return to the van."

"Sonja was loitering near the van. Maybe she slipped in when Beznik was busy with the engine."

"The van was locked."

"And she flew first class," Scarlett said. "Why would she steal a wallet?"

"Petra?"

"Beznik claimed he watched her the whole time she was in the van."

"And why would Petra steal from her father?"

"Rob?"

"Why steal when you're about to inherit?"

"Tide him over until the inheritance clears probate?" Scarlett asked. "What's a little theft after a murder?"

Chapter 9

Day 7: Friday, April 23

At breakfast on the pension's stone-paved terrace overlooking Navarino Bay, Scarlett suggested everyone sit with someone different than usual. Race sat with Chance at one of the circular metal tables set for two. Their coffee sent steaming columns into the still, cool morning air. A pair of brightly painted fishing boats chugged into the harbor, returning from a dawn fishing trip. As the crew cleaned the deck and washed pieces of bait and fish through the scuppers, gulls warred over the opportunity to snatch the choicest morsels.

Race and Chance talked about the trip thus far and what was coming up next as they sipped an orange drink and nibbled Melba toast, crumbs falling into their laps. Race started through a platter heaped high with crackers, using them to devour a bowl of garlic and red pepper hummus. Chance dribbled a spoonful of honey onto a bowl of rich, thick yoghurt in a white porcelain bowl.

"You eat a lot," Chance observed. He patted his stomach and added, "Unless I'm sailing, I have to watch my calories or the rigging will snap under me."

"With CF, just breathing can take 4,000 calories a day." Not wanting to discuss his disease, Race asked if Chance had noticed anything odd during their time at the Corinth canal. "You went back to the van...."

Chance stopped eating and his cold eyes focused on Race in a clear challenge. "True; I was alone in the van. Beznik let me in and then went back to the engine. The hood was up, so he couldn't have had eyes on me even if I'd emptied the van of everything on it and sold it all in the Corinth bazaar. But I did no such thing. I grabbed my camera and disembarked. I didn't steal a damn thing and if you were 20 years younger you'd be on your ass."

Race sipped the orange-flavored drink, which tasted more like water than orange, and switched to his steaming tea.

As Chance finished his yoghurt, the ex-fighter pilot said, "Why would I steal 1,200 euro? Wouldn't keep Sonja in makeup for a day. Besides, I didn't have the intel that anyone was stupid enough to leave cash in the van anyway."

"Any idea who stole the wallet?"

"Beznik's in jail for it."

"Not for long."

Scarlett announced it was time to prepare to depart. Everyone rose and Chance gulped down his coffee as Race asked, "Did you happen to notice anything on the flight to Athens?"

"I heard that woman dying and nobody doing a damn thing, except you." Everyone was starting back to their rooms when Chance added, his voice low, "Bravo zulu, by the way, even if it was for naught. Her son is some piece of work, eh? Can't be missing her much, given how little attention he paid her on the flight."

"I heard Rob tried to use the first-class bathroom."

"Stewardess sent him back to steerage, but only after Petra Fox tried to set him back on the true course. He ignored her; damn rude."

"Was he carrying anything when he tried to use the bathroom?"

Chance shook his head, no.

Race sighed; so much for that idea.

"But in those baggy shorts of his," Chance said, "he could have stowed an entire pharmacy."

As Race drove the tour down the abrupt hill into Pylos and along the waterfront, he said, "Navarino Bay, as Pylos was then called—"

"Its Italian name," Chance pitched in from his guidebook.

"Is 5 kilometers by 3," Race continued, ignoring the interruption, "and one of the finest natural harbors in the world. It was the scene of a one-sided naval battle in 1827."

"The British, French and Russian fleets blew 53 Ottoman Turk ships to hell and sent 6,000 men to their graves," Chance said. "Without losing a single ship."

"It was the last major battle fought entirely by sailing ships," Race said, eyeing Chance. Why couldn't the man stick to checking off destinations? "The battle wasn't meant to happen and the British regretted it. King George said it was a 'deplorable misunderstanding,' but it helped Greece win her independence."

"A misunderstanding?" Cohen asked from the rear of the van.

"The Ottomans and British negotiated a cease-fire, but the Ottomans were outraged when the Greeks, with British officers leading many of them, continued attacking," Race said. "The British commander didn't have authority over the British officers leading the Greeks; an unrivalled mess."

"Hard to imagine bloodshed in such a serene place," Sonja said. "Better setting for a coming-of-age family saga about an extended Greek family, with lovers divided by warring families." She eyed David.

"And a wealthy foreigner, who moves in to buy up all the fishing rights," David added.

"And impoverish the locals," Gayle said.

"No, he hires them, enriching the whole town," Dr. Lodge said. "Why are businessmen always the villains in movies?"

"Everyone hates the rich," Gayle said.

"You mean, envies them," Lodge said.

Leaving Pylos and its 2,700 inhabitants behind, Race drove 15 minutes south to Methoni Castle, which perched on a spit of land at the tip of the most southwesterly arm of the Peloponnesus. He parked in an unpaved lot just off one of Messenia's broad, sand beaches. He led the group through the town past shuttered cafes and tavernas, white single-story houses with blue shutters, and vacant lots with plane and olive trees. It felt dry and dusty, even so near the sea.

"I'm glad it was a short drive this morning," Race told Scarlett. His lungs were tight and sore.

"A longer one this afternoon to Kyparissia," Scarlett warned. "Are you up to it?"

Scarlett's cell rang.

"Should be Kanavou," Race said, "with good news."

Scarlett answered, nodded to Race, and listened for a few moments as they continued walking through the town. She said, "I understand," and clicked off.

"So, when will our Beznik be back behind the wheel?" Race asked.

"You're the one who asked Inspector Kanavou to look for oil on the wallet?"

Race nodded, awaiting praise.

"Kanavou said he inspected the wallet closely."

"And?"

"He found oil on the wallet."

Race stared at her in disbelief.

"Thanks a lot; you just sealed the case against Beznik."

Scarlett led the way across the 14-arch stone bridge to Methoni Castle's main gate. She elbowed Race none too lovingly to jar him out of his shock over Beznik. Refocusing, he said, "Methoni Castle was the Venetians first and longest-held fortress in Greece, and was a way station for pilgrims on their way to the Holy Land. The walls encompass a space the size of four soccer fields. The walls are relatively intact, but the inner buildings are mostly just foundations."

"More ruined ruins, then," Sonja said with a smile.

"A dry moat protects the landward side of the castle, while a rugged coast protects the other two sides of a rough triangle."

Shrubs sprouted from cracks and crevices in the intact stone walls, which boasted round towers at regular intervals. Race led the tour through the open gate. They turned left 90 degrees down a 300-yard stone-paved canyon between the outer and inner walls toward a second, inner gate.

"Hate to have to fight my way down this," Chance said. "A kill box if I ever saw one."

"Robbie! Robbie!"

Looking back, Race beheld an onrushing figure in blue shorts, neon red hiking boots, a bright yellow sleeveless T-shirt, and a tan Japanese soldier's cap with a trailing flap that protected the wearer's neck from the Grecian sun. The figure's arms flailed and waved like runaway windmills. Everyone stopped and stared as if at an apparition.

"Robbie!"

Race saw that the apparition was a man, probably in his early forties. He was in decent shape and sported bright red hair, which straggled out from under his cap, and pale, yet muscular arms, which protruded from his sleeveless shirt. "Rob!"

All eyes now switched rapidly between the newcomer and Rob, who raced back to meet the stranger, a look of joy on his youthful face. As everyone watched in shock, the two men hugged each other, slapping each other on the back as they alternatively lifted each other off their feet in exuberant bear hugs. The tour edged over to the joyous reunion. The newcomer was talking faster than an auctioneer. Race caught something about finally having found Rob, sympathy over his loss, and the difficulty of finding a decent dinner before 7 pm, although the ouzo and Retsina were rather fine.

"Rob," Scarlett finally was able to slip in. "Who's your friend?"

With his startling blue eyes dancing with delight, the friend announced, "I'm Rob's bestest friend in all the whole wide world. Allow me to introduce myself. My name is Benjamin 'Benny' Sartoros, and it's a pleasure to meet you, one and all." He bowed low, sweeping his hand across the paving stones at his feet.

As everyone was introduced, Benny looked the men up and down as if admiring prize stallions, even Cohen, who shifted uncomfortably under the blatant appraisal. The introductions made, Benny extracted a silver hip flask from his short's pocket and, after toasting the group with a long swig, offered it around.

"Ouzo," Benny announced. "The Greek national drink. When in Greece...."

Chance accepted a shot, but everyone else declined until Race, who also accepted.

Scarlett cast him a look as if he was about to drink hemlock. Race thought that one shot shouldn't affect the drugs he took for his lungs. And, if it did, maybe he wouldn't have to drive any more.

It quickly became clear that Benny was joining the tour.

"I'll just take Hilda's place, as it were," Benny said. "I'm sure she wouldn't mind, not now." He giggled. Scarlett looked aghast.

Rob hesitated only a moment. "He can take mom's place. It's fine."

At that, Dr. Lodge turned on his heel and stalked toward the inner castle gate, camera bag over his shoulder. Petra and then David hurried after him.

"Having a good time?" Benny asked Rob as they strolled toward the castle entrance past the remainder of the dazed group. "Apart from your mom, I mean."

Chance said, "Well, I'll be damned."

"I wouldn't have pegged Rob as gay in a million years," Gayle said.

"Maybe they're just friends," Scarlett said.

Everyone looked at her as if she was insane.

"Just what I need," Sonja said with a sour look and a tilt of her head, "more competition."

Chance shot her a dirty look, but she didn't notice as she hurried off after Dr. Lodge, Petra and David.

Scarlett watched Rob and Benny, both of whom were laughing raucously as they turned into the castle, and asked, "I wonder what he sees in someone so….so loud?"

Race considered a moment and said, "Fun."

While the others toured the castle, Race drove back into Pylos and found a doctor who prescribed a different type of antibiotics. Race hoped the new drug would kill what he feared was a budding lung infection.

When he returned to the castle, Scarlett arranged the picnic lunch Race had bought from a restaurant in Pylos. Two hampers contained iced water, thermoses of coffee, tea and orange juice, fresh bread, Kalamata olives, Greek salad, grapes, tomatoes, a selection of cheeses and hummus, as well as *baklava* for desert.

"Did you pay full price?" Scarlett asked.

"Course not," Race said. "The doctor referred me to the restaurant, which happened to be run by his brother. Gave me 10 percent off."

"Ten percent? They mark up everything 100 percent. You could have got 20 percent off just by opening your mouth."

"A feast fit for a king," Benny announced, helping to distribute the food with gusto, commenting on every dish as if he had created it himself. "What a lovely outfit, love," he gushed to Sonja.

"This old thing?" the actress said, glancing down at her floral print summer dress. "Just a little something Lisa Kline insisted I wear to Steven's Fourth of July party last year."

"Steven *Spielberg*?" Gayle asked, eyes wide.

"It's to die for," Benny enthused, moving on to offer grapes to Dr. Lodge. "Aren't you hot in that shirt?"

"Certainly not," Lodge said, shrugging off Benny's hand on the shoulder of his long-sleeved Navy blue dress shirt.

"I'd be sweating like a pig in Sumatra," Benny said, moving on to Petra and David with one of the food hampers, making small talk as if he was the host and had known them for decades.

Dr. Lodge rose with his plate heaped with food and said, "I will eat down on the causeway. I plan to take some pictures of the castle from the water side after lunch."

"I'll come," Petra said with a disapproving look at Benny, who sat beside Rob as they boisterously discussed how the ancient foundations would make for an exciting soccer match in the castle grounds. Benny was wondering whether they could recruit enough local kids to form teams. As she strode away, Petra called back, "Coming, David?"

Her husband looked down at the paper plate of food on his lap as he sat in the shade of the crenellated wall and sighed.

"Stay with us," Sonja offered.

"I better go," David said, rising. "Happy wife, happy life."

Sonja ate rapidly and Chance ignored her as she rushed off toward where Dr. Lodge, Petra and David were eating on a causeway that led to a tower at the tip of the peninsula. As Race finished his third crusty roll dipped in olive oil, he saw Sonja and David set off together toward a stone gate on the far side of the courtyard.

After lunch, Race intercepted Petra as she strolled across the castle's vast courtyard. They discussed the history of the castle before he asked about Dr. Lodge's stolen wallet.

"When I went back for my sweater, our bags, including father's, all seemed fine; and where we left them." Even her statements ended with an inflection, as if they were questions.

A sea breeze nicely compensated for the warmth of the sun, gently moving the ends of her shoulder-length blonde hair. "What's with the winged lions?"

"They represent St. Mark," Race said, looking up at a carving in the wall. "From when the Venetians ruled Methoni."

Petra walked across the uneven ground, avoiding foundation stones and sidestepping clumps of sage and broom. She sighed and said, "I probably wouldn't have noticed if anything had been moved anyway. I'm not really very observant. Hasn't David mentioned it?" After a moment she added, "I think Cohen took the money. He hates my father, has for years. Or maybe that Garcia woman. She just wants money. I wouldn't trust her with a newt."

Race frowned.

"I have a fire newt, Neptune, at home. He's 23 years old. I've had him for years; longer than David. Only eats live bloodworms, none of the frozen, which is probably why he's lived so long."

Race was about to ask how long fire newts lived, when he realized such a question might lead Petra even farther from the issues Race needed to focus on. "Did you know before the other day that your father and Gayle had a child together?"

Petra's habitually reticent expression vanished, replaced by ice. "I know no such thing, nor do you, Mr. Traveler."

"True," Race conceded. He stopped to look out at the sea, marveling at the way the sunlight dappled on its tranquil surface even as he gave Petra time to calm down. "I heard you alerted Rob on the plane that his mother needed help."

"He was ignoring her something awful. I couldn't believe it; watching some dumb movie while his mother was dying."

"Did you know they were related?"

"They boarded just before us. I saw Rob hand two tickets to the agent, so I knew they were together. Had to be mother and son, given their ages, although she was so elegant and he, well, he dresses like he's twelve and a poverty stricken twelve at that. Does he have no self-respect?"

They reached the southern end of the ruins with a view across a stone causeway to a three-tiered octagonal tower or *bourtzi* that sat solitary and serene on its own islet surrounded by the translucent, shimmering sea. Dr. Lodge was atop it, photographing the castle.

"He even had the gall to try to use the bathroom in first class, dressed like that," Petra said. "Can you believe it?"

"Did he have anything with him?"

"I couldn't really see his hands. They were jammed into his pockets so far I could barely see his elbows."

Deep in thought, Race drove the tour the few kilometers back to Pylos. Vivid red soil showed between the sage and shrubs. Once through the town, he drove up a steep hill to another castle.

"The Turks built the Neo Kastro or New Castle in 1573 to use as a base to invade Crete," Race said as he parked. A stand of pines guarded the castle gate.

As they entered the castle, Dr. Lodge said, "Much larger than the castles I've seen in Scotland, England and Wales. Could fit a couple of Conwys in here."

The Neo Kastro had intact walls but only the foundations of buildings remained within, save for two rebuilt structures. One building housed drawings from the Battle of Navarino. The keep was also intact, with thick stone walls and a hexagonal courtyard. From the walls the tourists were rewarded with views of the tranquil bay, although they could not fail to hear Benny chasing Rob in an enthusiastic game of tag in the main courtyard among the plane, pine, aspen, fir, and palm trees.

Race and Scarlett meandered through the trees. Race took Scarlett's hand, but she pulled it away.

"Your hand's oily," Scarlett said. "Is the van losing oil again?"

"No, it's just olive oil from lunch. Nowhere to wash at Methoni Castle."

"The citadel has restrooms; go wash up."

As Race turned to go, a thought struck him. He stopped dead and groaned. "I was so stupid. How could I....Why didn't I realize....I need your cell."

"You're not getting olive oil on my cell."

"If you want Beznik freed, I need your cell, now."

"But Beznik is guilty. He stole the wallet. I didn't believe it, but the oil—"

"The oil is the key. Your cell, now, please."

Chapter 10

Having told Kanavou about his latest deduction, Race hoped the inspector would release Beznik soon so Race could stop having to drive. Until then, Race drove. He sped north from Pylos up the coast past walled coastal towns with stone jetties that shielded snug harbors from the sea. Finally, after Rob had asked nine times, "Are we there yet?", they reached Kyparissia. Olive groves surrounded the agricultural center of 5,000 people. Two arcing rock jetties embraced a brightly colored fishing fleet that bobbed alongside a flotilla of sailboats and powerboats.

"Will there be time to walk up to the castle tomorrow morning to take some photographs at sunrise?" Dr. Lodge asked as the tour milled about the Hotel Akrogiali's lobby.

"It's largely ruined," Race warned as he looked out through the lobby's windows at Kyparissia Castle perched on a spur of Mount Egaleo amidst cypress and pine trees high above the town.

"Looks like it offers striking views," Dr. Lodge said. "I wanted to capture some photographs of the sun's first rays on the Ionian Sea. I have new filters with which I wish to experiment."

"There should be time," Scarlett said. "As long as you're back promptly by eight for the drive to Olympia. At dawn you should have the castle all to yourself."

"I will ensure that I return promptly by eight o'clock," Lodge promised. "Will you do me the pleasure of accompanying me, Petra?"

Petra pursed her lips. "I think I'd rather get some sleep."

"You always used to come with me on my early morning photography expeditions," Lodge reminded her with an encouraging smile. "Scotland, South Africa, Australia, Peru, Japan, remember?"

"I was a child then."

"I would greatly enjoy your company, Petra."

"I'm tired and I really don't feel 100 percent. I'm sorry, Daddy, maybe another time."

Lodge nodded, visibly disappointed.

"I wouldn't be tired," Sonja said, leering at David. "Ever."

"Would you please leave him alone," Petra screamed, exploding at the movie starlet.

"I really don't know what you're talking about."

"You've been after him ever since that silly pro-am."

"The silly pro-am that found you a liver donor?"

"Kidney; It was a kidney." Petra advanced on the actress and, rearing up to invade Sonja's personal space, roared, "Look, you slut, leave my husband alone. Do you understand?"

"I understand you're letting your sordid little erotic daydreams make you all hot and bothered, dear. Best keep them to yourself or someone is bound to get hurt, badly."

"Beznik!" Race exclaimed, relieved at the chance to divert the group's attention from the rapidly escalating confrontation.

"What is he doing here?" Dr. Lodge demanded as the young Romani-Greek ambled into the lobby.

"He's our driver," Race said, purposely obtuse.

"And thief," Lodge added as he glared at the new arrival.

"The police released me," Beznik snarled as he lunged at Lodge. Race grabbed Beznik's arm, deflecting him just enough to miss Lodge.

"More fool them," Lodge said.

"More like lack of evidence," Race said as he, Chance and David hauled the struggling Beznik away from Lodge, who stood tall and aloof, righteous and certain.

Frowning, Scarlett said, "But when the wallet was stolen Beznik had oil on his hands from working on the engine, and Kanavou said there was oil on Lodge's wallet."

"Kanavou did see oil on the wallet," Race said, "but he couldn't tell which kind just by looking."

"What difference does the kind of oil make?" Cohen asked.

"The difference between guilt and innocence."

"WD 30 or WD 40 makes that much difference?" David asked with a smirk.

"Not that type of oil," Race said. "Kanavou had the police lab test the oil."

Gayle asked, "Why didn't he use the lab in the first place?"

"It's just a stolen wallet, not a serial killer," Race said. "Lab tests cost money."

"What did the lab find?" Scarlett asked.

"Olive oil."

"So Beznik didn't steal the wallet," Scarlett exclaimed.

Lodge asked, "Ever hear of washing your hands?"

"Beznik did wash them, just before we had lunch, and he didn't go to the van alone after that," Race said. "He had motor oil on his hands by the time you exited the van, so he couldn't have stolen your wallet. If he had, the wallet would have had motor oil, not olive oil, on it."

Lodge glared at Race as he said, "You are not going to allow him to handle our bags are you?"

"I will never touch your filthy bags," Beznik yelled, still held at bay by Chance and David.

Lodge sniffed and with a look of utter disdain stalked off. Beznik broke free of David as he fought to rush after Lodge. Chance held Beznik for a moment until Lodge stepped into the hotel's elevator. Beznik glared at Chance, who met his glare with an even stare. Beznik straightened his shoulders and shoved past the ex-fighter pilot.

"Watch it, little man," Chance said, the ends of his lips turned up with just a hint of a good-natured smile, although his eyes carried a cold look of warning.

As the tour dispersed to their rooms, Scarlett told Race, "I can't believe Kanavou thought Beznik was a thief."

"He confused need with greed," Race said. "Even so, I still don't know who stole the wallet, and whether Rob murdered his mother or tried to murder Gayle."

"That will help me sleep well tonight; a possible murderer on the loose."

"I can join you, if that'd help you sleep better."

"That would definitely have the opposite effect."

Chapter 11

Day 8: Saturday, April 24

As the tour gathered at the van, Race took a deep breath. His lungs were improving with the new antibiotics from Pylos. Cohen emerged from the hotel hunched over, wearing sunglasses, and moving slowly and deliberately, as if struggling to make headway against a gale. He nodded at the others' greetings before clenching his mouth shut and rushing over to the side of the lot where he vomited into a mass of orange bougainvillea. Scarlett offered assistance, but he waved her away as he wiped his mouth with the back of his trembling hand.

"I wonder where Petra and Lodge are," David said as he sidled out of the hotel, his hair wet from a shower. He took a long swig from a water bottle.

Scarlett asked, "Did Petra go up to the castle with Dr. Lodge?"

"She told me last night she'd changed her mind and decided to go," David said. Everyone looked up at the Frankish ruins silhouetted above the coastal town. "Without meaning too, she woke me early this morning when she left. I'm tired, and sore from sitting in the van for so long the past few days." He took another long swig of water as he stretched his back and grimaced.

"It's almost eight," Scarlett said, eager to depart. "Maybe we should drive up to the castle and see if they're there."

"Let's wait a few minutes," Race said. "Don't want to miss them if they're on their way down."

Gayle, Benny and Race helped Beznik load the van. A distract-ed David stared up at the castle ruins.

With the van loaded, there was still no sign of Petra or Lodge. Beznik drove everyone up the switchback road past houses clinging to the steep slopes of Mount Egaleo to the castle. On the way, Race listened to *Pagliacci* in one ear as he started another novel, *A Kiss Before Dying*. At the castle's three-car parking lot, everyone exited the van and paused at a viewpoint sporting a blue and white Greek flag to take in the magnificent view of the Ionian Sea.

Chance announced, "It's padlocked," as he fiddled with the lock on a chain-link fence that ran across the ruined castle's main gate. A sign stated in Greek and English that it would open at 10 am.

"Petra!" David yelled. "Dr. Lodge!"

Chance added his booming voice honed on air strips and docks around the world. Save for a couple of startled barn swallows who swooped overhead from a nest in the castle wall to complain, there was no reply.

"I think there's an opening over here," Rob called, pointing at a well-worn path that led along the base of the castle wall to an oft-traversed breach.

"We shouldn't break in, should we?" Scarlett asked.

"What's there to steal?" Race asked.

"How can they be inside?" Cohen asked. "It's locked up, and it's posted."

"Rules are guidelines for having fun," Benny said with a devil-ish smirk. "Rules not to live by, as it were."

Race led the way along the foot-wide paths, scrambled over the jumble of ancient stones that had once formed a wall and into the castle. The interior was small, albeit with an amphitheater, where, Race knew, plays were performed in the summer for audiences of 40 or 50. Most of the walls had crumbled down to their founda-tions. Well-worn dirt paths formed a spider web through the waist-high dry grass and shrubs.

"No one here," Chance announced, hands on his hips as he surveyed the ruins. Birds called and the breeze ruffled the grass, but there was no sign of anyone else.

"Over here!" Cohen yelled.

Race and the others rushed to the western edge of the ruins where Cohen stood beside a camera tripod near the narrow landward entrance to a cannon embrasure. In the dirt beside the tripod sat Dr. Lodge's battered black camera bag. Turning sideways, Race slipped past the tripod and the bag. David rushed up to the edge of the cliff beside Race. Before Race could turn him away, David looked down. David's scream could be heard in the town below. Race knew because when David screamed Inspector Kanavou looked up from where he stood far below beside the two bodies.

Chapter 12

Race could see the bodies of Petra Fox and Dr. Peter Lodge amidst the poppies and cliff roses on the rocky white hillside at the base of the cliff. Petra lay on her back, one leg bent unnaturally to the side and her arms splayed out. In contrast, Dr. Lodge had landed on his feet. Although he lay on his stomach, Lodge was folded at the waist like a child's discarded doll. His feet and legs must have been compressed; the force of landing driving his legs up through his torso. Race felt ill at the sight of the ex-professor's body, foreshortened as if drawn by a demented cartoonist.

Having taken in the horrific scene in an instant, Race heard and then saw David. The golf-club salesman was slumped against the side of the gun embrasure, his face hidden behind his hands, sobbing. Rob stared down at the bodies, squinting, as if either not believing what he saw or wanting to see it better with a childlike curiosity. Chance's face was impassive, like a commander surveying a field after a battle he may have won or lost, while Sonja hid her face behind her hands fighting back tears. But when she lowered her hands, she had won the fight and her face was dry. Gayle remained far back, not looking, a trace of loss in her look. Cohen leaned against one edge of the embrasure with a look of contentment, as if a long battle was finally over; his nemesis was dead.

The police cordoned off the castle with red and white caution tape and after brief initial interviews, Inspector Kanavou moved the excursionists to a conference room in their hotel. As they sat waiting, Scarlett whispered, "A death on the plane, a stolen wallet, and now two more deaths. What's going to happen next, besides Traveler Excursions closing its doors forever?"

Race's dream of traveling for as long as his lungs supported him teetered on the precipice of disaster. "I'll figure out what happened," he said with more conviction than he felt.

Race whispered to Beznik, who sat nearby, "Where were you early this morning?"

Beznik's eyes narrowed, but he answered, "Asleep in my room."

Race's questioning ended before he even got started when an officer called Beznik to another room for further questioning. Race rose to saunter over to Rob and Benny.

"Please sit down, sir," the officer at the door ordered.

"Just checking on our clients. They are my responsibility."

The officer gave him a stern look. "Back to your seat, sir, now."

As Race sat down, Scarlett whispered, "And then there were five."

"We aren't ten little Indians."

"If we were, I'd know who did it."

"How? No judges on this trip."

After the police concluded their questioning, Race and Scarlett caught up to Kanavou on his way to a waiting police car in the parking lot. Race asked, "What happened?"

Kanavou paused, lit a cigarette, and said, "A deeply regrettable accident, Mr. Traveler." In his dark suit, Kanavou reminded Race of an undertaker.

"How'd it happen?" Scarlett asked, always eager for the gory details.

Kanavou glanced at the young officer waiting behind the wheel of his police car. "Dr. Lodge and Petra and David Fox had dinner last night together. The desk clerk saw them return at about 10 pm. At or about 5:30 am, Petra Fox and Dr. Peter Lodge fell from the castle. From interviews, we know Dr. Lodge planned to go up to the castle to take photographs of the sunrise. He probably went too near the edge, started to fall, his daughter tried to grab him, and they both fell to their deaths."

Race frowned. "I just thought it odd."

"What, Mr. Traveler?"

"When we stopped at the Corinth Canal, Dr. Lodge kept well back from the edge."

"He was afraid of heights," Scarlett said, catching on.

Kanavou took out his *komboloi* and started working the beads one by one between his fingers. "The reverse might have happened; Petra Fox went too near the edge, started to fall, her father rushed to catch her, and they both fell."

"Dr. Lodge's camera tripod was in the landward-side of the gun embrasure blocking the entrance," Race said. "If Dr. Lodge was behind his camera, how did he *and* Petra end up in the embrasure? And, if Petra was in the embrasure, she would be in any picture Lodge took. Why stand there?"

"A portrait?"

"They climbed all the way up there," Race said, gesturing at the castle far above them, "lugging camera gear and a tripod just to take a photo of her?"

"Against the rising sun on the Ionian Sea from Kyparissia Castle," Kanavou said, although he sounded as if even he didn't believe it.

"I don't think Lodge would ever go near the edge," Race said, "so he wouldn't be near enough to even try to save Petra."

Kanavou fingered his *komboloi*, like a child with an interesting, yet baffling toy. He dragged on his cigarette. "My wife hates heights. She never liked me going anywhere near the edge of castle walls when we toured Germany."

"Dr. Lodge would have warned his daughter to stay well back from the edge," Scarlett said.

Kanavou said, "Yet they didn't."

"Or someone helped them to the edge," Race said.

Kanavou said, "The tripod was still standing."

"Easy to right it, if it fell," Race said.

"It was undamaged."

"Any minor damage would be put down to normal wear and tear. Lodge bought a used camera bag, probably was a used tripod."

Kanavou worked his *komboloi*. "If you are right and this was not an accident, I may need to ask everyone on your tour to remain here until this matter is resolved."

Scarlett asked, her voice rising with worry, "In Greece or in Kyparissia?"

"Kyparissia."

Having successfully led Kanavou to the conclusion that Petra and Dr. Lodge might have been murdered, Race now saw his future destroyed: the tour detained in Kyparissia, tour members furious, and the good name of Traveler Excursions sullied forever—or at least for the rest of his short life. Scarlett's company, already struggling from the effects of the war in Iraq, would fold.

"If you let the tour continue, Inspector Kanavou, I can gather information for you."

"I think I can do my job with full competence, Mr. Traveler."

"I just thought American tourists would be more likely to talk when they're relaxed, enjoying a tour than answering questions from a police inspector while stuck in a foreign town."

Kanavou threaded his *komboloi* through his fingers.

"Tourism is down with the war in Iraq," Race said, desperate to save the tour. "I'm sure you don't want a group of American tourists who did come to Greece to have a worse experience than they have already been through after three deaths."

"Public relations do not concern me."

"Of course not, but..." Race saw his future destroyed—this was the end.

Kanavou worked his *komboloi*, clicking them like mini-castanets.

"I really need your help, Inspector," Scarlett said. "If my excursion has to remain here, my company may not survive....nor may I." She sniffled. "I can't believe Traveler Excursions is going to go under because of a crime that really has nothing to do with my little company." Tears wet the corners of her turquoise eyes. She snuffled again and wiped her eyes. "All I've ever tried to do is give people a fun experience in foreign lands, and what has it got me? A death on the plane, a missing wallet and now, murder. I don't think I can go on. I really don't." A sob escaped her lips.

Kanavou straightened as he stuffed his *komboloi* into his pants pocket. "I do not think it will be all that bad, Ms. Wynter."

"Of course it will. Who will want to take a tour from a company where people die and the police detain the survivors?" Another sob sent tears streaming down her face.

"I think, well...," Kanavou said as he looked flustered and glanced around, apparently seeking assistance with the hysterical American female—or maybe to make sure no one overheard what he was considering doing.

Scarlett sobbed again.

"Your tour members were not the most talkative during my interviews with them," Kanavou admitted.

Another sob.

"Possibly they would talk more to their tour guides," Kanavou said as he eyed Scarlett and Race. "Maybe, Ms. Wynter, your tour can continue."

As Race and Scarlett walked back into the hotel, she said, "Nice going; we could have been stuck here until the next Olympics." The tears had stopped.

"I'm sure Kanavou will solve the murders well before then."

"I doubt our clients want to be held in Kyparissia for four years."

"Your cascade of tears avoided that eventuality—good timing with the waterfalls."

"If a woman can't play the damsel in distress, what's the point of being a woman?"

Scarlett's deft handling of Kanavou aside, Race needed to solve the murders, fast. He spotted David standing at a picture window staring out at the sea. While Scarlett went to call their next hotel to tell them they would be late and change their flights to the Greek islands, Race walked over to express his sympathy for David's loss— and to start to try to figure out what had happened to Petra and Dr. Lodge.

"You go to sleep happy with a loving wife and in the morning she's dead," David said, shaking his head.

"I heard you organized a golf tournament to find an organ donor for Petra."

"It wasn't really to find a donor specifically for her. You can't do that. There's a registry and all that, but I organized a golf tournament to raise awareness and get people to sign up to be donors. Someone who signed up at the tournament was matched with Petra. Pure chance, but it was as if fate wanted her to live."

"You awoke this morning alone?"

"Not a living soul with me. Last night Petra said she wanted to talk to her dad about that boy he had with Gayle, so she decided to go up to the castle with Lodge."

As Race walked with David toward the elevator, Race asked, "No doubt it's his?"

"The good doctor loved women, all sorts, sizes and shapes; probably has a bastard in every state in the Union and enough overseas to fill a lecture hall. He usually hit on married women—safer. Both with a spouse to lose, and if a baby appeared, no problem; well, in most cases. As I said, Lodge loved all sorts of women."

The elevator arrived and they stepped in, their shoulders touching in the fridge-sized conveyance.

Race asked, "Do you think Petra and Dr. Lodge argued?"

"Petra was furious when she heard Lodge had a son. She never saw her beloved daddy clearly, but it must have been an accident; the cliff, no danger signs, and no fence or railing. I'll have to look into suing. I assume the government owns the castle? Small recompense whatever they pay, of course, but I don't want it to happen to anyone else."

Race could smell David's cologne as the elevator whirred and rose. Race said, "It may not have been an accident." Up close, Race could see that David's skin, which appeared tanned, was actually the color of cherry wood. The Greek sun had only darkened it a shade above his golf shirt's collar.

David stared at him. "Murder?"

"Possibly. Did you get along well with your father-in-law?"

"Better than some, worse than others. He was a lady's man, but he was a good father. He loved Petra. He raised her well after her mother died. Petra adored him."

"And your relationship with Petra?"

"Married 18 years. We had our differences, but we were happy." Then, as if coming out of a daze, he stared at Race and, a cold edge in his voice, said, "I don't like what your questions imply. I did not kill my wife and father-in-law. Why would I?"

"Your father-in-law was a wealthy man."

David's face hardened. "Lodge had had several strokes, and Petra was his only child. Why murder him?"

"Someone else might not have known his medical history."

"Gayle? She might have gone up to see Lodge to beg support for their kid, it turned violent, and Petra just happened to be in the way. Or it might have been Cohen over that dating company deal years ago or Beznik or…" David shook his head. "The more I think about it, the more I realize there were enough people who hated my father-in-law to hold a golf tournament."

The elevator stopped, the door slid open and they stepped out. David said, "If it turns out Gayle killed him, don't think he was a complete bastard toward her. He told Petra the other night that he offered to get a divorce and marry Gayle all those years ago. She turned him down; too old and too white, I guess. She's probably twisted it all in her mind after so many years and thinks it's all his fault."

Race nodded.

"And Cohen, I hate to say it, but do you want to know why Lodge ended their partnership?"

Race nodded.

"Cohen was an embezzler."

When Race returned to his room to get his bag before they left, Scarlett was waiting for him. "Thanks to you that vile inspector's arrested Beznik again."

Race cursed his own stupidity. He had convinced Kanavou that the deaths of Lodge and Petra were not an accident, which, he now realized, left Beznik as the prime suspect. Race said, "Beznik *was* angry over Lodge accusing him of stealing the wallet."

"Enough to kill him, and Petra?"

"No one thought Petra was going to be up there. She told her father in front of everyone she wasn't going with him."

"So Beznik goes all the way up there to murder Lodge and, finding Petra there, pushes them both off the cliff?"

"He is a strong young man."

"You sound like you think he did it, and to think, the last thing Beznik said to me as they led him away was to ask you to help prove his innocence."

"I did clear him of stealing the wallet."

"Only to convince Kanavou to arrest him for a double murder."

Chapter 13

"Why don't we just wait until tomorrow morning?" Gayle asked as they all stood in the hotel's parking lot late that afternoon. "We could have a nice dinner, relax over some ouzo or wine, and leave for Olympia in the morning. It's been a hellish day."

"We're already a day behind our itinerary because of the…," Scarlett said, her voice trailing off. "We need to leave now to be at Olympia tomorrow morning early before the crowds."

Everyone started talking at once but Scarlett soon convinced the remaining tour members of the wisdom of her plan. Race moved on to collecting everyone's passports for Kanavou; the inspector's condition for allowing them to continue the tour.

"This is the property of the United States Department of State," Chance declared, brandishing his eagle-emblazoned passport like a religious icon. "No way am I going to surrender it to some damn foreigner."

"Just for Inspector Kanavou to hold until the tour is finished," Race said.

"I really don't see the reason," Rob said, holding his passport against his chest. "A cop I spoke with said there was no sign of a struggle. It was an accident, wasn't it?"

"It's stone up there and windy," Chance said, "you could stage a fleet championship bout up there and there'd be no trace of it."

Seeking to head off a rebellion, Race said, "The inspector wanted to detain us here in Kyparissia."

"For how long?" Chance demanded.

"Yes, for how long do they intend to keep us cooped up here in this god-forsaken hole?" Sonja asked, her dramatic voice rising.

"Kyparissia is far from a hole," Scarlett said.

"Until Kanavou determines whether Petra and Dr. Lodge died by accident," Race said.

"Of course it was an accident," Sonja said.

"Didn't they arrest Beznik for the murder?" Gayle asked. "If it was an accident, why arrest him? And, in either case, why hold us?"

"Because this has been the worst tour in history," Chance said.

"You just need to look on the bright side," Benny said as he lounged against the van beside Rob.

"The bright side of three people dead, a stolen wallet, and being stuck in some town no one between here and Catalina has ever heard of?" Chance demanded. "Might as well look on the bright side of senility."

"If you're senile, at least you forget you're old," Benny said. "Besides, can't do anything about any of that now, but look to the future and have some fun—at least until we're all senile."

"Or dead," Chance said.

Benny stuck his tongue out at the ex-fighter pilot and blew a raspberry at him.

Race held up his hands for calm. He didn't want Chance to add Benny to the mounting death toll. "In any case, Kanavou agreed to allow us to continue the tour, if he holds our passports. Otherwise, we're stuck here for the foreseeable future."

"Oh, hell," Benny said, "It's only some pieces of paper with an unremarkable likeness." He tossed his passport to Race, who caught it. "Rob, give it up. A lot worse places to be stranded than Greece in the springtime with handsome men and beautiful ladies." He flung one arm around Rob's shoulders and the other around Gayle's, smiling broadly at each of them in turn.

"One thing is certain, I am not going to be stuck here," Sonja declared, handing over her passport, followed closely by Chance, who acted as if he was surrendering his sword.

The growing rebellion quelled, Scarlett asked, "Where are David and Cohen?"

David was with Kanavou, but no one had seen Cohen. Kanavou had an officer check with the hotel desk clerk. Cohen had checked out just after the police concluded their questioning. The desk clerk ordered a taxi for him, but did not know his destination.

"That solves it then," Scarlett said as Kanavou and David joined the group. "Cohen murdered Lodge over being taken in that dating site deal, and Petra just happened to be in the wrong place at the wrong time."

"Great," Gayle said. "Now there's a killer on the loose."

"Please do not worry," Kanavou said. "Every police officer in Greece will be watching for Mr. Cohen, and I will ensure we keep some surveillance on your party."

Scarlett asked, "So you'll release Beznik?"

"Beznik will be released if and when we determine that Mr. Cohen is the murderer, and that he acted alone."

Scarlett said, "He certainly fled alone."

Race, Scarlett and Gayle set to work loading the luggage aboard the van. David walked over to help.

"No, no, no," Scarlett said, shocked as David started to lift a bag. "We can do this."

David said, "I like to help."

"Are you even sure you want to continue with the tour?" Race asked.

David stopped after putting one of the smaller bags in the van. "I don't know what I'd do if I left. Go home? To what?" He sighed, rubbed his red-rimmed eyes and said, "May as well be useful." He lifted one of Sonja's mammoth Louis Vuitton suitcases, turned to put it into the back of the van and grunted in pain, his face twisted in agony.

"What's wrong?" Scarlett asked, rushing to his side.

"My back," David said, setting the bag down with a thud.

"My crystal," Sonja wailed, as if David had just dropped her newborn baby onto the blacktop. "Be careful!"

"Twisted wrong," David said, wincing. He tentatively massaged his lower back with both hands. He stretched this way and that, the pain appearing to ease, but not entirely. "I think I'll sit down." He moved with a rigid, straight back to the van's door and slowly, carefully and with extreme care climbed aboard and sat down, as if he was in slow motion. Sonja joined him.

"Mr. Traveler!" Sonja yelled. "Mr. Traveler! Help me, please! Now!"

Race boarded and found the source of her distress; towels strewn across the back bench of the van, several wadded up into a flattened ball.

"Can't you at least keep the van neat and tidy for the paying clientele?" Sonja asked, nose raised with hauteur.

Race grabbed the towels and, noticing they were from the hotel, headed inside to return them to the front desk as he wondered how they had ended up in the van.

Scarlett hurried after him and asked, "Do you think Cohen will want his money back?"

"I doubt he'll need much money in prison. Cigarettes maybe, if movies are to be believed."

Race returned the towels to the front desk.

"I hope you enjoyed your stay," the brunette clerk said with an engaging smile. Her dark eyes lingered on Race, even if she was half his age.

"We did, we did."

"Slept well?"

Race was about to answer when a thought struck him. "Can you check to see if a reservation was used last night?"

"I shouldn't, but..." She smiled at Race.

The drive to Olympia was uneventful—no one died. After a late *kreatopita* dinner of a meat pie with goat, rice and a light tomato sauce wrapped in a pastry, Race kissed Scarlett at her hotel room's door before he turned toward his room.

Scarlett grabbed his arm. "I'm scared, Race."

"Why? It appears Cohen was the murderer and he's fled."

"But he's still on the loose, and even if they catch him, that still leaves the murderer of Mrs. Rasmussen, and Rob is still in our group."

"If she was murdered and if Rob did it, I don't see any reason why he would want to kill you."

"Please stay."

With only a modicum of feminine convincing, Scarlett convinced Race to stay. With only one Queen bed, they got into bed and he rubbed her back to be friendly.

"Don't," she said.

"Why not?"

"I've told you."

Race lay back and stared at the ceiling. Why was she more worried about him dying than he was? "You should remember one thing."

"What's that?"

"You can't lose something you've never had."

"Maybe everything you have is just something more to lose."

Chapter 14

Day 9: Sunday, April 25

Deciding the early tourist avoids the hordes, Scarlett had everyone roused and down the hotel's coffin-sized elevator for breakfast by 6 am. Race was late, having to do his chest therapy and nebulizer treatments longer than usual. His lungs were worsening.

After breakfast they drove the short distance through the geometrically laid out town to the ancient site. Race recoiled at the tourist-trap nature of Olympia. The main street was a gauntlet for the eyes formed by stores selling miniature Greek helmets, red and black urns, postcards, glass coasters, figurines, and all manner of ancient, pseudo-ancient and modern kitsch, including playing cards demonstrating 52 sexual positions with a presumably Greek flavor.

Having crossed the Kladeos River, a tributary of the Alfeios, the tour disembarked at one of the most visited sites in Greece. Every tour visited Olympia, including boatloads of tourists from cruise ships calling at the newly enlarged port of Katakolo, a brief 15-kilometer air-conditioned bus ride from Olympia.

"Nine euros?" Chance asked, aghast. "Most of the other sites are three or four euros, some even free."

"Only because there's no one around to collect the cash," Gayle said.

"But nine euros? That's what? Fifteen bucks?"

"A great deal to see the birthplace of the Olympic Games," Gayle said.

"I'll cover it, if you like," David said. He was walking carefully, his back golf-club straight.

"How kind," Sonja said, beaming at David. "Such a generous man."

"I'll pay," Chance muttered.

"See, nobody here yet," Scarlett announced, happy that her dawn strategy had beat the tourist hordes, although March was wide open compared with standing-room-only June, July and August. "We have the site to ourselves."

"If I can pry my eyes open long enough to see it," Sonja whined, having gone from beaming to whining in less than a second.

"Wake up and see the stones," Benny urged her, rubbing her back with great enthusiasm. "Lots to see and lots to do today. Wake up."

"I'm awake. I just got up early to jog farther than usual this morning," Sonja said. "I need to get into peak shape to look my best; the parts will be rolling in by the time I return to the real world."

"It's far larger than I thought it would be," Gayle said, taking in the extensive grounds.

"Most people know Olympia as the birthplace of the Olympics, but it was actually a major religious center," Race said. "The public was only allowed on the site for the games."

"When were the games held?" Gayle asked.

"From 776 BC to 393 AD, and then not again for 1,500 years," Race said.

"The games were designed to teach young men the skills for war," Chance said with relish. "Wrestling and boxing."

"And to unify the Greeks, which they did for almost 1,200 years," Race said. "Over there is the original 45,000-seat Olympic stadium with stone seats for the judges; everyone else had to sit on the grassy slopes. Over there is a rectangular temple to Zeus with a few huge, manly columns still standing. The fallen columns show how the sections were put together with a notch and wood-peg system. The Temple of Hera, over there," he said, pointing through the widely spaced trees, "has about 20 slim, elegant, feminine columns still intact, while in the far corner of the site the Roman Emperor Nero had a house built for himself for when he visited."

"I hope he didn't bring his fiddle," Chance said with a grin.

David managed a smile through his grief and Gayle a chuckle. No one felt like laughing.

"The wrestler's school, although ruined, can be discerned over there by its foundations," Race continued. "Over in that direction is where they light the Olympic torch, marked by a small, rectangular foundation about the size of a Manhattan condo's bedroom."

Race stopped. David looked as if he had just returned from a combat tour in Iraq: dazed, exhausted and devoid of emotion at seeing one of the world's great historical sites. Gayle appeared excited, but her face was drained of color and her eyes had furrows beneath them. Only Rob with his irrepressible, boyish enthusiasm, and Benny, who always seemed up and ready for anything, showed any semblance of interest, let alone excitement. Sonja was smiling, but her mind was elsewhere as she inspected her nails—at least she wasn't on her phone.

"The museum is across the road, over there," Race said, conceding defeat to the sadness of the day. "You have a few hours, so relax, wander and enjoy."

His last word, as soon as he said it, seemed far from appropriate. The tour members drifted away. Olympia was in terrain vastly different from the dry, rugged coast. Poppies, wildflowers and grasses appeared in far greater numbers than along the coast. The grass glistened with dew and almond trees in full bloom had carpeted vast sections of the site with pink petals. Hard to believe, Race thought, that anyone could die within a thousand miles of such a serene place.

As Scarlett and Race walked down the grassy incline toward the ruins, Race spotted Gayle wandering off alone toward the Leonidaion, the lodging place for athletes taking part in the Olympic Games two thousand years ago. Race and Scarlett followed her at a distance and, when she sat on one of the round stones that were all that remained of one of the great columns, they approached her.

Gayle raised her lowered head and said, "I'm sorry, but I'd really prefer to be alone." She wiped tears away.

"Is there anything we can do?" Scarlett asked, crouching before Gayle.

Shaking her head, Gayle sniffled and said, "No one can help me now."

Race hesitated. He should remain silent, but the puzzle of the murders of Dr. Lodge and Petra was still missing pieces. "David said Dr. Lodge offered to help you before, a long time ago."

Gayle frowned. Scarlett cast Race a warning look; Gayle was a client.

Race had to ask. "Did Dr. Lodge offer to marry you when he learned you were pregnant with his child?"

Gayle laughed, deep, resonant and bitter. "The king of match-making leave his wife? You must be mad. It would have scuttled his company before it even got started. Who wants to join a dating website run by someone who's just divorced his wife?" Shaking her head, Gayle stalked off deeper into the ruined site.

"What are you doing?" Scarlett demanded. "Cohen's the murderer; case closed."

Wandering through the site, Race stopped to admire the temples, taking it slow, but not telling Scarlett he was tiring. He feared his lungs were harboring yet another infection, but hoped the new antibiotics from Pylos would allow him to finish the tour—and figure out if Cohen had murdered Dr. Lodge and Petra, not to mention discovering who stole Lodge's wallet and whether Rob murdered his mother.

Scarlett and Race crossed the road as the first buses arrived, but they were not tourist coaches; they were school buses. Children poured forth into the columned entrance of the Archeological Museum of Olympia. By moving into rooms before or after the classes of shepherded children, Scarlett and Race were able to see what they wanted: piedmonts from the temple of Zeus depicting battles, a chariot race and Heracles' 12 labors; vases; statues of Roman emperors standing like a receiving line at a royal wedding; hundreds of miniature horses and bulls, votive offerings to the gods; and the largest collection of bronze armor in the world, including the famous Greek helmets—properly called Corinthian after their origin in Corinth. Finally they gazed upon Scarlett's favorite, the 4th century statue *Hermes of Praxiteles*.

"Amazing how Praxiteles made stone appear to be cloth," Scarlett said. "Looks like you could reach out and crinkle it with your fingers."

Race put his arm around Scarlett's shoulders and held her close. In the room alone, the statue was stunning; the marble exuding an inner warmth as if it lived.

As a brood of schoolchildren flowed into the room like a tide, Scarlett and Race slipped outside. Workers were adding parking space amongst the firs and planting shrubs as they prepared for the expected Olympic-size crowds in August with the Olympiad in Athens. Race drank a nutrient rich shake he had bought at the museum's store as they crossed the road back toward the ancient ruins. His stomach had been upset from the antibiotics and he felt weak. He hoped the shake would help. In the distance they saw Inspector Kanavou with Chance and Sonja. The couple stood rigid, faces set, arms crossed over their chests.

"Three yachts in seven years," Kanavou said as Race and Scarlett approached within earshot. "Insurance paid out almost $26 million on those three claims alone."

"I move yachts during the off season," Chance said, an edge in his voice. His aviator sunglasses hid his eyes. "The weather's bad and the owners never want to pay for a full crew."

"So conveniently it is just you," Kanavou said.

"Sonja was with me."

"I had nothing to do with the sailing," Sonja said. "I was just along for the sail, as it were." Even from a distance, Race could feel the warmth of her smile as she beamed sweet innocence at Kanavou.

"She did testify at the inquiries about the weather and what happened in each case," Chance said, betraying a mounting anger that was creeping into his face, body and voice. "She was with me the entire time, on every yacht I lost."

Sonja shot a glare at her husband that would have frightened Ajax.

Race and Scarlett stopped near the trio. Even so, Kanavou continued his questioning. "Were there any other witnesses?"

"Two of the boats were lost at night and one off a remote part of Corsica," Chance said, his face now incredulous as he whipped off his sunglasses. "Who would be around to see?"

"Indeed," Kanavou said with a knowing nod. "Indeed."

"We barely made it off the *Lord of the Isles*," Chance said. "Once we made it ashore, it took three days without food or water to reach a town."

"We almost died," Sonja said.

"Indeed."

"I lost an F-16 over Iraq," Chance said. "No witnesses, at least on our side. You going to charge me with losing it on purpose, too? I'd talk to the Iraqi SAM crew first. They might want to hang onto their claim for shooting my tail off."

"We have divers going down to investigate the wreck of the *Lord of the Isles.*"

"That was almost a year ago," Chance said, his voice rising.

"You can't do that," Sonja said, her brow furrowed with concern, her mouth twisted with worry.

Chance said, "She was lost in deep water."

"The hulk has been pushed closer to shore by the current," Kanavou said. "I'm told it's amazingly well preserved. There's a cold-water current off Sicily in that particular spot; maintains wrecks as if they are in a deep freeze."

"That was all settled a year ago," Sonja said, as if remembering a nightmare. "The maritime court and the insurance company both ruled it was an accident. We almost drowned."

"Sailing's a risky business," Chance said.

"It is when you do it," Kanavou countered.

"I had nothing to do with those boats sinking," Sonja said, taking a side step away from her husband.

"Shut up, Sonja," Chance ordered.

"I wasn't the one sailing them."

"Shut up."

With a last long glare at her husband, Sonja spun on her designer heels and stalked away.

"Those boats went down in storms or were unseaworthy to begin with," Chance said. "That's what you'll find no matter how much time and money you waste investigating them."

"So you say," Kanavou said. "So you say."

Chance turned to pursue his wife, shouting after her as she headed farther into the ancient site, "Let's get the hell out of here, Sonja. We have better rubble back home; ever see Detroit?"

"Why are you questioning Chance and Sonja?" Race asked Kanavou. "Isn't Cohen the murderer?"

"Or Beznik?" Scarlett asked. "You're still holding him."

"We are still searching for Cohen, and Beznik still lacks an alibi for the time of the murders, while having a strong motive," Kanavou said. "As to Mr. Charles Stirling, when Dr. Lodge reported his missing wallet, he said he recognized Mr. Stirling as someone pointed out to him at a party in New York as someone who could 'lose your boat for a handsome profit.'"

"Any progress on the Petra and Lodge case?" Race asked.

Kanavou said the deaths occurred between 3 am and 7 am, when almost everyone except Sonja, who was out for a jog, was in their room. Therefore, everyone lacked an alibi or had an alibi supplied by a significant other, which amounted to the same thing—no alibi at all.

"David Fox found an organ donor for his wife a few years ago," Race reported. "Saved her life."

"Ruling him out as a suspect," Scarlett said. "Why save your wife's life, just to murder her?"

Race coughed, earning a concerned look from Scarlett.

Race asked, "Did you search the plane for Mrs. Rasmussen's missing inhalers?"

"We did; nothing. It is a large plane that carried 297 passengers. If Robert Rasmussen took his mother's inhalers, he could have slipped them into any one of the other passengers' bags during the flight or as everyone deplaned."

"Are you tracking down the passengers to find out if anyone found inhalers in their bags?" Scarlett asked.

"As much as we can. It is a time-consuming task and with the Olympics, resources are required elsewhere. You must remember, it is questionable whether Mrs. Rasmussen was even murdered."

Race started coughing. He dug out a tissue and, turning away, hacked out some phlegm. He coughed again, his lungs burning with pain as it felt as if his rib cage was squeezing his lungs flat.

"Do you need a doctor?" Kanavou asked, frowning with concern.

As suddenly as it started, the attack stopped and Race was able to say, "Probably, but right now I need to speak with Beznik."

"I already have."

"People tell different things to different people."

When Race arrived in the Kyparissia jail's tan interview room, Beznik hugged him. The hug hurt his lungs, but Race just grinned at the young Greek. After making sure Beznik was being treated well, Race said, "You slept in the van the night Dr. Lodge and Petra died, so I wondered if you saw anything related to their deaths?"

"How...?"

"Towels in the back row of the van were made up like a bed, and the hotel clerk said the room Scarlett reserved in your name was canceled."

His eyes downcast, his lips pursed, Beznik said, "I will return the money."

"It was your room to use or not; either way, it's your money."

Beznik stared at Race with a look of disbelief. "I must save money. My brother wants to buy a fishing boat to take tourists fishing. He knows about sailing. I am learning the tourist business, so I will send him clients."

"Please tell me what happened early that morning."

Beznik glanced at an intercom on the wall.

"The truth can only help you, Beznik, if you weren't involved in their deaths."

"The actress, Mrs. Weaver, went jogging early. I do not remember exactly when. It was still dark."

"Anything else?"

Beznik looked away as he considered. "I saw Mr. Cohen at about 4 am, before Mrs. Weaver went jogging."

"Cohen has fled."

Beznik frowned. "He had been at the taverna. I had to help him to his room or...." Another glance at the intercom. "A policeman was driving by. Stopped when he saw Mr. Cohen. I thought he was going to arrest Mr. Cohen, so I rushed out of the van in my bare feet and helped him to his room."

"Probably saved Cohen a night in jail," Race said, but the incident also placed Cohen out of his room when someone murdered Petra and Dr. Lodge. "Nice of you to help."

"Did me no good." Beznik scowled. "*Batsos* told me not to sleep in the van. At least he did not arrest me."

Race nodded, rose and as he reached for the door handle, asked, "If you were asleep, how did you see Cohen?"

"He woke me up; crashed into the van's hood."

Late that evening, Race turned the corner toward Scarlett's room to give her a report on the mounting evidence against Cohen when a door opened ahead. Sonja stepped out of the room. With a luscious smile, she said to someone in the room, "That was very gratifying and fun, dear. I hope our relationship continues along similar lines in the future." She turned, floated across the hall and entered her room. Sonja did not see Race.

When Scarlett answered her door, Race told her that Beznik had seen Cohen returning to the hotel at 4 am, although Cohen appeared drunk.

"An act?" Scarlett asked. "Maybe he thought Beznik had seen him as he returned from murdering Lodge and Petra, and decided to act drunk to try to show he was in no state to have murdered anyone."

"He threw up the next morning."

"Remorse over what he'd done? In any case, it sounds like it'll be all wrapped up once the police catch Cohen."

"Still leaves Mrs. Rasmussen and Lodge's stolen wallet."

"So Rob let his mother die by hiding her inhalers and Cohen took the opportunity of one death to try to mask his murder of Lodge."

"It isn't like Cohen left Rob's backpack at the scene of the crime or anything."

"Maybe he hoped the police would think Petra saw Rob dispose of the inhalers on the plane, so he killed her."

"No one knew Petra would be up at the castle that morning. She changed her mind, remember? Lodge was the target."

"So Cohen murdered Lodge over the dating website deal and Petra just happened to be in the way."

Race shook his head. "It's like one section of the jigsaw puzzle is complete, but all around it are missing pieces. I'm going to keep asking questions."

"Be careful, Race, someone might want to kill you if they realize you're investigating."

"Why? I'm dying anyway."

"You might get close to something the police don't notice."

Scarlett wanted him to stay, so Race undressed and slid into bed, nestling up against Scarlett's inviting curves. "Is it too late for some fun? And who's in 206?"

"Not the fun you're thinking, but that feels wonderful," she said as he massaged her back. She slid up her nightgown to allow him easier access to her back.

"Two-oh-six?"

"If I tell you, will you just shut up and keep doing what you're doing?"

"Of course, among other things."

"Race, let's just stick to massage for now. I still don't know if I want..." Scarlett moaned as he kneaded the tension from her shoulders.

"Don't wait too long to decide. The oldest CF patient lived to 81. I plan to beat that, but you never know. Who's in 206, across from Sonja and Chance?"

"Uhhhh...."

"Who?"

"David....Fox."

Chapter 15

Day 10: Monday, April 26

"It's not in my guidebook," Chance announced early the next morning as he slammed shut his bible.

"Chlemoutsi Castle is one of the finest examples of Frankish castle building in the world," Race said. "Scarlett agreed to let us see it, even if we are a day behind schedule."

"We should have it all to ourselves," Scarlett said, "especially since it's difficult to find."

"Just to add to the difficulty," Race said, "it's also called Kastor Killins, after the nearest town, and Castle Clermont, an anglicized name for the knight who founded it."

With low clouds and occasional gust-driven shower adding to the somber mood, Race drove the excursion back out to the coast and, at the Ionian Sea, turned north.

"There it is," Rob exclaimed, sitting in the back with Benny, who sucked regularly on his flask of ouzo and munched sour cream and onion crisps.

"Must you always drink?" Sonja asked Benny.

"Must you always whine?" Benny asked with a wicked smile.

The pair glared at each other.

"Wow," Rob said, staring out the window. "Cool."

Emerging from the low clouds in the distance atop a broad hill, an imposing castle stood mighty, strong and, from a distance, intact.

"That thing's 10 miles away," Chance marveled. "It must be huge."

"Not so much huge," Race said, "built on the most command-ing hill in the region to protect the port of Glarentza."

They wound through villages and olive groves as rain splattered the van's dust-filmed windows. Finally signs for the castle appeared, but by then they were at the foot of the castle's commanding hill. Race parked in the dirt area outside the main gate that could hold, at most, six cars. The castle walls towered above an empty hut where in the summer some lonely soul accepted the rare admission fee.

Race said, "The real gem is the keep, with a three-story, 600-foot long great hall that is still intact after 800 years."

Once inside, the excursionists marveled at the great hall's arched ceilings far above them. The keep rose from the highest point on the hill within the crenellated main wall, although it was the only building still standing. Clumps of yellow-flowered bushes, sage, rosemary, thyme, and a few stunted trees fought for life in the rocky courtyard.

"The Venetians called this place Castel Tornese, after silver *gros tournois* coins, which they thought were minted here for the Principality of Achaea," Race told Sonja as they stood on the castle's wall looking out toward the sea over the gentle hills covered with olive groves.

"Any gold coins to be found?" Sonja asked, peering with narrowed eyes back at the uneven, rocky ground of the outer keep.

"The mint was actually in Glarentza, just over there, not here."

"I've never had any trouble finding gold when the need arises," Sonja said. "Maybe I'll find my fortune even here."

Race followed her gaze. She was looking back over at Gayle, David and Rob, who stood at the entrance to the keep. Race eyed the stately actress and wondered if she would kill for love, if not for gold. Did she go up the mountain to kill Petra and Dr. Lodge got in the way, all so Sonja could pursue a love affair with David? It seemed farfetched, but how far would love and lust drive someone, especially a fading beauty grasping at one last chance for true love?

"Given how observant you were when the wallet was stolen," Race said, "do you have any theories about Petra and Dr. Lodge's deaths?"

"Cohen fled; he must have done it, although Beznik's still in jail for it."

"Doesn't mean he did it."

Sonja nodded as she posed as if for a magazine photo shoot. "Petra was furious over her father's bastard son," she said, turning her head so the sea breeze ruffled her long hair. "Maybe they argued and went over the cliff together in a terminal father-daughter embrace. Make a fabulous final scene, don't you think?"

David had mentioned the same possibility. Given that Sonja had been in David's room the night before, were they lovers who had agreed to blame the deaths on a father-daughter argument that turned violent? Would Sonja follow David's script and mention Gayle returning with euros for lunch after visiting the van at Corinth next, followed by Cohen's embezzling, as David had?

She didn't.

After watching her strike a range of model poses, Race asked, "Did you see anyone during your jog that morning?"

"Just David."

That was news. Had David told Kanavou he'd left the hotel that morning? Was it true, or were David and Sonja lovers providing each other an alibi, albeit a weak one?

Sonja said, "He took my picture."

That certainly would strengthen their alibis.

Sonja dug her cell out of her tight pants pocket and, after a few deft manipulations, showed Race an image of her at the beach in a jogging outfit. In the background was the easily identifiable breakwater at Kyparissia. "David was walking on the beach. Said Petra woke him when she left early. He couldn't get back to sleep, so he went for a walk. Date and time down in the corner: 5:06 am. Here's another from 5:58. We…ah…talked for a time. Isn't that about when Petra and Lodge died?"

They drove back down the coast and inland through Olympia and up into the rugged mountainous interior of the Peloponnesus. The road was built on a ledge blasted into cliffs, with steep jagged mountains above and narrow valleys below. With every turn, Race wished Beznik was driving. Race's chest hurt and he was exhausted. The anti-inflammatories and antibiotics he took for his lungs dried him out and he felt parched no matter how often he guzzled from his water bottle. He no longer listened to music as he drove. He had enough difficulty forcing his mind to concentrate solely on driving.

Glancing in the rear-view mirror, Race saw that Sonja had managed to sit next to David; far easier now without Petra. David seemed dazed, yet as they drove, he began to respond to Sonja's whispers. Chance sat in front of them, reading his guidebook and glancing out the window, apparently lost in his own thoughts—about missing yachts?

Gayle sat in the front row, leaning her head against a window, the picture of dejection. She seemed oblivious to the passing scenery, yet when David laughed at something Sonja had whispered, Gayle turned and eyed David for a long time.

Benny and Rob sat together, watching the scenery, giggling and laughing at private comments. Benny sucked from his ouzo flask and Rob munched on chocolate chip cookies he had procured somewhere.

The mountain roads were tortuously slow, even if there was almost no traffic. At one point, after hours of twisting mountain road, they hit a new section of wide, straight highway.

"Now we'll make up some time," Scarlett said.

Race sped around a sweeping corner only to hit the brakes. A detour led off the new road, a section of which had collapsed in a landslide. They were back on the old road, which consisted of hundreds of hairpin, steep climbing and abrupt downgrade turns, often narrowing on the corners with the ever-present shrines on the roadside to remind Race that an accident was only a millisecond away if anyone was coming the other way. When Rob asked yet again whether they were there yet, it only made Race miss Beznik more.

They drove past Langadia, a village perched on an abrupt hill with a cemetery so full of white crosses it appeared completely white. When they stopped to stretch their legs and buy gas, the tour took in the fantastic view down the deep, narrow valley. As Scarlett wrote down the amount for the gas in her budget book, Race took the opportunity to walk well out of everyone's earshot to make a call with her cell. It took him three tries to find the person he needed.

"We are interested in hiring Gayle Garcia at North Shore Sports Medicine," Race said. "Do you mind confirming her employment with you?"

"She was with us for almost six years," the US Olympic Team Chief Medical Officer replied from Colorado. "Dedicated, caring, and the athletes loved her. Many said they wouldn't have medaled without her."

"If I may ask, how did she injure her arm?"

"One of those freak things. She was treating one of our weight-lifter's backs. She had her hand under him and when she went to pull it out as she did a manipulation, her watch caught. The weight-lifter's entire weight came down on her wrist—snap."

"She said it would heal completely soon." Race bit his lip as he waited the response.

After a pause the doctor said, "I am sorry, but I can't comment on that."

They climbed to an alpine ski area with broad meadows, firs and mountains wearing snow caps where they joined a new highway built to facilitate skiers driving from Athens a couple of hours east.

"I didn't know they ever got snow in Greece," Rob said.

"Wait until we reach Kalampaka," Race said.

"There's no snow is there?" Sonja asked, horrified. "I didn't bring a single stitch of winter clothes."

"You'll be fine," Scarlett assured the actress. "It won't be that cold."

Two-hours after leaving Olympia they reached Tripolis, the largest city on the Peloponnesus with 200,000 people. As a light rain misted the van's windows and left a silver sheen on their hair, they disembarked at a taverna for lunch. Race sat with Gayle.

"I can see why you wanted help from Dr. Lodge," Race said as he blew on his *spetsofai*, a stew of country sausage, mild green peppers, onion, and wine.

Gayle stopped, a gyro bulging with grilled lamb, parsley, oregano, onion, tomatoes, *tzatziki* (strained yoghurt), and fries halfway to her mouth.

"I spoke with the Olympic Team's chief medical officer. He said he'd be happy to have you back when your wrist heals." Race watched Gayle closely as he added, "Not that he thinks it will."

Gayle set the gyro deliberately down in its wax paper wrap on her plate. She pressed her lips tightly together as her eyes narrowed. "He shouldn't have told you that."

"He didn't," Race said, his suspicion confirmed. Gayle not only needed money for her son, she was unemployed and, disabled, she was unlikely to ever work as a physio again.

Gayle frowned.

Before she could figure out what she had just done, Race asked, "Why approach Dr. Lodge now after so many years?"

Gayle sighed and said, "My son's been accepted to USC. I can't afford it." She glared down at her injured wrist as if it were a malevolent creature. "It's his dream to study computer engineering. Should he pay with his dream for a mistake I made 18 years ago?"

"You argued with Petra at Mycenae," Race said, savoring one of the big rounds of sausage in his country stew.

Gayle glanced over at David, sitting alone, lethargically poking at a layered *pastitsio* of Béchamel sauce, pasta and ground meat cooked with tomato sauce. "How would killing Lodge, let alone Petra, help my son?" Dropping her voice, she whispered, "You should talk to Sonja. I saw her going out at about 5 the morning Lodge and Petra were killed."

Race already knew Sonja had been out for a jog but he wondered what Gayle had been doing up so early to see her.

Gayle whispered, "Sonja hated Lodge."

It seemed everyone on the trip hated Lodge: Beznik over the wallet; Cohen over their dating business; Gayle over their son; Chance over the yachts; and now Sonja. "Why?"

"Sonja was slated to be the centerpiece of an ad campaign for his dating website. TV, radio, print, Internet, social media; the whole carnival of media offerings. It would have reignited her career; modeling, acting, even singing."

"What happened?"

"Dr. Lodge saw Sonja and nixed it."

"As an actress and model, I'm sure Sonja's had her fair share of jobs fall through."

"Not with Lodge telling her to her face in front of a boardroom full of top ad and media executives that she's too old. Word hit the tabloids and the label stuck: Sonja Weaver's too old. Do you know that part she's trying to land taking this tour?"

"How do you know all this?"

Gayle snickered. "My dirty little secret isn't murder; it's reading tabloids by the dozen. Sonja's up to play the *mother* of the star in some movie about a tour of Greece. The very thought must kill her, but now with Lodge and Petra dead, guess who's going to be making all the decisions at the dating company now?" Gayle glanced over at David.

"That seems extreme; murder for an ad campaign."

"Sonja would do it. She once starved herself to lose 30 pounds for a part. She was hospitalized and almost died. And she's been involved in deaths before." Gayle leaned across the table and whispered, "Her stunt double died filming *Transparent Waters*, a movie she produced and starred in years ago. The director wanted to film a climactic chase scene on a log boom in a soundstage and punch it up with CGI magic, but Sonja wanted realism, so they filmed it off Vancouver Island in the north Pacific. Sonja's stunt double slipped between two Douglas firs, the logs crashed together and crushed her to death."

Race winced at the thought of such a way to die and looked over at Sonja. Was the actress that cold-blooded? Or was it just tabloid exaggeration to boost sales? She did seem to be paying undue attention to David, and had been since the trip began. Had Sonja planned to murder Lodge all along to make David the decision-maker at the dating website?

"She's ruthless," Gayle said. "Did you read her tell-all book a few years ago? She accused her father of sexually abusing her. He denied it, as did his wife and Sonja's three older sisters and older brother. Fat lot of good it did him. He was fired and ostracized in his home town in Tennessee to the point where he had to move to Arkansas. Finally someone beat him to death outside a bar, supposedly for having despoiled the angelic Sonja Weaver."

"Why lie about something like that?"

"Publicity. Her career was at a low point. Her attempt at a comeback movie did less business than a documentary about McNamara and the Vietnam War. But after her tell-all book came out, she appeared on every tabloid's cover, every daytime talk show's couch, and she got a bunch of leading parts, at least until Lodge labeled her 'old,' killing her career again, dead, dead, dead."

David offered to drive. Race's lungs ached as if a little man was trying to strangle him from the inside and the new antibiotics made it feel as if an energetic gnome was gardening in his stomach with a metal rake, so Race agreed, but only after David assured him that driving wouldn't aggravate his injured back.

They sped out of Tripolis in the rain to the isthmus before turning north toward Thebes on a two-lane road that wound through rising hills. David often had to pass slow trucks. Most of the Greeks did not use headlights in the misty rain, which made it hard to judge when to pass. At first Race watched each dash around a truck, but soon decided he'd rather not know when David was risking their lives, let alone to what extent. The ex-golfer had an athlete's reflexes, taking far greater risks than Race would have— even if Race was risking a far shorter life.

The drive was broken regularly by Rob's question, "Are we there yet?" At least he always sounded excited when he asked, eager to reach the next site. If he had sounded whiney, there might have been another murder as Chance glared at Rob every time he asked his eternal question.

At Thebes, the valley opened into a broad agricultural plain. The promise of a flat road was brief and they soon climbed around Mt. Parnassos to Archehova, which clung to a steep mountainside. Chalet-style stone buildings topped with steep, red-tile roofs lined the street. David waited while two buses pulled in their mirrors to inch past each other in an intimate dance along the narrow street. More buses waited behind them to perform the identical minuet with the oncoming bus.

"Looks like an Austrian alpine village," Chance said. "Did you take a wrong turn, David and take us to Innsbruck?"

"Straight out of Disney," Gayle said, emerging from her depression for a moment. "Hard to believe there's room for a house, let alone an entire village on such a cliff."

"This is the Balkans," Race said, "which comes from the Turkish word for mountain."

The buses finished their dance and David drove another mile to Delphi, which was less filled with tourist and their buses than Archehova. Race found their hotel as the sun set, its glow masked by wet, cloying clouds. Scarlett insisted Race share her room. Cohen was still loose and she feared Rob was a murderer. From their room, Race could just discern through the shifting mist and shimmering rain the villages of Itea and Galaxidi far below in the precipitous Pleistos Valley. Swaying pencil cypresses poked through the mist and he could intermittently see a narrow river that snaked down the deep valley to the Gulf of Corinth and the harbor city of Kirrha 15 kilometers away.

Race set up his nebulizer and chest therapy devices. He lined up a row of pill bottles on a table making their room look more like an ICU than a hotel room.

"Are you going to ask the Oracle who stole Lodge's wallet?" Scarlett asked as she burrowed into the bed for a rest before dinner.

"The Pythia, as Delphi's oracle was called, last gave a response in 393 AD, when Theodosius I ordered pagan temples closed, so we're a tad late."

"And to think, I'm never late."

Chapter 16

After dinner, Race used his chest percussor and nebulizer as Scarlett tallied up the day's expenditures and then dozed on the bed. After finishing his medical ministrations, Race felt restless, so he pulled on his Goretex jacket.

"You aren't leaving me alone?" Scarlett asked, fully awake in an instant.

"I forgot my book in the van. I'll be right back." Race leaned down to kiss her as she lay coiled under a puffy comforter. The intermittent hum of the wind along the valley reached them even through the closed window and drawn curtains. "I'll lock the door."

"And the window?" Scarlett peered across the room at the drapes with fear-filled eyes.

Race strode across the marble-floored room. He parted the heavy drapes and peered through the rain-speckled, locked window. "It's 600 meters of slick rock to the valley floor. No one but a suicidal spider could climb up to the window."

"Some spiders bite. Please stay."

Race's head swirled with questions about a stolen wallet and three murders. He felt anxious, as if some unseen pressure was squeezing his brain. He was desperate for answers. Compounding his mental turmoil, his lungs felt tight and sore. He wasn't getting enough oxygen and he wanted time to think, alone; time to let his subconscious sort out what had happened to Mrs. Rasmussen, Lodge's wallet, Petra and Dr. Lodge, and Gayle at Palamidi Castle.

"Please stay," Scarlett repeated.

"Why?" Their relationship was yet another thing on Race's mind that appeared to defy resolution. Tired in body and soul from being sick, from the unsolved mysteries, and from his relationship with Scarlett, he said, "I'll be friendly, you'll say no and then we'll both be upset." As soon as he said it, he regretted it, but he had had enough of their dance that never seemed to progress.

Scarlett pursed her lips, hurt by his words, but she did not deny them. Her voice low, she said, "I need you."

"Not the way I need you., Race said as nicely as he could. Lacking the luxury of time, it was time to force Scarlett to decide.

"There's a killer on the loose, maybe two. I don't think it's the best time to discuss our future, do you?"

"What better time? When you can see the end, it's a great incentive to focus on what's important right now."

"So you agree, our lives are at risk. I need you. We'll both be safer together."

"I'm so weak I couldn't defend a BBQ at a vegetarian convention."

"Then go see a doctor."

"Too late tonight. A walk should help loosen up my lungs."

"I thought you were just getting your book."

"I'll be back soon. You'll be fine."

Scarlett's reply was stilled by her buzzing cell. Inspector Kanavou had identified the police officer on duty near the Kyparissia hotel the night Petra and Dr. Lodge died, but hadn't been able to question the officer yet about Beznik's account of that morning. Race thanked him and told Kanavou that Gayle had been awake in time to see Sonja jogging the morning Lodge and Petra were murdered. Other than that, Race had nothing more to offer.

After the call, with Scarlett upset but silent, Race said goodbye and let himself out. He was too tired for an argument. Keeping to the lee of the buildings and thereby largely out of the soaking rain that seemed to come direct from Norway, he plodded toward the van. The sidewalk glistened with moisture, making it slick. He decided to just grab his book and get back to Scarlett to make-up—or should he? There were other women in the world, ones who might want a relationship with him, even if he was a dying man. Wasn't every man dying?

"Race Traveler," a seductive voice called from behind him.

Race turned to behold Sonja striding through the mist like a goddess in white under a neon red umbrella glistening with a sheen of rain from the light of an adjacent taverna.

"Need some protection?" she asked, filling the last word with sexual innuendo as she stopped beside him and held the umbrella over both of them. Inches away, he could smell her citrus perfume with its strong undertone of mahogany.

Race patted his rain jacket and said, "I stay protected in this. Thanks anyway."

She remained right beside him. He realized that she was sexy the same way rain was wet; it wasn't anything she did, it was an intrinsic part of her. She stood beside you and you felt sexual attraction.

"Care to join me for a stroll?" Her eyes sparkled.

Race hesitated. Sonja was married, even if he wasn't.

"Chance ditched me; headache. After that interminable drive, I was desperate for air. Didn't want to risk a jog on the slick pavement. An ankle sprain would scuttle my chances for the part, not to mention any other work that happens along upon my return to the real world."

Race decided. If Scarlett didn't understand, she should marry him.

Sonja and Race walked on. They talked of the tour thus far, the sights they'd seen, and then Sonja said, "It's so dreadful what happened to Dr. Lodge....and Petra."

"And Mrs. Rasmussen."

"I really wish we hadn't all had to take that dreadful flight from New York."

"Cheaper fares as a group, although not much of a break in first class."

"If anyone ever saw me in coach, it'd be front page of every tabloid from here to Tokyo; finish my career." Sonja slid her arm into Race's and, drawing him even closer, said, "With the murders, I'm afraid to stay on the tour. Chancey says I'm silly, but still...."

"Petra and Dr. Lodge may have died by accident."

"Just like the boats Chance lost?" she asked with a sly grin, her head flicking around to catch Race's response.

What was she after?

"Didn't Cohen murder Lodge and Petra?" she asked. "He did flee, or maybe that Beznik did it. He's still in jail, isn't he?"

Race nodded as they strolled along the narrow sidewalk, arms linked at the elbows, shoulders brushing against each other.

Race asked, "Did you see Rob try to use the bathroom in first class?"

"No."

"Chance said he did."

"Chance may stare at the bathroom, I do not. Did that detective say anything to you about Chance...or me?" Her face tightened with concern, but just for an instant.

Race realized what she wanted. All innocence, he asked, "Why would he?"

"You seem to talk with him now and then, I hear. I just wondered if Chance has come up."

"Not once."

"And me?"

"Never."

Sonja threw back her head and twirled her red umbrella, spraying rain droplets around them in a delicate spiral. "Just as well; no gutter gossip to ruin my grand return." Her face relaxed back into a beautiful mask of confident serenity. "By the way, what do you think of David Fox?"

"I'm sure he's the first one to pick for a partner in any foursome."

"I didn't know you were into such adventures, but I'm game. Who shall we ask as the fourth? Scarlett?"

"I fear in such a scene, Scarlett would upstage you, at least in my eyes."

"I never could stand being upstaged, let alone in matters of the heart." Sonja smiled and said, "I wondered what you thought of David as a man. I mean, as they say, is he a man of his word?"

"I barely know him."

"True, but if you had to say, to rely on him or not?"

"I would say that for any man, trustworthiness depends on what you're trusting him with."

Sonja laughed a brief, lilting laugh. She looked up at Race, a smile spreading across her face with a hint of mischief behind it. Her eyes narrowed and she tilted her head as every starlet since

Lauren Bacall has been taught to do at such times. "Coy as ever. So what are you doing with the rest of your evening in mystical, magical Delphi? I thought I would find a taverna, have a few rounds of the local spirits and dance the night away with someone too handsome for words." She drew him along as he slowed at their hotel's front door. "A celebration of sorts."

"Of what?"

"My agent called. My career is about to return to its former, proper trajectory."

Race delicately extracted his arm from hers and stopped. She stopped, looking back over her shoulder at him, the picture of a model. Race stared. Who wouldn't?

"Sure you won't join me?" If he had taken a photograph, it wouldn't have required any retouching to achieve perfection.

"Enjoy your evening," Race said, forcing his mind to think of Scarlett as he tore his gaze from Sonja's flawless beauty.

"I'd enjoy it more with company."

"I think, like Chance, that I have a headache."

"I have the cure." Her smile and eyes turned lewd.

Race laughed. He could go. Why not? Sonja was beautiful. Sonja was fun. But his lungs were sore, he needed his rest, and Sonja… Sonja wasn't Scarlett. He wondered; did experiences require meaning to be worth living?

"With a murderer about, I could use a protector." She looked up at him with raised eyebrows. "Cohen's still loose, and who knows what other villains are lurking about."

"I'm sure you'll find a phalanx of protectors at any taverna you choose to frequent anywhere from here to Rhodes."

"None of them would be you." Holding his gaze, she said, "Please."

"I can't."

"Can't or won't?"

"Sadly, both."

"I really do need protection; famous movie star, alone in a small town full of horny Greeks."

Race laughed. "Enjoy yourself."

Sonja's face fell into the Actor's Studio version of a devastated frown. "You're missing out on the time of your life—not to mention leaving a beautiful damsel in the most horrid distress."

"I'm certain you will have the time of your life."

"Could be the end of my life, with a killer about. Maybe I should stay in." She smiled with mischief behind her eyes, as if talk of murder was just part of a practical joke.

"Life's too short to stay in; go, enjoy yourself, celebrate your good fortune."

Race convinced the night clerk to allow him to check his email on one of the hotel's computers. He shouldn't have bothered. An email said one of his friends from New York, Ellie Rogers, whom he had met in a CF support group, had died. She was 29 years old.

As he lay in bed beside Scarlett, Race thought about all of the friends he had lost: Sharon, Ailish, Devin, Cody, Jennifer, Coleen, Patricia, Shannon, Derek, Angie, Frankie, and… He stopped. It did no good. He would always remember them, every single one, but not tonight, not now.

Why did he have to have CF? Why did his family have to carry this genetic curse? Why? Would it ruin some vast eternal plan if he was healthy? If his brother had lived, would the universe be thrown irretrievably off kilter? If his grandfather had lived past 23, would it have been such a cosmic crime? He sighed. There were no answers, just reality. He had to face it. He had faced it since he was diagnosed.

He turned on his side and his mind drifted to other injustices: Why did enzyme pills work well for others, but not for him? Why did antibiotics upset his stomach so much more than other CF patients? Why was he so much older than Scarlett? Why had he met her so late in life? Why, why, why? All the unanswerables of life.

He lay on his back and thought about prayer. He was uncertain whether there was a god, but why not hedge your bets? If there was a god, He knew your mind better than you did and, Race hoped, would understand what fear could do to even the most devout non-believer, let alone to an agnostic who was uncertain and afraid—no, terrified. So, he prayed. But pray for what? Pray for courage? Health? Long life? Another year? Another month? A cure for CF? The love of a fine young woman? No. In the face of God, it all seemed so petty, so small, and so selfish. He could handle CF, or at least accept it. He could wait for Scarlett. He could live what was left of the rest of his life, however long that was with some degree of acceptance. But there was one thing he could never accept; just one thing.

"Dear God," he prayed, "please don't kill any more of my friends."

As he tried to sleep, depressive tendrils seeped into his mind, wrapping themselves around each and every cell in his brain. The psychological burden of losing friends worsened each year as more people he knew died—and always the victim of the same killer: CF. All prayers aside and regardless of what he had told Scarlett, he hated the thought of dying, not so much death itself, but the process of dying. It might be alright now, with little discomfort, as well as no mortgage, dentistry or long-term worries, but later, as his body failed, he loathed the thought of losing control, the loss of privacy and dignity, the end of all the things that brought him joy, let alone imprisonment in a failing body. He detested the idea that tomorrow would in all probability be worse than today. The future was supposed to be better, not worse.

Race looked across the dark room at the window. Open the window, step off the cliff and all would be ended, just like his father. No more lung infections. No more sinus headaches. No more twice daily tedious treatments. No more dizziness. No more nausea. No more hospitals. No more doctors. No more IVs. No more enzyme pills. No more hacking. No more coughing. No more spitting up blood. No more CF. No more anything.

He rolled over and looked at Scarlett's form beside him. He rested his hand gently on her hip through the comforter. Valletta. Dinners together. Back rubs. Kisses. Watching her. Thinking about her. Her.

Reasons to die and reasons to live.

He rolled onto his back. If Death was coming for him, he would not surrender. He would not just wait for death to happen. He would snatch as much happiness as he could before Death wrapped its dark fingers around his lungs and squeezed them flat. And, before he died, he would snatch something back from Death; give death some meaning, at least for some. He vowed that he would figure out why death had taken Mrs. Rasmussen, Petra Fox and Dr. Lodge, and he would do it before Death took him.

Chapter 17

Day 12: Tuesday, April 27

When Race looked out their hotel room window the next morning he could just discern through the shifting gray mist the village of Galaxidi. For centuries the villagers had been sailors and shipbuilders. Today, Race thought, would be a good day to leave the boat tied to the dock, whether or not you were a Galaxidiot. At least the weather didn't impede the search for a killer.

His feet cold on the tile floor, Race scampered back to bed. Scarlett squealed when his cold hands touched her back.

"You never give up, do you?" Scarlett asked.

"Can't when you're battling a terminal disease. It's just waiting for that one split second of weakness to sweep in and take you away."

"It's not the only one."

He caressed and kissed her, holding her tight.

"No, Race."

He stopped, sat up in bed and sighed. Silence descended on them like a shroud. Race felt Scarlett's warm hand on his bare shoulder.

"Don't be like that," she said.

"Like what?"

After a long pause, she said, "I love you, you know that....But I'm afraid."

"So am I." He got out of bed, ignoring the frozen floor, and, as he headed over to his chest therapy device and nebulizer, said, "We're just afraid of different things."

As he set up his machines, Scarlett said, "We're both afraid you're going to die."

Race stopped and stared at Scarlett. "No, I'm afraid I'll die before I see the world; you're afraid I'll die before you."

"Where are Sonja and Gayle?" Scarlett asked as they met David, Chance, Rob and Benny at the van after breakfast. "We should be at the site when it opens."

"Sonja isn't back from her jog, yet," Chance said. "Will it be busy with the rain?"

"Probably," Scarlett said. "Delphi's one of Greece's most popular sites."

"Sometimes Sonja goes farther than she planned," Chance said, "if she's feeling masochistic, fat or rejected."

Race hoped he hadn't sent Sonja on a jog to Thebes and back.

Chance peered up and down the two-lane road. It was empty now. The tour buses had not yet arrived to pick up their charges from the hotels to convey them to the ancient site or on to other attractions throughout Greece. "The morning we were in Kyparissia, she went farther than usual; might have again."

Scarlett glanced at her watch. Chance pulled out his cell and started pushing buttons. "Bloody hell," he muttered.

"What's wrong?" Scarlett asked. The only thing worse than falling behind schedule was an unhappy excursionist.

"Forgot the access code." Chance frowned and shook his head as he chewed a lip. Giving up, he stuffed his phone deep into his pocket. "It's just down the road, right? I'll leave her a note at the front desk to just walk over and join us when she gets back."

Race went in with Chance and called Gayle's room from the front desk. After seven rings Gayle answered. She said she was sick and asked whether she could skip Delphi and meet them at the van at 11, check-out time. Race agreed.

On the two-minute drive to the ancient archeological site, Race explained that the ruins had an amphitheater at the top that offered a wonderful view.

"In this weather?" Chance asked, eyeing the thick tumbling mist that rolled along the mountainside like an incoming tide.

Race said that a short walk down the road bubbled a Sacred Spring, which in ancient times was renowned for its healing properties.

"Maybe it'll heal what's ailing Gayle," Benny said, "and calm my tummy. That ouzo is smooth, but I ate one platter too many octopi last night."

"Yuck," Rob said. "You can't eat an octopus. They're smart, almost as smart as we are."

"Smart or dumb," Benny said, "they are tender and succulent."

Just below the road stood the remains of a gymnasium, 200 yards long, Race explained, which was ruined save for one massive wall built into the hillside. Just past it was a tholos to Athena.

"A what?" Rob asked.

"A circular temple," Race said. "The museum at the main site is free, although unfortunately it's largely closed for renovations in preparation for the Olympics. But a 5-foot gold bull sculpture and the famous charioteer statue, which I'm certain you'll recognize, are on display."

"Pay all this money and we see two statues?" Chance grumbled. "Says in the guidebook the museum is a 'don't-miss attraction.'"

"I would cancel the Olympics if I could," Scarlett said.

When they arrived at the ancient site, two tour groups were already filing off buses, their handlers, Race overheard, explaining the sights in Polish and German. Race suggested walking to the top of the site and working their way down so they would have most of the site to themselves as other tours started at the bottom and walked up. The ancient site stood in a bowl-like cleft in Mount Parnassus with cliffs on three sides, shielding it from the chill breeze. Through a shifting white mist that rose up out of the valley like smoke Race could see the valley below, which cradled a profusion of greenery that crept up the steep sides of the valley to the base of the cliffs.

As they set off up the wide paved walkway past carved stele, Race pointed at a bullet shaped rock sitting on a square pedestal and said, "This is the Sacred Way, and that is what the ancient Greeks called the Navel of the Earth. They believed it marked the center of the earth."

"An out-ee, not an in-ee," Benny commented with a grin. No one laughed in the somber group, although Rob smiled.

Chance stopped and looked back along the road. "Where the hell's Sonja gotten to?"

"She'll catch up soon," Scarlett reassured him with a pat on the shoulder.

"This is the Rock of Sybil on which the famous oracle made her pronouncements," Race said. He thought he might as well entertain everyone on the way up the mountain spur. "The Oracle was usually a woman in her fifties who was chosen by Apollo—the god of prophecy among other things—for her virtue. She would bathe in a special fountain, inhale a concoction of laurel and incense, and then gibber something out of which wisdom came.

"Here is the Temple of Apollo with its six columns still standing, and—we can take more time on the way down—here are the treasuries. One for each city-state. This one is for Athens, which was reconstructed from 1903 to 1906. It was originally built to commemorate an Athenian victory. The inscription near the base translates as: 'From the Athenians to Apollo as offerings from the Battle of Marathon, taken from the Mede or Persians in....'"

Race stopped. His mouth went dry as he stared past the twin columns that flanked the open doorway into the square, stone treasury.

"In 490 BC," Chance finished from his guidebook.

"What's the delay, Race?" Scarlett asked.

Race gestured into the Athenian treasury. In the shadows, her red cell phone shattered beside her and her splendid chest disfigured by multiple bloody slashes, lay Sonja Weaver, dead.

Chapter 18

"Do any of you recognize this knife?" Inspector Kanavou asked the sadly diminished tour.

As the remaining excursionists stood in a cordoned-off area, they stared at the 12-inch ornamental dagger glittering in the drizzle. Hundreds of tourists on the other side of the blue-and-white plastic police tape grumbled and complained to Hellenic Police officers who had sealed off the site, now a crime scene. Today sightseeing at Delphi would be delayed, if not cancelled altogether.

"Anyone?" Kanavou asked, holding the dagger higher in a clear plastic bag. As he waggled it, the point sliced through the corner of the bag and threatened to fall clean through. Kanavou grabbed the handle through the bag with his free hand.

Race noted the dried blood visible on its keen blade. He glanced at Rob, who frowned. Benny stared at the blade, a deepening frown creasing his forehead. David stared at Rob with a look of expectation. Chance looked confused, as if he couldn't believe what he was seeing. Scarlett opened her mouth to speak just as Rob blurted out, "It's mine."

All eyes fell on the boyish-looking man whose mother had so recently died—or been murdered.

Accepting what he had seen, but not at first believed, Chance barreled past Race and lunged at Rob. Race caught the ex-fighter pilot's arm, deflecting him just enough to allow Rob to slip behind Benny. Race clung to Chance's arm as David grabbed the pilot's other muscular arm.

"I'll kill you," Chance roared at Rob as he struggled to free himself from Race and David's grasp.

"Enough!" Kanavou ordered.

Kanavou turned his dark eyes and broad frame toward Rob and said, "It is my duty to ask you certain questions, Mr. Rasmussen."

"Rob, please."

"That's the knife he bought in Monemvasia," Scarlett whispered as officers led Rob toward a white police car.

Before he could answer, Race coughed, then again and again as a violent attack struck. He coughed and hacked, and felt light headed. He spat out evil-smelling phlegm laced with blood. His lungs felt as if they were being ripped into pieces. Through his coughing and pain he faintly heard Scarlett ask Kanavou for a doctor.

Confined to the hotel's dining room under the watchful eyes of police officers, Race, Scarlett and the remaining members of the tour waited for Kanavou to summon them for questioning. Race sat with his head down, arms on his knees. He felt bereft of the energy to do anything beyond breathe. Even with the new antibiotics a paramedic had given him, his chest felt as if it was in an ever-tightening vice. His throat felt like it was the size of a straw, dangerously limiting the air he could inhale. His sinuses throbbed. On top of his physical pain, his thoughts of Sonja battered his emotional state.

"It wasn't your fault," Scarlett whispered, placing a reassuring hand on Race's knee.

"I was the last one to see her. She asked me to protect her."

"She knew she was going to be murdered?"

"She was light hearted about it, but she knew there was a killer about." Race closed his eyes a moment and said, "I've been trying to figure out whether Mrs. Rasmussen was murdered, who stole Lodge's wallet, and who murdered Dr. Lodge and Petra. If I'd figured it all out, Sonja wouldn't be dead."

"You don't even know if they're related."

"If they aren't, we run the unluckiest tour on earth."

"Please don't tell anyone that," Scarlett said with a wan grin.

"I need to figure this out."

"Leave it to Kanavou."

"I need to do it."

"It's his job."

"The rest of his life isn't at stake."

Scarlett frowned.

"If I don't solve this and people keep dying, no one's ever going to take a Traveler Tour again. I'll end up broke and dying in some run-down pension in the least-visited corner of Greece."

"Don't you mean a Traveler Excursion?"

Race couldn't even manage a smile.

"I'll take care of you." Her smile filled his eyes.

Forgetting everything else, Race looked at her and said, "Marry me."

Scarlett took his right hand and kissed it. "Maybe after all this is over, after you've solved it all."

"Now there's a grand incentive."

Scarlett's smile widened, something Race didn't think possible. She said, "At least we know one thing."

"What?"

"We can rule out insomniacs; three murders before the sun was up."

"Is Rob an insomniac?" Race glanced at the boyish-man who sat by Benny in a corner. Kanavou had spoken to Rob and then sent him back to the hotel under police guard with the others while Kanavou investigated the murder scene. Chance, David and a newly arrived and ill-looking Gayle all sat by themselves, widely separated. An officer with about six-and-a-half feet of muscle ensured Chance did not attack Rob again.

An officer called Rob for an interview with Kanavou. An hour later another officer called Benny. Rob did not return. After having fended off Scarlett's demand that he go to a hospital, Race was finally feeling somewhat human. Another hour later, Benny returned and Race caught his eye. Benny hesitated before sitting near Race and Scarlett as an officer called Chance for an interview.

Frowning, Benny whispered, "Kanavou said when he searched Rob's bags, he found four kitchen knives wrapped in a towel."

"The kitchen knives would give the bundle roughly the same weight and shape as the dagger," Race said.

"Rob didn't have the foggiest notion it was gone," Benny said. "Kanavou said a tourist spotted the dagger in the Sacred Spring."

"Not the best hiding place, given all the tourists," Race said.

Benny sniffled and rubbed his eyes with both hands. "I don't believe this. Rob didn't kill anyone, but Kanavou's on the verge of arresting him."

Scarlett asked, "What does Rob say?"

"He refused to answer any questions."

"Was he with you this morning in your room?"

"Yes, of course."

"Why didn't Rob just tell Kanavou he was with you, then?"

Benny shook his head and wandered off to sit by himself, staring out the rain-streaked window as he snuck gulps from his ouzo-filled flask.

Scarlett asked Race, "What do you make of that?"

"Rob didn't want to tell Kanavou he's gay?"

"At least with Beznik in jail, we know he didn't murder Sonja."

"Cohen is missing, so he could have murdered her."

"Why?" Scarlett asked.

"Sonja saw Cohen murder Lodge and Petra when she was out for her jog."

"Or, if Rob did it, maybe Sonja saw Rob murder his mother. But Sonja was in first class. What could she have seen?"

"Maybe it's something Petra and Lodge saw when Rob tried to use the bathroom in first class and they mentioned it to Sonja?"

"It wasn't like Dr. Lodge or Petra were fast friends with Sonja," Scarlett said. "If anything, Petra and Sonja hated each other over Sonja's attentions toward David."

"If Lodge, Petra and Sonja all saw something on the plane that necessitated murder to silence them, then David, sitting beside Petra, probably saw it, too. Will he be Rob's next victim?" Race shook his head.

"What?"

"The first murders were clean and quick: let someone die of an asthma attack; shove two people off a cliff. But Sonja's, her murder was far more violent. There was fury behind all those slashes; a fierce, uncontrolled rage."

"Two murderers?"

"Or one murderer with two motives."

The other tour members returned. Kanavou strode into the room bearing clear plastic bags containing an empty wine bottle, a pair of wine goblets and a white candle burnt down to the thickness of a misshapen silver dollar. "Does anyone recognize any of these objects?"

Silence descended on the remaining excursion members.

"They were found at the Sacred Spring near where the dagger was recovered."

"A midnight rendezvous?" Chance asked. His angry gaze flashed over at David and then, after a second, at Rob. "If I ever find out who did this to Sonja—"

"The glasses were stolen from the hotel," Kanavou interrupted. "We are investigating the origin of the wine."

No one said a word.

Kanavou arrested Rob. As the excursion prepared to depart for northern Greece, Benny debated what to do. Race convinced him to stay with the tour. Race promised to stay in touch with Kanavou to keep Benny abreast of Rob's location and situation.

Before leaving, Race managed to speak by phone with their hotel's night desk clerk. "Did anyone leave the hotel early this morning?"

"The movie star left for a jog."

"Anyone else?"

"I told the police everything. They just left. I need to get to sleep. I'm on at 10 tonight."

"Anyone else? This is important."

"Let the police investigate it."

"If this murder isn't solved, I'll lose my job and my boss, who I happen to love, will lose her business."

"Oh," the clerk said through a yawn. "The bread delivery arrived. I went out to help with that. Marina appreciates it, and she can be so generous with her appreciation."

"Did you see any other hotel guests come or go early, before dawn?"

"It was hard to tell when dawn was, it was so dark and overcast."

"Not the sunny Greece of the travel brochures."

The clerk chuckled. "Don't tell anyone; I need a job."

"I will keep the secret until I give Charon his obolus."

"One guest did leave early; a man. Had to be from your tour."

"Why?"

"It's the off season. We only had six other guests—four are women and two are older than Socrates."

"What was he wearing?"

"All the guests begin to look alike, except the pretty ones."

"How did he walk?"

"Walk?"

"Did he stroll, march, amble, limp, saunter, stagger, stride, strut, trudge, waddle—?"

"I don't know....Uh....He walked with a slouch. And he was carrying something."

"What?"

"I didn't see. He was hiding it under his jacket. I thought he might be stealing towels, but it clinked, like metal or glass against something hard, maybe an ash tray on a belt buckle, not that any of you Yanks smoke anymore."

Back at the van, Scarlett told Race, "Pretty soon you won't need to solve these murders. The only ones left on the tour are going to be you, me and the murderer."

"Look on the bright side."

"The bright side of three deaths and a stolen wallet?"

"The murders could bring some publicity to Traveler Excursions."

"Not the type of publicity I'd ever want."

"Don't they say any publicity is good?"

"They're stupid."

Once aboard the van, Scarlett whispered to Race to say something about Sonja. Race hoped this announcement would be better received than his announcement about Mrs. Rasmussen. As the drizzle played a subdued tattoo on the van's roof and streaked the windows, Race stood and said, "If you please, may we have a minute of silence for our former tour member and all-too-brief friend, Mrs. Sonja Weaver."

A silent minute later, Race expressed condolences to Chance.

"I didn't even get to say goodbye," Chance said, wiping away budding tears. "She was off jogging before my feet hit the deck."

"She seemed happy," Benny said, placing a hand on Chance's shoulder.

Chance's head swung around as he shook off the consoling hand. "How the hell would you know, you silly ponce?"

Benny swallowed and for a moment appeared to be at a loss for words, which must have been a new experience for him. "I feel I got to know her somewhat after spending most of last night drinking with her."

"You?" Chance asked in disbelief.

"I think Chance expected me to fill that particular role," David said with a wan grin.

"I admit we didn't hit it off initially," Benny said, "but last night I ran into Sonja at a taverna. I figured we'd be together on the tour, so why not mend fences, proffer the olive branch and see if we couldn't at least get along for the sake of a fun trip? I bought her a shot of *tsipouro* and a Cretan *raki*. She reciprocated and soon we were having a nice tête à tête over some excellent and rather powerful ouzo. She seemed to crave the company, wanted to talk about men, her career and such."

Race asked, "When did you part company?"

"I crawled from her side at about 2 am."

"So you were the last person to see her alive," Chance said, his eyes narrowing.

"Not quite," Benny said. "Kanavou checked. The night clerk saw Sonja come in after me at about 2:30 singing loud enough to be heard in Rhodes, so I'm off the short list of suspects."

"So Rob must have gone out early this morning when Sonja went jogging," Chance said, his face as set as stone.

"Rob had no reason to kill Sonja," Benny said, "except maybe competition. Never enough handsome men around, and she attracted them like alcoholics to a bar."

"Probably some local low-life killed her," Gayle suggested, although Chance still glared at Benny as if he was the prime suspect and not his boyfriend Rob. "She shouldn't have been wandering around alone, late at night, wearing such expensive clothes. Who does that? Probably a robbery gone wrong, murdered for her money."

Chance laughed. The others froze at the strangeness of laughter at such a time. Noticing the others' appalled looks, Chance stopped laughing and said, "That's a joke. She was the poorest person here."

"No," Gayle exclaimed, her face the picture of shock. "I've read about her homes and cars and vacations, and her clothes. How could she be poor?"

"She lived in friends' houses. Our house—singular—was mortgaged thrice over," Chance said, a bitter tone creeping into his voice. "She wore jewelry loaned by designers who wanted it seen. Our vacations were comped so places could use photos of her in ads for their hotels and spas."

"The tour?" Gayle asked.

"Studio covered it."

"But she flew first class," Scarlett said.

"She was an actress," Chance said, breaking into the hint of a smile at the recollection. "She could convince Poseidon to give up his trident. Getting an upgrade from some airline desk clerk was as simple as background work to her. She spent her life getting what she wanted with a look, a toss of the hair or a few words, for what good it did her; probably got her killed. She never carried more than a few bucks, if that much."

"No shortage of men buying her drinks last night," Benny said. He paused, thinking. "If it wasn't her money, then it must have been…" His voice trailed off. Everyone in the humid van looked at him. "No, nothing, forget it."

"What Benny?" Scarlett asked. "It might help find Sonja's killer, and help Rob."

Benny's eyes flicked around the group like a nervous springbok amidst a pride of lions.

"Tell us," Chance ordered. He looked enormous and muscle-bound beside the pudgy Benny. "I want to know who murdered my Sonja."

Pursing his lips, Benny looked down at the floor and said, "Sonja had an argument with someone at the taverna."

"She started it," Gayle spat out.

Shocked, everyone stared at Gayle in the back row.

"What the hell happened?" Chance demanded.

Gayle glared at Benny but remained silent.

"Tell me what happened." Chance rose from his seat, stooping to avoid hitting his head on the van's ceiling.

"It's personal," Gayle said and turned to stare out the window, her shoulders hunched defiantly against the others.

"They are going to find out," Benny said softly. "A dozen people at the taverna must have overheard. You two weren't exactly demure in your disagreement."

Gayle maintained her silence as she glared out the rain-speckled befogged window.

"Please Benny, Gayle," Scarlett pleaded, "what happened?"

"I'll find out," Chance vowed, as he loomed over Benny.

"Sit down, please," Race said.

"I doubt smashing my teeth in will make it any easier for me to talk," Benny told Chance.

Even as David rose to defend Benny, Scarlett said, "Chance, please let Inspector Kanavou sort it out."

"Sit down, Chance," Race ordered.

Realizing everyone was against him, Chance hesitated and, with the greatest of reluctance, sat down.

Race started the van, switched on the wipers and paused to let the fan clear the condensation from the front window. A white compact car sped by and a couple hurried past, black umbrellas held at an angle to combat the sideways rain that was blowing in along the valley. Race was saddened as he remembered Sonja's vibrant red umbrella of the night before.

The window clear, the street free of oncoming cars, Race took his foot off the brake and started their drive north to Meteora. Before he had driven three feet, he slammed on the brakes.

"What's wrong?" Scarlett asked from the passenger seat as the van rocked from the abrupt stop.

Race stared out the driver's side window. "Beznik."

"Here?" Scarlett asked, shocked. "Did Kanavou finally release him?"

Race was already out of the van, leaving the driver's door open. The rain combined with passing cars and buses muffled his footfalls as he raced after the man he had just spotted. Race clapped a hand on the shoulder of the man's rain-sodden gray hooded sweatshirt. The man spun around, sliding back into a fighter's pose.

"Beznik works with me," Race said as he stared at a man who could have been Beznik's twin. "How's the navy?"

The drive north to Meteora was as somber inside the van as outside it. A funereal pall settled over the remaining four tour members; a pall mixed with fear. David and Chance mourned. Benny worried about Rob, dampening even his perennially high spirits. With Dr. Lodge dead, Gayle had apparently lost all hope of securing her son's collegiate future and it showed in her gloomy demeanor. A chill, misting rain fell, filming the van's windows. A cloying smell of sweat and dampness mixed with Race's salty snacks permeated the air. Race's sinuses ached and his lungs felt as if they were packed tight with cotton. At least no one wanted to hear any tour guide speeches.

At a stop for gas, Race told Scarlett about his talk with Beznik's brother, who said he had come to defend Beznik against the wallet accusations, only to learn Beznik had been arrested for a double murder.

"Do you think Beznik's brother helped Beznik kill Dr. Lodge and Petra because Lodge accused Beznik of stealing the wallet?" Scarlett asked. "Family honor sort of thing?"

"His frigate just docked in Pireaus yesterday, so that's impossible, but he could have made it up to Delphi by early this morning to murder Sonja."

"Why?"

"Sonja was up early for her jog that morning in Kyparissia, so maybe she saw Beznik kill Dr. Lodge and Petra."

After filling up, Race, ill and his strength failing, accepted David's offer to drive. David said driving helped take his mind off Petra. They drove through several mountain ranges on roads that wrapped around peaks like carelessly thrown-on scarves and finally, after a couple of hours, reached the broad Thessaly plain. The road was two lanes and straight as a map edge. Greeks sped along at 140 kilometers an hour through the misting rain with no headlights. David soon followed suit to avoid being run over from behind, although he did use the van's headlights.

"You're becoming a Greek driver," Scarlett told David. Race wasn't sure if it was a compliment or a warning.

They sped past a Romani camp and then another, which only added to the somber mood. The camps were indescribably sad. Rusting metal campers tilted alongside ramshackle huts made of salvaged sheet metal and lumber odds and ends knocked together with no coherent design. The camps were sited in the worst of locations. One was in low-lying ground near a meandering garbage-strewn muddy creek. It looked like a Third World slum in the depths of the rainy season.

At dusk they arrived in Kalampaka, which nestled beneath the towering monasteries of Meteora. Race directed David up through the narrow irregular streets to the top of the town of 12,000.

"We're staying here?" David asked as they disembarked at the Koka Roca Rooms in the gathering gloom.

"If Sonja weren't dead," Chance said, "the prospect of staying here would put her in her grave."

At the end of a street, the Koka Roca Rooms were above a rustic taverna. Two stories of unpainted wood and whitewashed plaster, the building looked like a poor aunt's farmstead. Once inside, the efficient proprietress showed them to their rooms. Scarlett insisted on sharing a room with Race. Their simple room offered a view of the base of one of the monasteries' striated rock pinnacles, which was so abrupt that all they could see was a cliff face.

When they returned to the ground floor for dinner, the owner and her son set to work. The taverna's main room had a stone fireplace large enough to roast a sheep in, a rough-cut stone floor, and wood tables that varied in size, shape and finish, if they still had any. A fire crackled in the hearth, keeping the evening's chilling dampness at bay. Two men with faces like crumpled brown paper sat at a table drinking, smoking and playing backgammon. One of the men took up a *bouzouki* and played a few bars. The kitchen was right off the main room, open, and clearly the owner's kitchen. A stuffed bird, shepherds' crooks and local knickknacks completed the worn, yet homey décor. A new computer sat incongruously in one corner on a narrow table with a cardboard sign stating, "Internet service available." Race decided not to check his emails; death could wait, although he hoped his prayer had worked for at least this long.

The owner's fortyish son strolled over and placed a clean, red-check tablecloth on each table and took orders. Scarlett and Race, feeling somewhat better with his new antibiotics and from the rest while David drove, ordered a green salad, *souvlaki* and, at the son's suggestion, homemade white wine. The son cooked the lamb *souvlaki* over coals in the fireplace. The salad was from the landlady's garden. The wine was from land the family owned on the Thessaly plain. Race also ordered a Greek salad and spinach pie. The meal was one of the best Race had ever savored.

After dinner, as David rose after picking at his meal, he bumped against Chance's table. Chance's copper cup of wine fell over, spreading a red sea across the table. Although Chance had been in a daze staring down at his untouched food, he grabbed his cell phone from where it sat beside his plate before the wine flood engulfed it.

"I'm terribly sorry," David said. "Let me clean it up."

The owner's son, however, was already using a towel to mop up.

"It didn't get your phone wet, did it?" David asked.

"No. No harm done."

"Let me check. Make sure it's okay." David reached for Chance's phone.

"It didn't get wet."

"If it did, let me know. I'll be happy to replace it."

"No battle damage done."

As dinner was cleared away, Scarlett chatted with the landlady while Benny and Gayle thumbed through a couple of the taverna's many guest books. Race perused one of the books filled with scribbled notes in a rainbow of inks and photographs of visitors from across Europe and around the world. Hundreds of people had penned glowing reviews in every language from English to French, German to Japanese, Korean to Spanish; at least Race assumed they were all glowing based on the samples in the eight languages he could passably read.

"Rick Steves recommends us," the proprietor's son said as he carried a load of dishes almost licked clean to the kitchen.

Race wrote a brief note about the dinner in a guest book as David penned a comment in another book. David walked with Race toward the door. As he slowly opened the heavy wood door, David asked, "Have you heard if Kanavou's made any progress? He hasn't told me a damn thing."

"As far as I know Kanavou believes Rob murdered his mother on the plane, stealing her inhalers and hiding them. Petra, Dr. Lodge and Sonja saw Rob dispose of them, which led Rob to murder them."

"And Beznik?"

"Even though Beznik didn't steal Lodge's wallet, Kanavou thinks Beznik murdered Lodge over his accusation of theft."

"So Rob and Beznik murdered Lodge?"

"Rob or Beznik, I guess."

"What about Cohen?"

"Fled after murdering Lodge over the dating website?"

"Not exactly clear as Waterford crystal."

As they started up the exterior covered stairs a driving rain lashed the side of the taverna. David stopped short. "I think I remember..." His voice trailed off, deep in thought. He took a step up the worn wood stairs, which creaked under his weight. "No, wait a minute, it was...no, I remember now. Petra said something about Rob having several inhalers."

"When?"

"One night when we were going to sleep."

"I mean when did Rob have the inhalers?"

"I assume on the plane, but I don't remember. I really wasn't paying much attention. I was half asleep. Petra only noticed because she thought it odd he had more than one."

"Did she tell Kanavou?"

"I don't think so." Noticing Race's skeptical look, David added, "She hated talking to people in positions of authority." He chuckled. "She once worked for a woman who called her Pauline for six months before her boss overhead me call her Petra at a company party. I pray to God her reticence didn't get her murdered."

Chapter 19

Day 12: Wednesday, April 28

As Race awoke, he saw Scarlett sitting up in bed, the covers wrapped around her as she stared down at him. From her red-rimmed eyes and slumped shoulders, it appeared she had got little sleep. She said in a small voice, "Let's send everyone home."

"You've already changed all our flights."

"I can convince the airline to refund them all."

"I have no doubt, but Kanavou won't let anyone go home until he solves the murders."

"You can convince him. He likes you."

"He just wants someone to get information from the crazy foreigners."

Scarlett clutched the blankets closer. "I'm scared, Race."

Race sat up and, ignoring the chilly morning air on his bare shoulders, held her close. He glanced at the door, against which during the night Scarlett had wedged a wood chair.

"I need this gig, boss," Race said. "No one else will die."

"Is that a promise or a prayer? Cohen's still on the loose and who knows if he committed one, two or all three of the murders—or none of them. Maybe it was Rob or Beznik or his brother or Chance or Gayle or some stranger or...." She stifled a sob and said, "I just want a quiet life. I want to settle down with someone and live the rest of my life without being anywhere near another murder."

"We can."

Scarlett looked into his eyes. "I don't want the 'rest of our lives' to be so short."

"No one knows how long they have."

"The average male CF patient lives to 36."

"I've already beaten the odds, then."

"For how long?"

"For as long as we have." A few nights ago, Race would have been hard pressed to reply with even a hint of optimism, but he had beaten Death's specter back that night, at least for however long his optimism lasted in the face of his executioner.

Scarlett swallowed hard and kissed Race. "You always taste so salty, my saltine." She sighed. "I know I've been awful at times recently, but please give me some time about you and me. This is the most difficult decision I've ever had to make."

"Time's my most valuable possession, but I'd give it all to you."

Scarlett was right; Kanavou did like Race. After only ten minutes Race convinced the inspector to let him talk to Rob on the telephone. The police escorting Rob to Athens had stopped the night before in Thebes on the Boeotia-Attica border. Race sat in their room in Kalampaka using Scarlett's cell. After making sure Rob was being decently treated, Race asked, "You were with Benny the morning Sonja was murdered?"

Silence.

"After his night at the taverna, Benny was probably well and truly passed out that morning."

"I guess."

"Where were you that morning?"

"What does Benny say?"

"That you were in bed with him, but I don't think so."

Silence.

"The night clerk at the hotel saw a man going out early, just after Sonja left for her jog. I think it was you."

Silence.

"Rob, I want to help you. If you didn't do it, talk to me, please."

A long pause. Finally Rob said, "I didn't see her when she left." His voice was flat, without a trace of his usual boyish enthusiasm.

"Did you see anyone else?"

Silence.

"Would your mother want you to remain silent after someone was murdered?"

Race heard a sigh. "I saw her, later."

"Who?"

"Sonja."

"Where?"

"She was jogging along the road from Arehova back toward the hotel."

"What time?"

"I'm not sure."

"Where were you?"

A long pause. Their room was cold and Scarlett, napping, shifted, reached down and pulled up the comforter.

Race said, "I know you were at the spring saying goodbye to your mother."

Silence.

"The night clerk said the man who went out early was from our tour."

"Could have been Chance, David or Cohen."

"The clerk said he walked with a slouch."

"So?"

"Chance, an officer, would never slouch. David is an athlete, so he doesn't slouch, especially with his bad back, and Cohen had already left, so that leaves you. The clerk also heard a clink as you left; a bottle of wine? The bottle Kanavou found at the spring?"

The silence lasted so long Race was about to give up and ring off when Rob said, his voice wavering, "Wine to drink to her memory, and a candle." Rob sniffed. "She would have loved being memorialized at the Sacred Spring at Delphi, just as the ancients were."

Race didn't have a clue whether the dead were memorialized at the spring but the living should be allowed to memorialize the dead any way they wanted.

After the inspector replaced Rob on the line, Race told Kanavou, "The wine, glasses and candle you found at the spring support his story."

"Or supports a tryst with Sonja that went terribly wrong."

"A most unlikely couple." Rob was gay, but Race didn't mention it, although he guessed Kanavou already knew.

"Robert Rasmussen refused to tell us where was that morning. If he was at the Sacred Spring, he was where the dagger was found."

"Found quickly and easily."

"Either a nervous murderer who wanted rid of the weapon and didn't think of throwing it down into the valley or—"

"A murderer who wanted the weapon found to cast suspicion on Rob."

"I spoke with the owner of the taverna in Delphi where a loud, somewhat overweight American and a tall American woman drank ouzo until 2 am, acting as if they were the best of friends."

"Benny and Sonja," Race said, "another unlikely couple."

"It supports Benny's story about drinking with Sonja, and probably meant he slept in, hung over and dead to the world."

"Leaving Rob free to go off and pay his respects at the Sacred Spring."

"Or murder Sonja for having seen him steal his mother's inhalers on the plane."

"Was Mrs. Rasmussen's death Thanatos or the Keres?"

"Still undetermined. I'm not sure we'll ever know. In the other case, we found a fisherman in Kyparissia who saw a beautiful American woman jogging along the beach early the morning Petra Fox and Dr. Lodge died."

"How'd he know she was American?"

Kanavou chuckled. "Simple to identify an American."

"Sonja said she met David."

"The fisherman doesn't remember him."

"Would you, if she was in your field of vision? She has photos on her phone." Race leaned over to look down at Scarlett as she napped after her early morning attack of nerves. The auburn streak in her hair glistened in the morning light through the window. He turned and coughed. His lungs were bad this morning.

"We discovered why Gayle Garcia was up early enough the morning Petra and Dr. Lodge died to see Sonja," Kanavou said. "She was on the phone in her room for 45 minutes starting at 5 am to her son in Los Angeles, where it was 7 pm."

"Or she called, left the line open, ran up to the castle, murdered Lodge over their son, and Petra, who she didn't know would be up there, and then ran back to hang up."

"You can do it in 45 minutes, if you're in shape. I had one of my young officers check."

"Better him than me."

"Rank has its privileges. Gayle is in shape, except for her arm. Can you shove two people off a castle with one hand?"

"If you're angry enough."

Race sat doing his chest therapy and nebulizer while Scarlett exercised. He hoped his lungs would clear, but he knew from past experience that such an outcome was unlikely without a hospital visit. He was running out of time. He had to stay upright long enough to solve the murders and finish the tour. Then he could go to a hospital, recover and then see more of Europe.

The group breakfasted in the Koka Roca Rooms' taverna on crusty bread with olive oil, spicy salami and Kefalotyri cheese before Race drove the tour the few minutes around the mountain to the monasteries.

"I miss the sunny Peloponnesus," Gayle said with a sigh as she peered out at one of the rock pinnacles piercing the clouds of another gray, sodden day.

"The pinnacles were formed when an ancient sea receded," Race explained. "Monks started building monasteries in the 11th century. The name Meteora means 'suspended in the air.' You can still see wood platforms jutting out of some of the caves where solitary monks once lived."

"Unless it clears, we won't see a bloody thing," Chance said. His guidebook was at his side; for once, closed. "You'd think God would shed some light on his own monasteries."

"He's probably too busy in the south of France," Benny said.

"Probably with Cohen," David said. "I can just see him, sipping an aperitif on the beach near Cape Ferret with a new mustache, beard, and some tanned, bikini-clad local babe on his arm."

"Cohen?" Gayle asked in disbelief. "More likely hiding in a library in Cleveland."

They parked at Moni Agiou Nikolaou Anapafsa. Through the ever-shifting mist, Race glimpsed a double-decker wood balcony wrapped around two sides of a stone structure.

"Sweet," David said, admiring through the van's window not the monastery, but a blue Ferrari 458 with Italian plates incongruously parked on the shoulder of the twisting, lonely road.

Once out of the van, David and Chance admired the sports car.

Chance said, "Wish I could have one of these to tour around Europe in."

"Need to borrow a fortune just to rent one like her," David said, longing in his voice.

"Maybe I'll come into some money soon." Chance patted David on the back and added with a hope-filled grin, "You never know."

The excursionists climbed the steep path and then stone stairs up to the monastery, hundreds of feet above the road. Gayle had to don a skirt the monastery provided, since women in pants or anyone in shorts were required to cover their legs and shoulders. Race led everyone on a tour of the main floor of the monastery and then climbed yet another set of stairs to the top of the monks' circumscribed domain. The clouds obscured their view, but the monastery was still impressive as it clung to the pinnacle of the rock tower like a ladybug atop a wheat stalk.

As they drove to the next monastery, Race pointed out an abandoned monastery atop another rock pillar, silent and eerie. "The locals say it's haunted."

"I'm beginning to believe in ghosts," Chance said. "I saw Sonja last night, curled up in a chair reading one of her old, thick novels. On my honor, she was there, real as life."

"When I wake up, I still see Petra asleep beside me," David said. "Always turns out to be just a jumble of blankets, but I reach over to her every morning just to be sure—hoping."

Race drove on and said, "Six monasteries are open to the public of the 26 that once existed. Before the bridges were added to some of the monasteries fairly recently, the monks used ropes, pulleys and wicker baskets to haul up supplies and priests. When asked how often they replaced the rope, one monk famously replied, 'Only when it breaks.'"

They walked across a stone pedestrian bridge to visit Saint Stefanou, a 3-story structure overrun with cats, and then drove the short distance to Rousanou.

"Wish I had the orange roof tile franchise for Greece," David said, eyeing the tiles on the monastery's roof—the same color tiles as on almost every building in Greece. "Make a fortune."

Nuns had restored Rousanou and it was the most photographed monastery, since it sits by itself on two pinnacles beside the road. Atop the first pinnacle, Race led the tour past a flower garden and then inside to marvel at the nuns' intricate lace, which was for sale. As the clouds cleared, they saw dozens of rock columns, six topped with monasteries, and far below a river curving across the green Thessaly plain.

Next they visited Agious Triados or Holy Trinity; the least accessible and therefore least-visited monastery. They parked, walked down a cliff on a zigzag dirt path and started up hundreds of stairs cut into the rock, passing through several short tunnels. Race insisted he come, although Scarlett's worried looks increased in duration and severity with every cough and brief rest stop he took.

They eventually reached a metal-studded, thick wood door, which stood open. At the top of the final flight of stairs just inside a towering bearded Greek Orthodox priest in a black cassock met them with a warm welcome and a box of sweets. He spoke English without even the hint of an accent. He had been to America twice—to Los Angeles and Eugene, Oregon—for conferences, and mentioned that the James Bond film, *For Your Eyes Only* had been filmed at his monastery. He was a physician who practiced in Kalampaka. Unlike many monks elsewhere, Meteora monks were involved daily in the world beyond their monastery walls.

Benny returned from the toilet brimming with the enthusiasm only a good story could produce.

"That's some toilet," Benny said. "A hole in the floor with water running down it from a black hose."

"A Turkish toilet," Race said.

"Freeze your ass off in the winter," Chance said, "and hopefully nothing else."

"If you look through the hole," Benny said, "you can see a thousand feet down to the base of the cliff. You're hanging out over nothing. I prayed the whole time I was pissing."

Gayle said, "Maybe that's what the monks intended."

Like the other monasteries, Agious Triados had a museum displaying illuminated religious books, priest's garments, and gold and silver treasures dating back to the 1200s, as well as a church with dark medieval paintings portraying fiendish views of hell.

"They liked to show you what might happen if you took the wrong path," Gayle said, looking up at a painting of devils pitchforking burning sinners in the flames of hell.

"I think they meant to show what *would* happen," Benny said.

"I hope they were wrong," David said.

"Don't we all," Chance agreed, "Don't we all."

As they neared Varlaam monastery, which covered every inch of the top of a broad butte, Race said, "It's said it took 21 years to transport all the building stones to the top of the pinnacle and then 21 days to build Varlaam."

The typical orange tile roof covered an expansive sprawl of buildings that seemed to grow out of the rock, as if the rock and monastery were one.

Once inside, Race gave a short overview and then everyone went exploring. With few tourists so early in the year, they had the monastery to themselves, save for the few monks.

Kanavou called Scarlett's cell and reported that he had obtained photos from the airport ATM's security camera showing Cohen and Gayle using the machine.

"So they withdrew money?" Race asked.

"Yes, but I don't know how much. The camera isn't keyed into transactions. But even if they did, either one still might have stolen the wallet for some extra cash."

Race and Scarlett were discussing the theft of the wallet and looking out across the Thessaly plain when someone screamed. Race rushed toward the origin of the primeval sound as it echoed throughout the monastery. He sprinted around the corner of a stone building, down stairs, through a courtyard, and around another stone building to a wood balcony. Chance hung by his hands from a rough rope over an abyss. The rope ran through a pulley and was tied to a beam in the ceiling of the balcony, which had a hole cut in the plank floor.

"Help me," Chance yelled. He kicked his feet to the side, trying to reach the side of the gaping opening over which he hung. "I can't reach the edge."

Spreading his feet wide, Race reached across the 6-foot opening that the monks used to winch up supplies from the valley floor, 1,224 feet below. He grabbed Chance under the arms. Chance's shirt was soaked with sweat. Race pulled, but as he pulled, he teetered, lost his balance and almost fell. He let go to regain his balance.

Chance yelled, "Don't let go!"

As Scarlett arrived, Race stepped around the side of the opening. He grabbed Chance's right arm and pulled. It did no good. Chance barely moved. Race could barely reach Chance. He had no leverage. If he reached any farther, he would fall. He let go of Chance.

"Race!" Scarlett screamed.

"Help me!" Chance yelled. "I can't hold on."

Race's mind was swirling with ideas, but what could he do?

Race used his left foot to catch the rope below Chance and then grabbed it.

Chance slid an inch down the hemp rope. Blood speckled the fibers where his hands had been.

"Do something!" Chance yelled.

Race lined up the rope between Chance's legs.

"Slide down the rope," Race ordered as he leaned back and held the rope taut at an angle from the pulley to the side of the balcony. The rope gave Chance something to grapple with his legs.

As he squirmed, Chance's aviator sunglasses slipped out of his jacket pocket and fell into space, falling down, down, down, and finally out of sight.

"Slide down the rope," Race yelled.

Chance did not loosen his grip. He clung to the rope as if his hands were entwined with its rough fibers.

"Slide down the rope! Now!" Race yelled as Scarlett joined him to hold the rope steady.

Chance, inch by inch, slid down the rope; inch by inch, inch by blood-stained inch. Finally, Chance was over the wood floor. He let go and collapsed in an exhausted, sweat-soaked heap. Race and Scarlett let go. Race's lungs screamed. His hands were torn and cut by the tough, fibrous hemp, which was stained with his blood. Scarlett stared down in pain at her rope-burned hands.

Between gasps, Chance said, "Some bastard shoved me. Lucky I caught that rope or I'd be down there, flatter than Lodge." He swallowed as he peered down through the opening in the plank floor.

"Who pushed you?" Race asked.

"Didn't see the vermin; attacked me from my six."

Race hadn't seen anyone. As he grimaced at the pain in his hands, he saw that there were three ways to the balcony: the way he had come, the other way around the stone building, and a set of steps that led down onto a lower rampart.

"Did hear a grunt though," Chance said.

"From hitting you?"

"Didn't sound like a grunt from the impact," Chance said, regaining his composure as he inspected his bloody hands, clenching and unclenching them experimentally with the greatest care. "More like a squawk of pain."

The Kalampaka police interviewed everyone about Chance's near-death experience, but Race held little hope they would unravel the mystery of who had tried to murder the ex-fighter pilot; the mystery went far beyond the environs of Meteora.

That evening at dinner, which Race had easily convinced everyone in the interest of safety to eat at the Koka Roka Rooms taverna, Gayle sat at David's table. A paramedic had bandaged Chance's hands after his abrasive encounter with the rope, so he struggled to even hold a knife and fork, let alone cut anything. Much to the Chance's chagrin, Benny took it upon himself to feed the ex-fighter-jock.

The son of the owner of the Koka Roca Rooms brought everyone a gratis metal wine goblet filled to the brim with his excellent homemade white wine.

"Just the resupply we requisitioned," Chance said, grasping his goblet with both bandaged hands as if he was a monk released from his vow of sobriety after 40 years.

"Alcohol may not be the answer," Benny said, grabbing his own goblet, "But it sure helps you forget the more irritating questions."

"Gayle is flirting with David," Scarlett whispered as she speared a forkful of green salad, fresh from the taverna's garden. Her hands were blistered and burned, but she was still able to heft a fork.

"That's nice," Race said as he dug into a flavorful Greek salad of tomatoes, sliced cucumbers, green bell peppers, onion, cubed feta cheese, and meaty Kalamata olives flavored with oregano and extra virgin olive oil. His hands sported bandages, but nothing compared to Chance. "Nice to see David with someone."

"He just lost his wife," Scarlett said, aghast.

"All the more reason; life can be unexpectedly short."

After dinner, someone knocked at Scarlett and Race's door. Scarlett picked up one of her hiking boots, brandishing it like a mace. Race opened the door. Benny stood outside holding a bulging black backpack and a coffee-table book.

"I had some things for Rob," he said. "I can't find that damn Inspector Kanavou's card, and I don't know if they've kept Rob in Delphi or Thebes or moved him to Athens or…." He angrily wiped away tears.

"I have Kanavou's card," Race said. "Come in."

Benny hesitated, then, as if he was a child waiting to be told what to do, when Race asked him again, he finally stepped inside. Scarlett lowered her boot-mace. Benny stopped short and stared at Race's nebulizer, a metal box with tubes and cords that stood beside his chest percussion device with its hoses and gray vest. Benny stared as if he was in a daze. To fill the silence, Race explained that he used the therapy vest for 20 minutes twice a day. The vest filled with air and then vibrated, shaking loose the mucus in his lungs. He could set the pressure so it would be comfortable, and the frequency. He often used the nebulizer at the same time.

"CF steals less time out of my life that way," Race said.

The nebulizer, Race said, turned liquid medicine into an aerosol, which he inhaled. The medicine looked like steam or white smoke. He used the nebulizer for five minutes twice a day. He added a bronchodilator to open the airways in his lungs, then mucolytics to thin the mucus, followed by salt water to loosen the mucus or antibiotics, if required.

"Sounds like a lot to remember," Benny said, emerging from his daze. "I'd probably put the medicine in the vest and shake the nebulizer."

Race explained that the order was crucial, so the medicine could reach deep into his lungs. He said that after he was done, he hacked out the phlegm.

"Not to be done in polite company," Scarlett said with a thin smile. The phlegm came out in ugly, green clumps, sometimes blood spotted, and it reeked.

Reading the coffee-table book's title, Scarlett asked, *"Weapon: A Visual History of Arms and Armor?"* She looked aghast at Benny's choice of reading material in view of recent events.

"It's Rob's."

A look of fear and concern spread across Scarlett's face. She raised her boot-mace a few inches.

"A fascinating topic," Race said, hoping Scarlett would relax.

"Rob loves it," Benny said. "I never had much interest, but he certainly makes some beautiful pieces."

Race and Scarlett frowned.

"Odd to think of weapons and armor as beautiful, given they are used for war, but they are," Benny rambled on, apparently happy to talk about something other than Rob's incarceration. "When I first met Rob I was appalled at what he did and didn't see a damn bit of beauty in any of it, but now I see it."

"What exactly does he do?" Scarlett asked.

"His reproductions are in dozens of museum gift shops from London to Tokyo," Benny said, pride in his voice.

"Reproductions?" Scarlett asked, setting down her boot-mace.

"Rob makes 100 percent accurate reproductions of arms and armor focusing on the 15th through 17th century. He's been consulted by the Tower of London, the Graz Armory in Austria, and the Prado in Madrid, and dozens of others."

"Hence his purchase of the dagger in Monemvasia," Race said.

"Not the wisest purchase given how things turned out," Benny said, setting the backpack down on the corner of the bed. "But he loves such things, he truly does."

Race promised to try to get the clothes and book to Rob.

As he let Benny out and said an early good night, Race spotted Gayle sneaking out of David's room.

"What are you staring at?" Scarlett asked from her perch on the bed in their room.

"Just someone trying to do something for someone they love."

Chapter 20

Day 13: Thursday, April 29

Race struggled to get up early enough to finish his treatments before they had to depart. His lungs were worsening. The antibiotics were losing the battle against the infection. He fought to keep the depression on the fringes of his mind from occupying his soul. Whatever his mental state, his body would need intensive medical help, soon. The nebulizer and chest therapy for his lungs, and a hot shower to clear his sinuses alleviated his discomfort enough to get him to breakfast and behind the wheel in time to beat the crowds to the one monastery that had been closed the day before. Built in the 14th century, the massive Holy Monastery of Great Meteoron covered the top of a towering butte of striated rock. A zigzag set of stone steps snaked up and then through the cliff. The church and museum inside featured a vast collection of Medieval paintings, and gold and silver artifacts.

"Funny," Scarlett said as they descended the stone stairs after their visit. "The monks live such simple, Spartan lives, as if they are the poorest of the poor, yet they have museums with enough silver and gold to let them all live like kings for the rest of their lives."

Race said, "Some people would rather have wealth than spend it."

David, his sore back improved, offered to drive the 420 kilometers south to Sounion. Race was relieved to be able to rest, read and listen to music. The road across the Thessaly plain was straight and they flew past fields of white-tufted cotton.

Benny asked with a wan smile, "Are we there yet?"

After crossing two mountain ranges they joined National Road 1, a modern highway, which took them south along the rugged east coast and then inland across Attica to Athens. Under a warm sun in Athens they passed the swimming, fencing, field hockey, and sailing venues for the upcoming Summer Olympics. David struggled through endless construction detours. Eventually they hit an open road on the west coast, passing communities set along broad sandy beaches with mixtures of new homes and crumbling huts. Gayle said one of the nicer areas reminded her of Malibu.

An hour south of Athens they rounded a bend in the coast and beheld the Temple to Poseidon perched atop a bluff marking the southernmost tip of Attica: Sounion. With 16 columns standing, the temple was a vision from antiquity. After stopping for pictures, David drove on and found their hotel, the Sauron. The tour settled into their spacious, sunny rooms. Race and Scarlett's room offered a view of the pool, palm trees and, over a whitewashed stone wall, the sparkling Aegean.

At 6:30, after a brief rest, the tour met at the van and drove the mile to the temple.

"Guidebook says the setting sun makes the Temple of Poseidon's columns look an 'amazing pink,'" Chance read.

"That's why we're going now," Scarlett said.

Race was happy Chance had returned to his guidebook; a sign of some sort of normalcy.

They walked up the path, past the fallen ancient stone wall that protected the site and there, looming above them, stood the temple. It was the first and last thing Greek mariners saw as they sailed to and from Pireaus.

As the sun set over the Aegean, they walked around the rectangular temple and marveled at it and the sea views on three sides. The cove on one side with a crescent sandy beach, two fishing boats bobbing in the gentle swells and a white-washed taverna on the beach summed up the popular tourist image of Greece.

After driving down to the taverna, they sat on the tiled deck with a view of the cove and the temple above. They ate under the shade of a vine-covered trellis as they watched a white sailboat putt-putt into the cove and anchor. Race had a seared white fish, Greek potatoes, hummus, and balsamic chicken while Scarlett munched on a Greek salad sparkling with olive oil.

When an emaciated stray dog loped along the beach, David convinced Gayle to donate some of her *souvlaki* to the stray, which the mongrel wolfed down.

"Petra would have wanted it fed," David said with a sad smile of loss.

Race watched Chance sitting alone on the stone sea wall staring out at the clear, green sea. Chance had declined dinner—grief or guilt? Had Chance feared Sonja would tell Kanavou something about the yachts Chance had lost and murdered her? Or was Chance jealous of Sonja's flirting with David and murdered her in a jealous rage? Or was Chance truly grieving for his dead wife?

Race moved during the desert of *baklava* to ask to sit with Gayle, who had been dining alone, while Scarlett went to talk with David. The group, with the rash of murders, had segregated into isolated individuals. Gayle took a long drink of red wine as she motioned that it was alright for Race to join her.

After chatting about the beauty of the Temple to Poseidon, Race asked, "Did you see anything the morning Sonja was murdered?"

Gayle hesitated, then slipped a sweet baklava into her mouth. After munching it down, she said, "I was sick that morning."

She offered him some of the desert, which Race accepted.

"You seem down," Race said. "Scarlett and I hope it's nothing related to the tour."

Gayle shook her head. She held up her splinted right arm. "Can't practice anymore."

"Any other options?"

"I had hoped Lodge would help my son, but...."

Race took another *baklava*. "Benny said he was with Sonja the night before she died. You were there?"

Gayle pursed her lips. "Hard to miss her and her mouth—or him. Sonja was talking endlessly about Chance being a crummy sailor and losing yachts. She complained he wasn't making money anymore. She had to do it all, not that she's had a hit movie, let alone a decent one, in years." She paused, considering. "It was odd, though, she kept talking about David. Love struck, I guess, or in her case, lust struck."

"You didn't like her."

"She was always acting; never a real person. She seemed to drink a lot at the taverna, but she really didn't. Kept ordering drinks for Benny and accepting drinks from men, but she always nursed her own like it held the last drops of water on earth. Still, even if she'd been drinking, it's no excuse."

"For what?" Race asked with a supportive, caring look.

Gayle's face tightened with anger. She hesitated, but an encouraging smile from Race was enough to release her pent-up fury. "She had the gall to tell me how hard it was to raise a baby. For a second I thought she might actually be at least part human. Then she says if it hadn't been for her night nurse and her nanny and her chef and her personal assistant she never would have survived having a baby. The bitch didn't know a damn thing about real life or men or anything. Her life was one story after another; none of it real. And telling me I couldn't keep a man. What did she know? That was 20 years ago. And 'I shouldn't have had him.' What a thing to say."

It clicked; what Benny had been so reluctant to mention in the van. "Your son?"

A look of utter hatred hardened Gayle's features into marble. She held her anger in check for just a second before it burst forth like an eruption. "An abortion. She said I should have had an abortion. My son, my boy, my baby? How dare she? What could she have been thinking to presume to…to…?" Gayle, breathing heavily, pursed her lips, drummed her good hand's fingers hard on the table top, and added as she regained her composure, even though her voice was still filled with icy hatred, "I do hope she's in a better place, but I doubt it. Given where she is now, I guess I should do the Christian thing and send her a fan."

"The hotel in Kyparissia left a message," Scarlett said in their room that evening as she clicked off her cell. Race did his treatment as he sorted his drugs into a pill container for the next day. Scarlett's brow furrowed and the tip of her tongue showed at the left corner of her mouth as it always did when she was thinking about an especially challenging issue. "They're charging us for sheets. They say a set was so dirty from one of the tour's rooms they couldn't get them clean."

Race yanked out the nebulizer mouthpiece. "Whose room?"

"Didn't say."

"Call and find out."

Scarlett called. While Race waited, eager for the information, Scarlett asked first one person, then another only to be finally told something that caused her to hang up.

"Well?" Race asked.

"The woman who handles the linen isn't in until tomorrow."

As they prepared for bed, Scarlett was unusually friendly. She rubbed Race's shoulders and as they got into bed sidled up against him. Normally Race would have accepted the surprising offer, but his head ached from sinus pressure and he felt weak and light-headed. He rubbed her back for a time, but then announced he was tired and should get some sleep. She gave him a look that mixed surprise and disappointment with a trace of anger, but she said nothing as he settled in. A part of him felt that at least now she felt some of what he felt when she repeatedly rejected him. It was childish, he knew, but with his head pounding and chest aching, he felt as if he was entitled to at least some childish behavior.

Maybe as payback, Race had trouble sleeping. Thoughts of missing wallets and murdered tour members flitted through his mind like bats. Checking his watch and seeing it was 4 am, he quietly rose so as not to awaken Scarlett. His chest felt worse. The infection was spreading. He hauled his nebulizer and chest therapy device out onto the balcony so his treatments would not awaken her. When he was done, huddled in his jacket in the cold morning air, he felt somewhat better.

He scribbled her a note and slipped outside, locking the door and double checking it. He couldn't replace the chair Scarlett had wedged under the doorknob during the night, but figured she would be safe from murderers until he returned.

Thinking through the various crimes that had plagued the tour, Race meandered down the deserted road to the Temple of Poseidon. The site was closed, but he snuck over a part of the fence that sagged near a convenient marble block. On the south side, he slipped under a rope strung to keep tourists back and found, on the lower edge of one of a column's sections, five letters carved into the stone by a poet: BYRON.

"Beautiful, isn't it?" a voice asked from behind him.

Race spun around. Benny stood looking east out across the Aegean. His eyes were red and he looked exhausted.

Race nodded. The horizon was just tinting the faintest orange with the first glimmer of sunrise. Gentle waves caressed the rocky shore below as the sailboat they'd seen at dinner, all buttoned up, bobbed ever so gently in the cove.

"Rob didn't murder Sonja," Benny said. "I know you all think he did, but he didn't. He couldn't. Why would he?"

Benny sat on one of the marble blocks that were being used to restore the temple. Race sat on a convenient flat-topped rock and said, "I believe Kanavou is working on the theory that Sonja saw something on the flight that Rob didn't want her to tell the police."

"What? Did he steal an extra bag of pretzels?"

Race looked down as the hatch on the sailboat opened and a man emerged in red bathing trunks. The man stretched, set a white towel and steaming coffee mug on the deck and dove into the water with minimal splash.

"There is a possibility that Rob withheld asthma medication from his mother," Race said. "Then hid her inhalers on the plane."

"Impossible."

"Kanavou learned that Rob and his mother argued at the airport."

"I know, I was there to see Rob off."

"Was it about money?"

"No."

"Witnesses said it was about money."

Benny looked down at his hands, looked up and said, "Sort of, but it was really about me."

"Was his mother uncomfortable with," Race hesitated, "her son's lifestyle?"

Benny let out a long, loud laugh that caught the attention of the swimmer who had surfaced down below. "You mean she didn't like him being gay? No, she had no problem with that, except maybe not having grandchildren."

"Then why were they arguing?"

"Over me."

When Race frowned. Benny laughed again. "Rob had dated men before; some she liked, some she didn't. But she had a big problem with me—personally; couldn't stand me. You might have noticed I have a fairly outgoing personality. Some have even said obnoxious."

"Some, such as Rob's mother?"

Benny nodded with a wry smile. "She called me far worse."

Race turned to see the top of the sun appear over the horizon, casting its rays across the glittering Aegean. He glanced over at the islet of Patroklou, rearing up out of the sea like a rocky wave off the end of the cape. Keeping his tone neutral, he said, "Mrs. Rasmussen had some nice clothes, rings, and shoes, and a new DVD player."

Benny's gaze flicked over to Race.

"Did Rob need money?"

Benny shook his head. "You've got it all wrong. His father was frugal, but conservative beyond reason. He never invested in anything other than savings bonds. When he died, his mom had enough money to get by, but nothing extra. Rob gave his mom her rings, the DVD player, luggage, and the clothes. He even paid for this trip."

"He makes that much money?"

"Just one of his suits of armor sells for 15 or 20 grand and his swords are minimum five grand. Rob helped his mom out financially after his father died. She said she hated how frugal his father had been, but she didn't exactly like to spend money either. Likes attract likes, I suppose."

"Rob supported his mom even though she disliked his relationship with you?"

"That was what the argument at the airport was about. Rob still wanted me to come along—Rob was paying for all our trips—but in the interest of giving them a chance to mend fences, I bowed out. Rob was furious about it, as much with me as with his mom."

"Furious enough to not help her when she was having an asthma attack?"

Benny shook his head, seemingly appalled at the suggestion. "He didn't like her trying to run his love life, but he still loved her. No question. He doted on her."

As the swimmer returned to the sailboat and climbed aboard for his coffee, Race asked, "I hate to ask, but what happened to Rob's father?"

Benny sighed as if he detested going over an oft-told story yet again. "The roof was leaking during a storm. His dad never wanted to spend money, so he called Rob. Middle of the night and Rob has to get out of our warm bed and go over to their place to fix the fucking roof in the cold and pouring rain. Rob didn't want to go. It was windy, and Rob's terrified of heights. I offered to go, but Rob knew his parents loathed me, so he ended up on the roof with his old man. If I'd gone, his dad might have shoved me over—he detested me. They started patching the roof with tar and had to climb up along a dormer. The roof is steeply sloped, like a black diamond ski run. They were fine until they were done. Rob said he slid down on his ass to make sure he could stop on the wet roof before he went over the edge. Ruined the seat of a new pair of jeans. He was just climbing over the railing back onto the balcony when his father came down standing up. Must have misjudged his speed or slipped. It was slick. Rob said he didn't even have time to reach out a hand before his father disappeared over the edge, God rest his soul."

Back at the hotel, Scarlett was furious that Race had abandoned her, but he calmed her down. Then he told her what Benny had said.

"Seems that Rob isn't our murderer," Race said.

"Maybe Benny's lying about Rob and his mom's relationship. If so, hatred's as good a motive as greed."

Chapter 21

Day 14: Friday, April 30

The next morning, Race was thankful David offered to drive again. Race's lungs were struggling to deliver enough oxygen to his brain and his sinuses pounded. He was even more thankful after it took two hours to drive the 50 kilometers through heavy traffic to the airport. They returned the van and Scarlett dutifully recorded that they had driven 2,432 kilometers in 12 days.

While they waited for their flight to Santorini, Race asked Scarlett to call the hotel in Kyparissia about the ruined sheets.

After the call, Scarlett reported, "They don't remember which room it was."

"Just one of our group's?"

"We occupied all the rooms on the second floor and the ruined sheets were from the second floor. The maid just doesn't remember which room. She didn't notice the sheets were ruined until she got to the laundry."

"Didn't she notice when she took them off the bed?"

"She told the manager they were in a heap on the bathroom floor, sopping wet."

Race tried to fit that piece of information into the jigsaw puzzle in his head, assuming the piece was from the same puzzle.

"Isn't that Inspector Kanavou?" Scarlett asked, surprised.

Race looked over to see the broad-shouldered inspector showing his identity card to an airport security officer. The tour members watched Kanavou with great interest as he entered the lounge.

"Ms. Wynter, Mr. Traveler," Kanavou said. "May I have a word?"

While David, Chance, Gayle, and Benny stared, Scarlett and Race followed Kanavou over to a vacant corner of the lounge.

"I have news," Kanavou said with a grim smile as he took out his *komboloi.* "A maid entered Gayle's room in Delphi the morning Sonja was murdered. She said Gayle appeared gravely ill."

"I spoke with Gayle on the phone from the front desk that morning and she sounded awful," Race said.

Kanavou nodded. "Yet she still called her son."

Scarlett said, "Makes a nice alibi for that morning, and the morning Dr. Lodge and Petra were murdered."

"If so, one worked out far in advance," Kanavou said. "We checked the phone records at the other pensions on your excursion. Gayle called her son every morning at the same time." Kanavou paused, glanced over at the remaining tour members and said, his voice low, "We also learned that Petra Lodge suffered a stroke."

"Before, during or after she fell?" Race asked.

"Before."

Scarlett said, thinking out loud, "She had a stroke, fell off the cliff and Dr. Lodge, trying to catch her, fell with her."

"Possibly," Kanavou said.

"But?" Race asked, sensing the inspector's lack of commitment to Scarlett's theory.

"The senior pathologist agrees with Ms. Wynter's interpretation."

Scarlett beamed.

"Is there a junior pathologist?" Race asked.

"There is."

Scarlett's beam turned into a look of chagrin.

"What's his view?"

Kanavou took a sharp intake of breath. "His view is that Mrs. Petra Fox suffered a terminal stroke and died at an unknown location. Then her body was moved."

"What's his evidence?" Race asked.

"Blood had pooled in Petra Fox's hands and feet consistent with the body having been moved shortly after death by someone carrying the body, probably slung over a shoulder with the legs and hands hanging down. The pooling did not match the position of the body when it was found."

"How long does it take blood to pool?"

"The body would have had to have been moved some distance," Kanavou said. "If he's correct, we are looking for a strong murderer with great endurance. She weighed 59 kilos."

Scarlett asked, "What does the senior pathologist say about that theory?"

"There is some slight pooling in the extremities, but far from enough to overturn the theory that Petra Fox had a stroke at the top of the cliff and fell. He said something about preferring simplicity over complexity."

"Ockham's razor," Race said.

Kanavou frowned.

"Father William of Ockham was a 14th century Franciscan friar and logician. He argued that the simplest explanation that fits the facts is the best. What's your view?"

Kanavou worked his *komboloi* through his fingers. As they clicked and clacked, he said, "I respect the senior pathologist, but Dr. Lodge's body suffered far more broken bones that Petra's, and had an entirely different blood-pool pattern than his daughter's body. The senior pathologist believes the difference is the result of how often they struck the cliff face as they fell, but to me the findings suggest that Petra Fox and Dr. Lodge did not die at the same time or even in the same place. There's also the way they landed."

"What do you mean?"

"If you're alive when you fall or jump, you can usually control the way you fall, at least to some extent, especially if it is a long fall."

"Such as off Kyparissia castle," Race said.

"Yes, so suicides and those who are alive when they fall usually land on their feet. It's easy to tell because they shatter their legs and spine when they hit the ground."

Scarlett asked, "And if they aren't alive when they fall?"

"If an unconscious or dead body is dropped, the body tumbles in the air and is likely to land on the stomach, back or head. The skin may even be intact when they hit the ground because the force of the blow is distributed over a larger area than if they land feet first, but every organ and bone may be broken inside."

Race asked, "Dr. Lodge landed on his feet?"

Kanavou nodded.

"Petra on her...."

"Back."

Race said, "So Dr. Lodge was alive when he fell, but Petra was already dead."

Kanavou shrugged. "The senior pathologist says that some people who are dead land on their feet and some who are alive land on their back. They are probabilities; it's not 100 percent."

Scarlett asked, "Did Petra have a stroke and fall, and then Lodge, trying to save her, also fell?"

"But Petra's body was moved," Race said. "Why, especially if she died naturally of a stroke? And who would have the strength to move her to the top of the mountain?"

Kanavou glanced over at David, Chance, Gayle, and Benny. "We still have not located Mr. Cohen."

"How strong is a black belt in Taekwondo?" Race asked. "Even a meek one?"

"Can someone with a bad wrist carry a 130-pound woman up a mountain?" Scarlett asked, eyeing Gayle.

"Depends how hurt it really is," Race said. "And how fast she healed. What about Chance? He's strong."

"Beznik?" Kanavou asked. "He was released from jail the night before the murders."

Beznik was the youngest and strongest of the group by far.

Kanavou said, "All strong suspects with motives. I hope no one plans on leaving your little tour."

"Excursion," Scarlett corrected him with a faint smile.

After 35 minutes aboard a 60-seat, twin-engine turboprop, the excursion landed on the eastern flat side of Santorini in the southern Aegean. They caught cabs to Fira, the main town, since buses only run from the airport in the summer. Scarlett and Race rode with another couple whom they had never met. Such doubling-up is common in Greece. To make extra money, taxi drivers yell their destination to see if anyone else is going the same direction.

Once everyone arrived, Race led the way a hundred yards down pebble-paved walkways between whitewashed homes with blue-framed windows and colorful accent tiles to the Hotel Keti. Like almost every building in Fira, it perched on the side of the caldera, built into the cliff with balconies and terraces on the near vertical slope. The view was spectacular down to the sea 700 feet below, where a cruise ship was moored. Santorini, Thera, and the smaller islands of Aspronisi and Therasia formed a ring delineating the ancient collapsed caldera. Two barren, low islands stood in the center of the ring; the remains of the volcano that rent the island called Strongili, the Round One, about 1650 BC, collapsing the middle of the island and sending tidal waves across the Mediterranean destroying Crete's Minoan civilization. The caldera's cliff face was charred black in bands from successive eruptions, alternating with red and pink bands. Sightseeing boats carried tourists out to Nea Kameni and Palea Kameni, the two uninhabited volcanic islands in the center of the caldera.

Race and Scarlett's room was down a flight of uneven, whitewashed stone stairs from the hotel's office. Cut deep into the cliff, their room was long, arched and narrow, entered from one of the ends. Outside their door, a table and chairs sat along a walkway that served as a balcony for three adjacent rooms.

Race bought bottled water, since the water on Santorini tasted like pool water or worse. Scarlett insisted on taking a sip. She regretted it.

The tour rode a cable car down to the waterfront so they could marvel at the views of the town hanging above them on the caldera lip. They rode donkeys back up the narrow zigzag paved path. There were no turnoffs, so handlers loaded tourists aboard at the bottom and sent the donkeys and their human cargo on their way. Race's donkey stopped beneath an overhanging plant to nibble a snack. A handler above yelled at the donkey to move on. The donkey reluctantly abandoned its snack and trudged on up the path. Even so, Race's donkey stopped several more times to snack, but always out of sight of the boss above. Race noticed that several repeat offenders had muzzles to prevent such clandestine snacking.

At the top, with Scarlett on a donkey behind him, Race spotted someone he thought he would never see again. As he had seen many a movie cowboy do on screen, Race leaned forward and kicked in his heels. Much to his surprise, the donkey lurched forward, past the outstretched hand of its owner, who had been about to help Race dismount.

"Race!" Scarlett yelled. "What are you doing?"

Race snapped the reigns and kicked in his heels again. His donkey bolted along a narrow walkway between two white-washed buildings. The donkey's owner ran after Race trying to catch the donkey thief, while Scarlett cantered along behind with her donkey's owner chasing her and her purloined donkey. The hooves of Race's donkey skittered on the walkway's smooth pebbles as it turned a corner. Race spotted his prey and urged the donkey on, yelling for him to gallop—can donkeys gallop?

Race gained on his quarry. He leaned over to the side and half-fell, half-slid off his donkey. His arms outstretched, Race's fingertips brushed the back of his prey's shirt, but that was all he could reach. Race fell to the unforgiving pebble-paved path. His lungs screamed from the exertion. He felt dizzy, nauseous and ill. His sinuses pounded as if a tsunami was trying to rupture his skull. Even before he could gather himself, the donkey's owner had retrieved the now stationary beast and was screaming at Race in most-expressive Greek.

"I was trying to catch a murderer," Race managed to gasp. "Contact Inspector Kanavou, he'll tell you. It's Michael Cohen."

Twenty minutes later, a liberal tip to the donkeys' owners for the extra-curricular chase, and the police summoned, Scarlett, Race and Cohen sat having Greek coffee in a restaurant overlooking the caldera. Scarlett said it was as good a place as any to question Cohen; plenty of witnesses if he tried something and, besides, if he ran again there were few ways off the island.

"Why'd you disappear from the excursion?" Scarlett asked. Battered, wheezing and aching, Race was more than happy to leave the questioning to Scarlett.

"Three people were murdered," Cohen said. "Wouldn't any reasonable person realize it was the safest course to get as far away from your tour as possible?"

"Where have you been?"

"Athens, but it's too smoggy to spend two weeks in, so I came here to see some more of Greece before my flight home."

"I doubt you'll be going home any time soon."

"Why?"

"Inspector Kanavou believes you murdered Dr. Lodge for swindling you in that dating company deal years ago, and Petra got in your way, so you murdered her, too. Then you fled the scene. I assume you were on your way to Turkey."

Cohen looked dumbfounded. "Fled? I did not flee."

"What do you call disappearing from the excursion without a trace?"

"Is leaving a message at the Athens police station for Inspector Kanavou fleeing without a trace?"

"He didn't get any message."

"Must have been misplaced."

"A likely story. It lacks verisimilitude."

Race winced; Scarlett loved her Jeeves and Wooster.

"The Greeks aren't known for their efficiency, are they?" Cohen asked. "I also ran into David before I left and told him I was leaving."

"Probably not the best person to leave a message with after he just lost his wife and father-in-law."

"Not many other people left to tell on your tour, if you don't mind me saying."

"Excursion." Scarlett met Cohen's gaze with a level stare. "In any case, I'm sure Kanavou will want to talk to you."

"Why? No one else has been murdered, have they?"

Chapter 22

Day 15: Saturday, May 1

In the morning, Race was in bad shape. Bruised and sore from his donkey chase, his lungs were barely functioning and his sinuses throbbed with a constant dull pain.

"You might have pneumonia," Scarlett said, peering at him with eyes brimming with worry.

Race did his chest therapy and nebulizer treatment, as well as his antibiotics. He dragged himself into the shower, which helped clear his sinuses a little. Even so, he still felt awful. His head throbbed with a sinus headache and he couldn't seem to catch his breath. He felt light headed and faint.

"I'm calling the front desk for a doctor," Scarlett announced. Race was too weak to argue.

The doctor arrived and diagnosed sinusitis, a lung infection, and possible pneumonia; an x-ray was needed to be certain. The doctor gave Race yet another type of antibiotics and ordered him to the hospital.

"What will they do at the hospital?" Race asked.

"Give you fluids, if you need them. Confirm the pneumonia diagnosis. Mostly you need rest, fluids and antibiotics."

"I have antibiotics and I promise to drink plenty and rest."

"A hospital would be better."

"A better place to catch some other infection."

Just after the doctor left and before Scarlett could argue with Race over going to the hospital, someone knocked at their door. It was Inspector Kanavou holding a padded Manila envelope. After greetings and enquiries about Race's health, Kanavou reported he had found the officer who spoke with Beznik the morning Petra and Dr. Lodge died.

"The officer said he leaned on the hood of the van as he wrote a note in his duty book after speaking with Beznik," Kanavou said. "The hood was cold. He checked to make sure Beznik had been sleeping in the van and not out doing something nefarious."

"So Beznik hadn't just driven back from the castle after killing Petra and Dr. Lodge," Scarlett said, casting a smile of vindication at Race as he lay in bed.

"Could have run," Race managed to croak.

"The officer reported Beznik was in his bare feet; apparently asleep until Cohen fell against the van's hood. The officer saw Cohen stumble. Beznik was also not winded or sweating. In fact, the officer reported, he was wiping sleep from his eyes."

"So you'll release Beznik?" Scarlett asked.

"I want to investigate further, but he appears to be innocent of the murder. In the other case, Cohen is not the murderer, at least of Sonja," Kanavou said. "Based on airline tickets and hotel witnesses, he was on Santorini when Sonja was murdered in Delphi. We also learned that Rob's mother was worth about $550,000; mostly equity in her house and the rest in government bonds and CDs."

"Ah ha," Scarlett said. "I told you so—motive. Rob murdered her for the money. She's rich, he's poor."

"Rob is actually worth far more than his mother, just over $1.5 million."

Scarlett frowned, but said, "He probably wanted to bolster his net worth."

"I do not believe so," Kanavou said.

"They did argue over Benny at the airport," Scarlett said.

"Speaking of the airport." Kanavou held up the padded Manila envelope. "Security in Seattle searched Mrs. Rasmussen's bag and whoever searched it removed everything. When they put everything back, they left some things out by mistake." He dumped the contents of the envelope onto the bed.

Race and Scarlett stared down at three reddish-brown asthma inhalers.

After Kanavou left, Scarlett lost the argument over Race going to the hospital, but won the argument over who would lead the tour. Scarlett led the tour and Race would rest in bed for the day.

When she returned that afternoon, she asked how he felt. Race said he felt fine.

"Fine as a cadaver," Scarlett said.

He asked about her day.

She shook her head at his cavalier attitude toward his illness, but said, "The Museum of Pre-Historic Thira has finds from an ancient civilization that was at Akrotiri on the southern part of Santorini. But you already knew that. You've been here before. You should rest."

Race asked her to continue anyway. "I'm bored, and I love hearing your voice."

"The Thiran civilization is 4,000 years old and had sewers, paved streets, and bathtubs," Scarlett said, excited. "They traded with Crete, the rest of Greece and lands even farther afield. They had frescoes of monkeys and elephants, so they had contact with Africa and Asia. Then one day in 1650 BC Santorini's volcano erupted and ended it all."

"Life is precarious, even in the best of times."

Scarlett said she marveled at frescoes of flawlessly drawn bare-chested maidens dancing, fishermen carrying their catch to market, and boxers exchanging blows that were so bright they looked as if they have been created four weeks instead of 4,000 years ago.

"One pitcher in the shape of a chicken looked exactly like the one our waiter used in Delphi," Scarlett said. "Just a completely different time."

Scarlett continued talking, but Race stopped listening; a different time...times...timing. Yes, he had been focused on where Petra's body might have been moved from, when the timing might be just as important. Timing...timing....

They got take-out *souvlaki*, balsamic chicken, Greek potatoes and Greek salad for dinner. After they ate, as Race lay on the bed and pondered the timing of things, Scarlett walked to one of the many dessert places that are common in Greece. Scarlett returned with a chocolate mouse, complete with a fancy box, a red bow and a tiny red plastic spoon. She said she loved how the Greeks took dessert seriously with all manner of pastries, chocolates, *baklava,* semolina pudding, *galaktoboureko, finikia,* honey cakes, and *vasilopita.* Taking a break from thinking about the murders, Race joined Scarlett to enjoy the sunset from their balcony with her dessert and a bottle of white Retsina wine, which Scarlett forbade Race from even sipping, given his condition.

After she finished her mouse, Race said, "The ancient Greeks claimed Santorini was perfectly situated for conception."

"I doubt you're in any shape for conception," Scarlett said, "besides, you're getting things out of order; marriage, then kids. Although it doesn't mean we can't snuggle some." She kissed him, but he wasn't paying any attention to her.

"Hey, I'm here," she said. "I thought…."

"The order of things," Race mumbled, deep in thought. "The order of things."

Chapter 23

Day 16: Sunday, May 2

Back in Athens after their flight from Santorini, Race faced a challenging battle to convince Scarlett to let him come to Rhodes, but he managed to win it before boarding started and, more importantly, before he started to wheeze. For 55 minutes they flew over the Aegean's sparkling waters and past a few scattered barren islets. At Rhodes' airport they hired a taxi van for the 20-minute drive into Rodos past palm-shaded white beaches with aqua green water that turned a deep blue a hundred yards offshore. The van took them along the harbor, around the imposing walls of the old town and through a stone gate. On the old town's narrow streets pedestrians climbed into recessed doorways to let the van pass. Finally the street was so narrow the driver could go no farther.

As they walked with their bags along the stone-paved street, Race summoned the energy to do his job. "Pension Andreas was converted from a Turkish harem dating back to 1494."

"The man who owned it just had more than one wife," Chance read from his guidebook, his bag in his other hand, "so the owners call it a converted harem."

"Never let the facts get in the way of a good sales pitch," David said.

"Sonja never did," Chance said with a sad smile.

The Pension Andreas was ramshackle but boasted rich, varnished wood ceilings, a resident turtle in a courtyard pond, and views from the roof-top patio of the old town with its minarets and, on the horizon, the coast of Turkey.

Scarlett warned her charges to pay attention to the pension's location, since tourists often got lost amidst the old town's maze of streets.

"If you get lost, find the city wall and follow it along until you reach the pension," Race advised as the group dispersed to explore.

Race still felt far from well and the new antibiotics upset his stomach, but he refused to miss seeing the town—a World Heritage site. He had a hard time convincing Scarlett, but in the end he succeeded. They walked in the dry moat—100 yards across—between the 36-foot-thick walls and the raised ground lined with trees outside the medieval city.

Race said, "The defenses on the land side of Rodos were built first, before the seaward-facing defenses, by the Knights Hospitaller in 1309 and have a scarp, moat, counterscarp, glacis, and bastion."

"What is a scarp, let alone a counterscarp?"

"A scarp and counterscarp are the inner and outer sides of a ditch or dry moat."

After 40 minutes they were two-thirds of the way around the old town and with Race weary from the heat they reentered the town to stroll up the famous Avenue of the Knights. A long and gently sloping street, it housed the Knights of St John divided into seven tongues or houses with intricate coats of arms above each door for England, France, Germany, Italy, Aragon, Auvergne, and Provence. The buildings were used by Greek government departments now, although Italy's served as their consulate. At the top of the avenue stood the Palace of the Grand Master, where the Grand Master of the Knights of Rhodes resided in what was once the citadel of the Knights Hospitaller.

Scarlett and Race strolled past colorful tiled mosques with bubbling fountains and the ruins of a Greek temple to Aphrodite. The streets were paved in smooth river stones turned on end in intricate patterns. Stone arches supported homes over the narrow roads, evoking a far more Middle Eastern ambiance than on mainland Greece.

Leaving the city, they walked across the street to the old harbor, which now berthed sailboats, yachts and excursion boats offering day trips to Turkey. Along the breakwater stood three abandoned, yet picturesque stone windmills. At the end stood a *bourtzi*. The crenellated walls of the Palace of the Grandmaster stood tall over the old harbor. A stag and a doe, the symbols of Rodos, stood on columns guarding the 100-yard entrance, where once stood one of the Seven Wonders of the Ancient World: the Colossus of Rhodes.

For dinner, Gayle arrived at the same restaurant as Scarlett and Race. She rushed over and asked, "Did you hear about David and Cohen? A yacht's owner found Cohen aboard his sailboat and called the police."

"What happened?" Scarlett asked. "Is he alright?"

"When the police arrived, a crowd gathered and another owner found David on his sailboat."

"The same one?" Scarlett asked.

"Different one."

"Were they arrested?"

"David managed to talk their way out of it—something about just admiring the yachts—or they'd both be in a Greek prison right now."

After dinner, Scarlett and Race returned to their room. With closed windows, the room was hot and stuffy, but Rodos has a large feral cat population and the cats would destroy a room if the windows were left ajar, let alone open.

"So did you solve the murders?" Scarlett asked as she undressed for bed.

Race came up behind her and held her close. "I need to check one thing."

"Then check," Scarlett said as he held her hips and nuzzled her neck.

"Too late tonight."

"Luckily not too late for some things," she said as she turned and started to undo his shorts.

Race coughed. She looked up, concerned. He coughed again and a third time, but then the fit passed.

"Are you recovered enough for….activities?"

Race was confused. "Is this a one-time thing or…."

"Or," Scarlett said with decisiveness.

Race frowned.

"What's wrong? I thought you'd be happy."

"You seem…You're confusing."

"I'm a woman."

"What changed?"

"After seeing you so ill, it finally sank in." She kissed him, her body relaxing into his arms.

He cast her a questioning look.

"I realized you're worth losing."

Race smiled, then coughed again.

Chapter 24

Day 17: Monday, May 3

In the morning, Race felt horrible. His lungs felt as if they had ceased to function and his sinuses felt as if they were full of concrete. He was ready to capitulate and go to a hospital, but he had to hang on just one or two more days. He had to solve the mystery of the murders. He was so close. He forced himself through his morning treatments, which helped, as did a hot shower, which cleared some of the green mucus from his sinuses so his head just hurt, instead of pounded.

After a call to Kanavou to ask him to find out the answer to one question and to request a covert team of bodyguards for one of the tour members, Race staggered up to the roof terrace. He wanted to keep an eye on everyone, even though he longed for sleep. He slumped onto a well-used Greek key sofa in the corner while the others broke their fast. Scarlett checked on him several times, offering tea, coffee, melba toast, or sympathy, but he was too ill to consume anything.

Kanavou appeared just as the tour finished breakfast. He waved a greeting to Scarlett and Race as he approached Chance and said, "Our divers have inspected the *Lord of the Isles.*"

"I still don't know why you went to the expense and bother," Chance said, setting his bowl of honey-laced yoghurt down heavily on the table with his still-bandaged hands.

"I thought you murdered Dr. Lodge."

"Why on earth would I murder a withered old professor?"

"He recognized you as someone he had been told was a man who could 'lose a yacht for a profit.'"

"Absurd," Chance roared, standing before Kanavou.

"You killed in the air over Iraq to protect your country—"

"In combat."

"Why not kill on the ground in Greece to protect your freedom?"

Chance stood glowering as he said, "I did not kill anyone."

"Even Sonja, who seemed on the verge of telling Kanavou about the yachts that appear to routinely sink under your command?" Scarlett asked.

"I did not kill her," Chance yelled, biting off each word in succession.

"And I believe you," Kanavou said.

Chance opened his mouth to roar a reply, but a shocked look came over his face and whatever he was about to yell died deep in his throat.

"In investigating the yachts, we have learned that the *Lord of the Isles*, which floundered off Sicily, did have engine problems," Kanavou said. "It was one of the reasons why the owner did not want to sail it himself. We also investigated one of the other yachts, the *Jana*, and found no evidence that it had been sunk on purpose."

"Which means I had no motive to kill Dr. Lodge, Petra or Sonja," Chance said as he sank back into his chair as if he had just fought a 10-round bout.

"Then who murdered them all?" Scarlett asked. She looked over at Race and, with Chance eliminated as a suspect, Race finally knew the identity of the murderer for certain—but he lacked one key piece of evidence and one piece of information to ensure the murderer would be convicted. He needed that piece of information from Kanavou, but could obtain the evidence himself.

As they left the converted harem for their day of sightseeing, Race caught up to Chance. As they chatted about the yachts in the harbor, Race slowed his walk so they fell behind the others, which was easy, given how ill he felt.

"Damn," Race said. "I forgot my cell. Mind if I borrow yours? I need to confirm our dinner reservations."

Scarlett overheard him and frowned. He didn't have a cell, and she had her cell, but Race cast her a look of warning and she remained silent.

"I still can't remember the bloody security code," Chance said. "Can't hit any buttons with my hands bandaged anyway."

"Can I take a look? I have some experience with codes."

"I have it written down back home; probably won't need it until then, but what the hell, give it a try. You can sure deep-six crossword puzzles."

As Race fiddled with the phone, he told Chance, "Scarlett wondered if, while I call, you'd tell the group about the history of Rhodes."

His ever-present guidebook in hand, Chance grinned like a twelve-year-old at the gate to an amusement park. Scarlett shot a confused look with a trace of chagrin at Race.

A few minutes later after returning Chance's cell to him, Race said he felt too ill to continue. As he turned back toward the pension, Scarlett led the tour onward while Chance babbled on about this and that historic building, statue or event.

That evening Scarlett told Race that Chance had done well until the Palace of the Grand Master, when he read in his guidebook that the whole castle was a fanciful recreation built by Mussolini.

"Mussolini?" Chance had asked. "That fascist bastard had a hand in this place?"

"Without him," Scarlett said, "it'd be ruins. The Italians rebuilt it in 1935 for him. They did a marvelous job."

With a subdued Chance tagging along, Scarlett said she led the tour to a free Arab library, established in 1794, and then back to the pension. She said the tour passed a family of Romani begging on the sidewalk. Gayle and Benny dropped euro coins in the beggars' plate, while David dug in his pocket and handed the wizened father a pair of 20 euro notes.

"David entertained the children with some sleight of hand," Scarlett told Race with a smile at the memory. "The kids barely let him go; they wanted to see more of his magical hands."

Race smiled; another piece of the puzzle fit into place.

Chapter 25

Day 18: Tuesday, May 4

Race awoke feeling even worse than the day before. When would Kanavou call back? He needed the answer to his question to be certain about his solutions to the excursion's mysteries.

Scarlett insisted on calling a doctor. Race refused.

"I'll pay," Scarlett said.

Race cringed; if Scarlett was willing to pay, he must be about to see the River Styx.

The physician recommended Race go to the hospital immediately. The lung infection was life-threatening. Even so, after a 25-minute debate, Race convinced the doctor to let him stay with the tour one more day. He had to solve the mystery. He promised to stay in bed, take his antibiotics and get to the hospital immediately if his condition worsened in the slightest.

Reluctant to leave Race, Scarlett finally agreed to lead the tour to Lindos, 47 kilometers down Rhodes' east coast.

Race was glad he stayed home; he desperately needed the rest and Scarlett didn't have the best time. Lindos was beautiful, with white houses above white-sand crescent beaches. The acropolis was striking but it was hot and muggy, and so crowded with tourists they were unable to get much if any feel for the ancient site.

"Meneleus and Helen stopped in Lindos on their way home from Troy after that nasty Homeric war," Race said.

"I didn't know that. That's why I need you along, as soon as you're healthy. Oh, and you won't believe this, we have another mystery to solve: Someone stole Chance's cell."

Race just smiled.

Chapter 26

Day 19: Wednesday, May 5

Race hoped Kanavou would call with the final piece of information he needed to solve the mystery of Petra, Dr. Lodge and Sonja's deaths, as well as the stolen wallet, but in the pension, Scarlett's cell refused to get a signal. After Race took longer than usual to do his treatments, they were late for their flight to Athens, so Race had no time to call at the airport. When they landed in Athens, Race had already borrowed Scarlett's cell and was dialing Kanavou's number when he passed out.

Drifting in and out of consciousness, Race felt an IV in his arm. A monitor hummed above his head. The bed was cool, almost cold and a hard piece ran across the mattress at the bottom of his spine. Was he in the hospital? No, he couldn't be. He had to see Athens, and he had a murderer to unmask. He knew who did it. He had the evidence. Had he told anyone? He had to tell someone—Kanavou, but he needed the answer to one question. No, he couldn't go to the hospital. He and Scarlett had argued about going. Had he won the argument? No, lost it when he passed out. He could smell the dry air with a hint of disinfectant that could only be in a hospital. Then the smell, the bar pressing into his spine and everything else was gone again, like a light switch turning off his consciousness.

Chapter 27

Day 22: Saturday, May 8

Race struggled to wake up as Scarlett told him she had to leave to bid the tour farewell at the airport. Had he missed two days? He tried to form the words to tell her what he knew about the murders, but he couldn't. His mouth would not function. She could not leave. He had to tell her. Be careful. The murderer....He felt her kiss his forehead. No, don't leave! Her footsteps receded. No, no, no. The faint scent of Penguin peppermints slowly, oh so slowly, dissipated.

An hour later, in the waiting area at the airport terminal, a pretty young nurse pushed Race in a wheelchair toward Scarlett, David, Chance, Cohen, Gayle, Benny, and Beznik. An IV bag was attached to a pole on the chair, a catheter inserted into Race's left forearm to provide him with much-needed fluid and antibiotics.

A none-too-happy Scarlett rose to meet Race in a fury. "What are you doing here?"

"Just a temporary jail break," Race said, wheezing heavily. If he focused and exerted what felt like superhuman concentration, he could talk, but it got harder each time he did it, as if he was slipping back down into a deep well of sleep. "I convinced Angeliki here to be my accomplice. Where's Kanavou?"

"Right here, Mr. Traveler." Kanavou approached with six officers escorting a confused looking Rob. "You said on the phone to bring Mr. Rasmussen and you would solve the cases of the deaths of Petra Fox, Dr. Peter Lodge and Sonja Weaver."

"He's too sick to find a single word in a child's word search," Scarlett said, glaring at the young nurse.

"Don't be angry with her," Race said. "The doctor authorized a three-hour sojourn."

"To solve the murders?"

"To be in on the finish. I solved it all on Rhodes, but I needed one more piece of information to be certain, which Kanavou provided me this morning when I finally reached him."

As everyone began to ask questions at once, Race raised his voice as best he could and said, "We are dealing with an especially evil murderer."

"Aren't all murderer's evil?" Cohen asked.

"Most murderers are content just to murder their victim," Race said. He was tiring but he had to do this; Death must know that he could fight back—he would fight back. Death would not win, at least not today. "Our killer has murdered, but has also tried to cast blame on an innocent man. Let me tell you a story." He coughed, struggled to regain his breath and, after a coughing fit, recovered enough to continue, even as Scarlett shouldered the nurse out of the way and assumed command of the wheelchair. "One more cough and you go back to the hospital immediately," Scarlett whispered in Race's ear. "Murders solved or not."

Race nodded. Sucking in a deep breath, he said, "Some time ago, a young man decided to marry a young woman. Things went well for a time. She was from a wealthy family and he most strongly desired to be rich. But soon they realized that they had differences. He liked to travel, she did not. She loved dogs, he did not. He liked spending money, she did not. She liked a quiet life, he craved excitement."

"Sounds like my parents," Rob muttered as he slumped almost horizontal in one of the airport lounge chairs.

"Or me and Sonja," Chance said, sadness lacing his words.

"The man realized he was nearing the limit of his financial resources living the lifestyle he craved."

"Going broke," Chance said.

"So this man staked his future on one hope."

"If you're going to dredge up those lost bloody yachts again," Chance said, rising from his chair.

"It has nothing to do with yachts."

"How about jealousy?" David asked, eyeing Chance.

"It is true that Sonja had a liking for you, David, which Chance couldn't fail to notice," Race said.

"The names of men and women she had affairs with would fill a London phone book," Chance said. "If I cared, would I have stayed married to her for twelve years?"

"These crimes do not have anything to do with lust," Race said. "They have everything to do with a much nobler emotion: hope. The murderer staked all hope on one thing: inheriting a fortune."

Everyone looked at Rob.

"Didn't Kanavou discover that airport security took the inhalers?" Cohen asked, frowning. "So didn't Mrs. Rasmussen die of natural causes?"

"She did," Race said, "as did Petra Lodge."

Everyone stared at Race.

"Petra Fox died of a stroke," Kanavou said.

"Then how did Dr. Lodge die?" Gayle asked.

"And Sonja?" Chance asked.

"Sonja was murdered because she had something the killer most desperately wanted," Race said. "On her cell phone were images of the murderer moving Petra's body."

"How could you possibly know what was on Sonja's phone?" Chance asked.

Race took a deep breath in an attempt to lessen his light-headedness and said, "Sonja thought she could use what she had to re-launch her career. Besides, as you all know, she and Chance desperately needed money."

Chance shrugged. "Who doesn't?"

"Once Sonja approached the killer, whom she thought was not a murderer but the kindest, most caring of spouses, she was in mortal danger. But at least she thought she had insurance: the images on her cell phone."

"Fat lot of good that does us," Chance said. "The killer smashed her cell when he murdered Sonja."

"Indeed. But the killer didn't know that Sonja had switched sim cards with your phone, Chance, for insurance before she went jogging that fateful morning in Delphi. When you tried to call her on your cell in Delphi, you couldn't remember the code to unlock the phone, but you hadn't forgotten the code. Your phone contained her sim card, so it required her code."

"The murderer figured out the sim cards had been switched," Scarlett said, catching on.

"That's why someone tried to kill me at the monastery in Meteora," Chance said.

"The killer realized before I did that you had her cell's sim card in your phone and, hence the evidence of the crime," Race said.

"You knew and left the murderer free to try and kill me?" Chance asked, his voice rising.

"I wasn't certain who did it, then," Race said, "but Inspector Kanavou kept a team on you from the time we left Meteora." Kanavou had acted well before Race had asked in Rhodes for the bodyguards for Chance.

"Didn't keep my cell safe, did it?" Chance said.

"We were protecting you, not your phone," Kanavou said.

"Why not just steal the phone in the first place?" Benny asked. "Why try to murder Chance?"

"The murderer didn't know whether Chance had seen the photos or if Sonja had confided in him. At the foot of the first monastery we visited, while admiring that Ferrari 458, Chance mentioned he might come into some money. That statement worried the murderer greatly; Was Chance going to blackmail the murderer? So the murderer first tried to ruin Chance's cell in a wine bath, and then concluded that with just one shove, Chance, the phone, its images, and any possible knowledge of them would be destroyed in the 900-foot fall from the monastery. Only when that attempt failed and Chance appeared not to have seen the images because he said nothing, the murderer seized the opportunity to steal Chance's cell."

"Which he did," Chance said. "So now we'll never know who killed Sonja and Dr. Lodge, and tried to murder me."

"Yes, we will," Race said. "It was someone who stood to gain a great deal, but only if Petra and Dr. Lodge died in the right order."

"Order?" Cohen asked, perched on the edge of his chair. "What order? Order of what?"

"You seem to be making a par five out of a par 3," David said. "Mrs. Rasmussen died of natural causes after airport security mistakenly kept her inhalers, and Petra died of a stroke. So the only mystery is who murdered Dr. Lodge. Even if Chance didn't lose those yachts on purpose, Beznik, Gayle or Cohen might have murdered Lodge. They all have motives—an accusation of theft, an abandoned illegitimate son, and a morally lopsided dating website deal."

Race stifled a cough. He glanced at Scarlett, but she was too engrossed in the story to stop him now. "At first I also focused on motives. Everyone had a motive and almost everyone had an opportunity. But Scarlett got me thinking about the timing and the order of things."

Silence descended as all eyes stared bewildered at Race.

"Petra died peacefully and naturally in the middle of the night," Race said, "in bed."

"How could you possibly know that?" Cohen asked.

"The sheets."

"The hotel billed the tour for a set of sheets from one of our rooms, so soiled they couldn't be cleaned," Scarlett said.

"When someone dies, their bowels loosen and make a mess," Race said. "The murderer used the sheets to move the body and, even though the killer tried to clean the sheets, they were ruined. A hotel maid found the sheets wet, stained and filthy on a bathroom floor."

"Why move a body of someone who died naturally?" Chance asked.

"Because Petra had to appear to die after her father, Dr. Lodge."

"How did Sonja get involved?" Chance asked, frowning.

"Out for her early morning jog. Sonja saw and photographed the murderer carrying a body to Kyparissia castle. The murderer shoved Dr. Lodge off the cliff and then threw Petra's body over the edge."

Rob asked, "What difference does it make what order they died in?"

"Millions of dollars of difference," Race said.

"Mr. Traveler asked me to investigate wills in the United States," Kanavou said. "In cases in which two people die at roughly the same time or in the same accident, the elder victim is deemed to have died first for purposes of insurance and inheritance."

"Precisely. Isn't that correct, David?" Race asked.

"I don't have a clue what you're talking about," David said.

"Of course you do. You mentioned your father was an attorney who specialized in wills and property law."

"So what?"

"Your father-in-law was a wealthy man, founder of not one, but two extremely successful dating websites. As you and your wife drifted apart, you had eyes only for his money."

"I didn't care about his money."

"I think not. When Petra and her father had a falling out in Mycenae over his illegitimate son, you did your best to mend the rift between them."

"I didn't want my wife and father-in-law at war with each other. Who would?"

"You also didn't want to risk your father-in-law cutting his daughter, your wife, out of his will. When he died, you and your wife would inherit a royal sum, as well as his online dating company, so you stuck it out in a dying marriage. After several strokes, how long could Dr. Lodge survive? You dragged Petra on a trip now and then, but she hated trips. She missed her dogs. You liked the high life of ease, while she preferred a quiet life at home. But you were patient. Golfers must be, playing a game that can take six hours. You could wait until your ill father-in-law died of a stroke. Then you could take half her inherited money in a divorce: you'd be rich and not have a boring wife to drag all over the world."

"Even if such an outlandish tale were true," David said, "why murder Dr. Lodge? As you just said, he was going to die soon anyway."

"One thing changed the entire equation."

"What was that momentous event?"

"You awoke in the early hours that morning in Kyparissia to find that your wife had died of a stroke. Your father-in-law would leave you nothing. You have no children, so why would he favor you with even enough money for a trip across town? So you had to make it appear that Dr. Lodge and Petra died at the same time to cement her inheritance and, thereby, your inheritance."

"You have no proof."

"The sheets."

"Could have come from anyone's room."

"Your back."

David frowned.

"You helped load the van at every stop until the morning Petra and Dr. Lodge died. Then you conveniently hurt your back as you lifted the first suitcase you picked up that morning."

"Sonja's bag was as heavy as an anvil."

"So was Petra's body when you lugged her up to the castle. When you shoved Chance at the monastery, he heard a grunt. You grunted because shoving him hurt your injured back." Race coughed, stifled an attack and swallowed hard as his head swam. "I also saw Sonja coming out of your room in Olympia, late at night."

"So we knew each other; proves nothing."

"Except two days later in Delphi she was dead."

"With Rob's knife, which was found in the Sacred Spring, where Rob admitted he was that morning."

"Everyone knew the knife was in his bag in the van, anyone could have stolen it to frame him."

"As you say, anyone."

"Sonja saw you carrying Petra's body to the castle, but you, David, you are frighteningly devious. In lying to Sonja to buy her silence, you used as much of the truth as you could. You told Sonja that Petra had gone up to the castle to confront her father. They had an argument about his illegitimate son with Gayle and Petra fell off the cliff. You told Sonja that Lodge hit his head during the struggle with Petra, returned to the hotel, passed out and died in his hotel room. You said that since Petra died well before Lodge and in a different place, you would inherit nothing. Therefore, when she saw you carrying a body in sheets, you told Sonja you were carrying Lodge's body to the castle to make it appear they died together, in which case the elder person, Lodge, would be ruled to have died first, and you would inherit. It would look like an accident. You also probably said you didn't want to sully the name of your wife and father-in-law by telling the police they had killed each other over an illegitimate son. It would not only hurt their good names, but also the dating company's fortunes."

"Sonja was many things," Chance said, "but she'd never agree to something so....so....sordid."

Gayle shot him a knowing look.

"It wasn't like she was helping a killer, or at least she didn't think she was. She thought it was all an unfortunate accident, a fight between father and daughter that got out of hand. And to sweeten the deal, I'm certain David promised Sonja that he, as the new owner of Lodge's dating company, would use Sonja as the centerpiece in the company's next ad campaign."

"Sonja already lusted after him," Gayle said, glaring at David.

Race nodded. Gayle, he guessed, had tried to latch onto the soon-to-be wealthy David as the last hope of securing her son's college future. But she was unable to bring herself to do what was required, which explained the night in Kalampaka when Race saw Gayle leave David's room so early. Race said, "The story worked, but David began to worry. Would Sonja figure out what really happened? And she was celebrating her expected boost to her moribund career, attracting attention, which could only put him at risk."

"Bullshit," David said. "Sonja murdered Lodge and Petra."

"What?" Chance roared, bolting from his chair at David. Two officers intercepted him just before he could tear the ex-golfer apart.

"It's true Sonja and I were having a fling," David said, coldly calm. "Sonja hated Lodge over the cancelled ad campaign and she asked me to help her murder Lodge. She thought if he was dead and I owned the company, I would sign her to the ad campaign. I refused. I was out walking that morning in Kyparissia and saw Sonja returning from the castle. She had pushed Lodge over the cliff. Petra unluckily got in the way, probably had a stroke from fright as Sonja attacked them."

"Sonja never killed anyone," Chance yelled, struggling in the grasp of two officers. "If she killed Petra and Lodge, who murdered her?"

"David killed Sonja," Race said. "She was slashed by someone who viciously swung the knife like a golf club. David was angry, furious that she was, even subtly, blackmailing him. David always helped with the bags, so he had ample opportunity to steal Rob's knife from his bag and replace it with kitchen knives. He went to meet Sonja in Delphi, murdered her, and then saw Rob coming from the Sacred Spring; the perfect situation to square the frame David was constructing around Rob."

David hung his head and said, "I had feelings for Sonja, so I didn't want to turn her in. I was in shock when I realized what she had done to Petra and Dr. Lodge. In Delphi I thought I'd be able to convince her to turn herself in, so I agreed to meet her early that morning. But she had Rob's knife. She attacked me, trying to eliminate the only witness to her crimes. I had to defend myself."

Frowning, Gayle asked Race, "Is that what happened?"

"How do you explain your injured back, the sheets, the inheritance, Sonja coming out of your room in Olympia, and the fact that you had no wounds from when Sonja allegedly attacked you with Rob's dagger?" Race asked.

"I've had back spasms, sprains and strains a dozen times over the thirty years I've played golf. You said you don't know which room the sheets came from. They weren't from mine. Sonja was an adult. She could visit whomever she wished, whenever she wished. No evidence of a crime at all. And she was an actress, not a black belt in taekwondo. I disarmed her fairly easily, but I was lucky. She was in a fury, not me. In sum, you have nothing."

"Except for one thing," Race said. "Chance, may I borrow your cell phone."

"It was stolen on Rhodes, remember?"

"Ah, yes," Race said as he turned to David, who wore a self-satisfied smile. "Luckily I borrowed it the day before on the excuse of making a call."

"I couldn't use the damn thing anyway," Chance said.

"I couldn't either, but I switched sim cards with you."

"Not much use; I don't know Sonja's security code."

"I know, so I gave it to Inspector Kanavou to break the code."

"Which our computer experts were able to do," Kanavou said. "The code was 1860, which Mr. Traveler pointed out was the year George Elliot published *The Mill on the Floss.*"

"She loved that damn book," Chance said. "Barely fit in her bag; half the time I had to yomp it all over the world for her."

"After breaking the code, we found....this," Race said and held up the phone to display an image of David carrying a sheet-wrapped bundle. "Dated the morning of the murder. It's David carrying Petra's body to the castle."

"Lodge's body," David said.

"Petra's body," Race said. "There was blood pooled in her hands and feet from being moved. Dr. Lodge's body had not been moved. There is no doubt. You moved Petra's body and murdered Dr. Lodge."

David closed his eyes for a moment and opened them to glare at Race. His voice hard, having lost all trace of its easy going timbre, he said, "I've been waiting for Lodge's will to mature for 20 years. Lodge with his penny pinching, his refusal to take me into the dating business, his puny gifts on birthdays and at Christmas. You'd think he was poverty stricken. I gave him expensive gifts, and he gave me a sweater, a box of golf balls, and a bag of fucking tees."

"And Petra?" Scarlett asked.

"When I met her I thought she was perfect," David said, softness returning to his voice at the memory. "She'd been to Paris for a semester in college, and she'd traveled with her mom all over the world. Her mom loved to travel, probably to get away from that womanizing bastard Lodge. I thought Petra would love traveling, would like the finer things in life. Then we married. I got her two dogs, she wanted them so much, but then she refused to leave home; hated to take a trip, even a weekend away. No one was good enough to care for her dogs. Turned out she hated traveling; had done enough of it as a kid. Hated staying in hotels. Hated eating out. Lived like a shut-in. I couldn't stand it."

"Except for the dream that one day, soon, you'd inherit," Race said.

"Lodge had two strokes. He never got any exercise. He screwed around at every opportunity. The old bastard should have been dead years ago."

"But Petra died first," Race said.

"I couldn't believe it." David rose to stalk about the airport waiting area as he ranted. "How could she die? My life was ruined, everything gone. I had to fix things, make it just, fair; find a way out." In an instant, David had pushed open a fire door and was gone as an alarm blared.

Kanavou's officers rushed after him. Kanavou stood serene and confident, not moving.

"Go after him," Scarlett yelled at Kanavou over the wailing alarm.

Kanavou said, "My men will catch him."

They didn't.

"Where are we going?" Scarlett asked as she pushed Race in his wheelchair onto the metro at Syntagma station. "The hospital?"

"Pireaus," Race said.

"No, no, no."

"We have to catch David."

Scarlett argued with Race the entire, thankfully brief, ride to Pireaus.

Race urged Scarlett to push him quickly in the wheelchair out of the Pireaus metro station. They cut through the heavy traffic across the main street to the harbor, where passenger ferries sailed to points all over the eastern Mediterranean.

"Why here?" Scarlett asked, as Race scanned the harbor. He wheezed and his eyes ran as he wiped them to see better.

"Airport security is tight and this is the closest port."

"Do you see him?"

"I'm not looking for him."

"Who are you looking for then?"

"Not who, what."

"What?"

Race stopped. "That." He pointed at a freighter flying a Turkish flag.

"Turkey and Greece dislike each other historically and are in a dispute right now over oil drilling in the Aegean. If David boards a Turkish ship, he's unlikely to ever be extradited back to Greece." Race shielded his eyes from the sun. "There he is!"

Race rose from his wheelchair, pulled out the IV, which stung, teetered, dizzy, but managed to start running along the jetty. Through blurred vision he kept his focus on David's back as the murderer sprinted toward the end of the jetty where a rowboat was tied up.

Even as he ran, Race knew he would be too late. He was too sick and David too fast. The ex-golfer was in the rowboat and rowing away before Race was within 50 feet of him.

Race reached the end of the jetty, wheezing, and fell to his knees. He would have screamed at David, but he lacked the oxygen to talk, let alone yell.

"He's getting away!" Scarlett yelled as she arrived with the wheelchair.

Race fell over on his side. He was going to die.

"No worries, Mr. Traveler," Kanavou said, his face appearing above Race in a blurry, shifting montage of distorted images and sounds.

"Yes!" Scarlett yelled. "A police boat!"

"You're not the only one who realized David was thinking about fleeing to Turkey when he was found on that yacht in Rodos," Kanavou said with a grin.

Race smiled and passed out.

Chapter 28

Saturday, May 15

"And how's your father doing?" a resident asked Scarlett at Race's bedside.

Race was hooked up to an IV and had been monitored, stuck with needles, scanned, and thoroughly drugged with more medicines than would fit on the hospital's form listing the drugs a patient was prescribed.

"My father is feeling somewhat better," Scarlett said, then cast a wicked little grin at Race.

"That's excellent." The resident proceeded to chat with Scarlett about the weather, local restaurants, tavernas, and beaches.

Race watched as Scarlett played with the ends of her hair, tilted her head to the side and then, the fait accompli, touched the young resident on the arm as she laughed at one of his jokes.

"Maybe I could call you some time," the resident said. "I mean, for coffee or dinner. There is an excellent taverna near my apartment which happens to have a panoramic view of the Acropolis; wonderful views, especially at night with a full moon. How about Friday?"

Scarlett gave him an expression of pure crestfallen remorse. "I would love to, but with my father so ill, I've fallen so far behind at work, I just have no time for myself, regardless of my own needs and desires."

The last word was so full of sexual innuendo that Race saw the resident swallow as his face reddened.

The resident slipped out and as the door closed, Scarlett laughed.

"Very funny stringing along an impressionable young man," Race said. "Probably scare him off older women for the rest of his life."

"Serves him right; my father. Really. You don't look a day past 60."

"Thanks. At least he didn't think I was your grandfather."

Race took a sip of orange juice and said, "Quite the trip. Great to see Nafplion, Epidavros and Monemvasia, Meteora, the Diros caves, the castles on the Peloponnesus, Methoni and Killins, Santorini and Rhodes; wonderful."

Scarlett popped a Penguin peppermint into her mouth. "You talk as if you'd never seen them before."

"I hadn't."

Scarlett stared at him. "You told me you knew all about Greece."

"I do."

"But you've never been here?"

"I read about a dozen guidebooks and a bookcase-full of histories."

"I don't believe you. I hire you as a guide for a place you've never been?"

"I only have a short time to live, why would I go to a place I've already visited? Besides, I did a good job, didn't I? Everyone learned a lot on the tour."

"Everyone who survived."

"At least I figured out who murdered Lodge and Sonja."

"A little late. And who stole Dr. Lodge's wallet?"

"David Fox."

"Why would David steal his father-in-law's wallet?"

"He was short of cash. At the airport, he was about to buy Petra a snack when he noticed the store only took cash. He begged off and Dr. Lodge bought her a snack. At the Corinth Canal, David was in the van and took Dr. Lodge's wallet. After that, he paid for everything with cash, including big tips. He was greedy, though. He took the cash, but also the Bloomingdales card, which eliminated any suspect who wasn't an American. No Greek, such as Beznik, would take the card, while a professional thief would have taken the credit cards, leaving only the people in our tour as suspects."

"Excursion. How did olive oil get on the wallet?"

"David ate crusty bread dipped in olive oil at lunch at the Corinth Canal. It was on his hands when he later emptied the wallet of the cash and Bloomie's card, and then slipped the wallet into Beznik's bag."

"How did he do that?"

"You told me how David showed you his sleight-of-hand skills with the Romani children in Rhodes. He also helped unload the van, so it was easy for him to slide the wallet into Beznik's bag when we arrived at the Pension Marianne in Nafplion."

"I still don't understand why he did it. David is rich."

"Nope."

"He was a professional golfer. He has nice clothes. He's traveled. He's got an expensive watch."

"All on credit, according to Kanavou. David owes more than most people earn in a decade. Just like the monks at Meteora, who look poor as church mice but have gold and silver galore in their museums, looks can be deceiving. Rob's mom looked rich, but was poor. Rob looks poor and is rich. Dr. Lodge was rich and had a second-hand camera bag. Sonja and Chance came across as millionaires, but didn't have a million pennies between them."

"Why's it always so hard to see how people really are?"

"Petra was the first to realize that David stole the wallet. She tried to get her father to drop the matter, questioning whether it'd been stolen. She even offered to cover the loss."

"But why would she think her husband had stolen her father's wallet?"

"David gave us a hint. He said he'd worked for every golf club company in the country. My guess is he kept getting dismissed for petty thefts at the country clubs he visited. No one would want to charge him with a crime and bring negative publicity to a club, so instead they quietly fired him."

Scarlett nodded. "I heard Kanavou asked Beznik to arrange a policeman's tour of Rhodes."

"Not all Greeks distrust Romani; few, actually."

Scarlett leaned back in her chair. She looked tired, her worries about the tour and Race's health had worn on her.

"Ironic," Race said. "David should have just left Petra dead in their bed and went up and killed Lodge. Since they would have died at about the same time, the older, Dr. Lodge, would have been deemed to have died first. Petra would have inherited, everything would have gone to David, and we never would have caught him."

"Sonja might still have seen him."

"But not lugging a body. He could have said he was just out for a jog. He wouldn't have been any more of a suspect than Sonja, who was also out jogging."

"And there wouldn't have been any photo to give him away."

"None, nor any need to murder Sonja or to try to murder Chance. But, then again, what's a clue but a mistake by another name?"

"You should have known it was David much earlier."

"Why?"

"As I mentioned long before you solved the mystery, the murders were committed so early in the morning, the killer had to be a golfer. They get up so early to play. How much time will David get?"

"Greece doesn't have the death penalty, but he'll probably miss 10 or 12 Olympics."

Scarlett stared at Race, then wiped the corners of her eyes with the backs of her hands.

"What's wrong?"

"He doesn't get the death penalty, but you do."

"We all do, just some of us know the name of the executioner."

Scarlett snuffled. "At least Benny said it was the most exciting tour he's ever been on, and Gayle was ecstatic. Kind of you to arrange a DNA test."

"With all the tests I've had done at Mount Herman, they owe me." The DNA test had proved that Dr. Lodge was the father of Gayle's son. Lodge's will bequeathed his estate to his children and grandchildren, if any. David could not benefit by law from his crime and, besides, Petra had died before Dr. Lodge, cutting David out of any inheritance through her. Dr. Lodge's dating empire would go to his first born: Gayle's son.

Scarlett kissed Race.

"I have enough money now for the summer," Race said. "By the way, will you marry me?"

"No; will you lead another excursion?"

"Of course, if you'll marry me after it."

"Where to? Somewhere nice, safe and quiet; Britain? The Wiltshires, Stonehenge and London?"

"London? Ever hear of Jack the Ripper?"

"Lot of history there."

"Maybe; I'll have to get some guidebooks."

"Or you could actually go there first. Maybe we could stay in Athens a few more days, then you can actually see some of the sites."

"So, will you?"

"What?"

"Marry me."

"Give it some time."

"I don't have a lot of time. Marry me."

"When you're rid of all this," she said, gesturing at the IV drip and monitoring machines by his bedside.

"I'll never be rid of it; it's in my DNA."

"Depressing to think your murderer's in your DNA."

"Luckily I'm pretty good at besting murderers."

About the Author

K. Scot Macdonald is the author of eight books. He has traveled extensively in Greece, Scotland, Wales, England, Ireland, Canada, and the United States. He lives in California with his wife, daughter, and a spoiled wheaten Scottish terrier. To find out more about him, visit KScotMacdonald.com.

About Kerrera House Press

Kerrera House Press is an independent press dedicated to producing the books you keep. Visit us at KerreraHousePress.com for more information about our authors and our latest books.

Reader Resources

For more about the story and writing of *A Plunge Into Evil* and the Traveler 'n Wynter Mystery Series, as well as photographs of the locations on Scarlett and Race's excursion, please visit KerreraHousePress.com.

www.ingramcontent.com/pod-product-compliance
Lightning Source LLC
Chambersburg PA
CBHW020747250626
47155CB00003B/966